N

D.J. McCUNE
DEATH
&CO.

D.J. McCUNE
DEATH & Co.

HOT
KEY
BOOKS

First published in Great Britain in 2013 by Hot Key Books
Northburgh House, 10 Northburgh Street, London EC1V 0AT

A CIP catalogue record for this book is available from the British Library.

ISBN: 978-1-4714-0092-6

1

Typeset by Palimpsest Book Production Limited, Falkirk, Stirlingshire
This book is typeset in 10.5pt Berling LT Std

Printed and bound by Clays Ltd, St Ives Plc

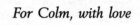

For Colm, with love

Prologue

athanial Mortson stood in the darkness, hands thrust into the pockets of his camel-hair coat. In the physical world it was freezing, the road glittering with ice, but here in the Hinterland he couldn't feel it. It was the middle of the night and he was tired. Usually he had company but on a job like this he preferred to work alone.

He stared at the car – or what was left of it, on its roof in the ditch. There were two people inside, teenage boys in a car that wasn't theirs; racing along a road they didn't know. Only one was still alive and he was hanging on by a thread, groaning softly in the wreckage. He didn't have long. Nathanial made no attempt to help him; there were rules about these things. The groans were trailing off into ragged breathing. It was only a matter of time. His friend's soul had already been taken care of.

Nathanial shifted from foot to foot, surprised at the pang of sadness the job was giving him. Usually one of his sons would be with him, learning the ropes, but there was something about a young person dying . . . He gave a rueful smile. His sons were hardly typical teenagers – and yet he still wanted to protect them while he could. He could handle two souls himself without help – or at least that was his excuse for coming alone.

On the other hand, no one knew better than him how tough his sons' lives were going to be. Maybe he needed to throw them in at the deep end more. Aron, his eldest, was calm and steady, able to cope with anything. Luc, quick-witted and fast to learn, took everything in his stride. But Adam . . . Nathanial sighed and shook his head. Adam struggled with the life he was born to live – and Nathanial felt powerless to help him.

The breathing stopped, jolting Nathanial out of his thoughts and back to the present. It was shocking how quickly silence fell in the still night air. The soul appeared suddenly, blinking at him, scrawny in his tracksuit and baseball cap. Something about his wide, bewildered eyes reminded Nathanial almost painfully of his youngest son. It gave him a little chill but he ignored it, said the words he had to say and watched the boy's soul disappear into his Light.

Usually Nathanial would have left immediately, but that night something made him stay. On the horizon he could see the dull haze of car lights. He stood in the Hinterland waiting as the lights approached, an invisible sentry standing guard over the twisted metal and broken bodies inside. He watched a shocked driver and passenger slow down as their headlights illuminated the wreck, steam still rising gently from the cooling engine. The driver, a middle-aged man, rang the police with a shaking voice while his wife wept into her hands.

I should be weeping, Nathanial thought wearily, but no tears came. There was no room in his world for tears. He stood rigid and listened to the dull wail of sirens in the distance.

It was time to go home.

Chapter 1

t had to be a disaster. Nothing else would have raised the whole household, dogs barking, his brothers bellowing, Auntie Jo squawking downstairs.

Adam Mortson groaned and rolled over. 'Keep it down, will you? Some of us have school in the morning.' When the door opened he tried to play dead – but then nobody here was going to be fooled.

'Adam. Get dressed.'

He squinted up at his mother's shadowy outline. 'Why?'

'Because you are needed.' Elise's voice was husky, which somehow made her light French accent more distinct. She cleared her throat. 'Your father will need your help tonight.'

He wanted to pull the pillow back over his head and pretend this wasn't happening – but she wouldn't be waking him if it wasn't major. 'What happened?'

'An earthquake.' She sounded calm but her fingers clutched at the front of her dressing gown. 'A city in South America. It will be a busy night.'

He closed his eyes, trying to swallow his anger and guilt. 'I have a test tomorrow. For science.'

'Adam.' There was a world of reproach in that word.

He groaned and threw the cover aside. 'All right, ALL RIGHT! Don't worry about me, whatever you do. I'll just fail another test and fall asleep in class *again* and do yet *another* detention but apart from that . . .' He groped about for the lamp switch and the room came alive with light.

His mother turned and walked to the door, then paused, resting her slim fingers on the frame. Her voice was very quiet and very cutting. 'Sometimes I am ashamed of you.' The latch snicked into place behind her.

Adam stared at where she had been standing just a second before. 'Sometimes I'm ashamed of you too,' he whispered.

Downstairs Morty and Sam were barking like hellhounds, chasing each other along the gloomy hall. The front door was ajar, cold air wafting in from the garden, making Adam shiver. The dogs came over and nipped at his elbows but he pushed them away, not feeling friendly.

Staring at his reflection in the hall mirror, he was confronted by a savage-looking figure – bloodshot blue eyes and tousled sandy hair standing on end. He looked, quite appropriately, like someone dragged kicking and screaming from his bed. Adam thought about Chloe, his younger sister, dozing upstairs. *She* didn't have to go on call-outs. Lucky her.

Ducking into the kitchen, he found Auntie Jo sitting at the scarred table, drinking whisky and surfing the Internet on her purple laptop. As usual her generous curves were swathed in a voluminous kaftan, and her short black hair stood askew. Her dark hair was the only thing she had in common with Adam's father; otherwise they looked completely unalike.

She glanced at him. 'Hasn't hit the web yet. Fresh in. Good chance you'll be one of the first ones there.' She sounded almost gleeful.

He shrugged, throwing two slices of bread into the toaster. 'Yeah, well, hope it's not as bad as everybody thinks. I wouldn't mind a couple more hours of kip before I go to school.'

Auntie Jo snorted into her whisky. 'I thought you would be growing out of all that by now.'

Adam watched the toaster and tried to ignore her but she wasn't to be deterred. 'I know you like pretending to be *normal* but you know you're going to have to leave school soon. I've argued for you for as long as I can but your father is losing patience. He won't let you stay there much longer, no matter what I say.' Her voice turned wheedling as the bread hopped out of the toaster and onto Adam's plate. 'Butter me a slice, will you?'

Adam gritted his teeth and smeared butter on as if it had attacked him in a past life. He slid the plate across the table to Auntie Jo and crunched his slice as he walked back into the hall. His older brothers were already there, arguing over how to divide up the souls when they got there. As usual their argument had spilled over into something a little more physical. Aron, his eldest brother, had Luc in a headlock. 'Listen, moron, I am older than you and I get the bigger zone. That is the way it's going to be.' His face was flushed beneath his blond hair.

Luc's shock of dark hair could just be seen through Aron's meaty arm. He was slight but wiry and he was wriggling like an eel. 'I can guide three times as fast as you.' He escaped the headlock with a *pop* and grinned at Aron. 'You can't do anywhere bigger than a school playground! I can guide a whole *town* in the time it takes you to do a *supermarket*!'

'Boys.' His father's voice could have frozen lava. Adam felt a powerful urge to shrink back into the kitchen and hide under the table. Maybe Auntie Jo wouldn't rat him out if he bribed her with the rest of his toast . . . 'Adam, stop lurking. Get over here.'

He was cornered. He dragged his feet forward until he was standing beside his brothers. Aron shot him a disgusted look. 'What's *he* coming for?'

His father ignored him. He was pulling on a camel-hair coat over his charcoal suit, smoothing his dark hair in the mirror. Nathanial Mortson was a tall, thin man with surprisingly broad shoulders and a very straight spine. He wore a suit to every job, whether it was in a crack den or a war zone. He said it reassured people that they were in safe hands. Adam glanced down at his jeans and trainers with a surge of resentment. He'd much rather be wearing his pyjamas . . .

He felt Luc's elbow in his ribs and jumped. 'Huh? What?' Luc rolled his eyes and looked away. Adam blinked straight into his father's even gaze. 'Sorry. What was that?'

Nathanial sucked air in between his teeth, his only sign of irritation. 'I *said*, do you remember the sequence? You haven't been on a job with us for a while. Can you remember everything?'

8

'Yes, Father,' he muttered, fidgeting. He could have said a lot more but he didn't trust himself. He had too many bad memories of chanting the long roads, over and over again. He was sure at that age most kids had still been learning how to spell their own names.

'Have you all got your keystones? Good. We're ready then.' Nathanial paused and fixed Aron and Luc in his pale stare until Aron's cheeks flushed afresh. 'I expect you to behave with dignity, not squabble like rats over bread. We are Lumen. The people there are relying on us. Remember what we're there to do.'

'Yes, Father,' all three of them chorused. Adam swallowed hard. He hated this bit.

Arriving, he had the usual sensation of having been turned inside out, dipped in ice water and squeezed through a very narrow pipe. 'Swooping' was the traditional name for what they'd just done – stepping through an invisible doorway from the physical world into a very different world – the Hinterland. They had just travelled thousands of miles in mere seconds. Swooping was fast – but frankly the name made the whole process sound much nicer than it really was. 'Only way to travel,' he muttered and swallowed, tasting blood at the back of his throat. He dabbed at his nose and pulled away red-stained fingers. At least his ears weren't dripping blood this time. Even so, he wasn't exactly going to be a reassuring sight – more like a scruffy, bleeding teenage ghoul.

Apparently his father felt the same. Muttering, he produced a pristine white handkerchief and flung it in Adam's direction. Adam pressed it gratefully to his nose, trying to stem the flow of blood. He felt stupid. Most Lumen got the hang of swooping fairly quickly. Everyone found it tricky at first but Aron and Luc had picked it up in no time. Not Adam though.

He knew it was all about perception. He remembered sitting in Nathanial's study while his father patiently explained the whole thing over and over again. 'Everything is energy, Adam. Your body, the world we see around us – it's all just energy. We just *see* it as physical. So now you have to shift your focus and experience a new world, a new way of seeing. It's already there, right where we're standing. The Hinterland exists on top of the physical world – it's just a different form of energy. Look at this picture. When you first look you see an old woman with a crooked nose. But look again – see her? A beautiful young woman with a fur hat. Both of them are there at the same time, just like our world and the Hinterland. And when you learn to see both worlds you'll be able to use your keystone and move between them with ease.'

Adam shook his head, snapping back to the present. In the physical world the air was thick with smoke. It had been the middle of the night at home but here it was early evening. What should have been a beautiful sunset was turning the scene before them a ghastly red. They stood in silence, getting their bearings among the shattered buildings and bodies, watching survivors staggering through the remains of their homes. One woman stumbled past, wearing an apron and one shoe, still clutching a wooden spoon. Of course *she* couldn't see *them*. For Adam the effect was like looking through a one-way mirror.

His father had made it sound so easy, stepping between two levels of reality. The Hinterland, the place of souls, lay like a pale shadow on top of the physical world, like a clear film placed over a map. It was freaky seeing both worlds at the same time. His eyes could see the physical world but they could also see the Hinterland. It was like being sandwiched between two panes of glass, watching the normal world pass by him – and through him – unaware that he was even there.

He felt pleasantly detached from the chaos in the physical world. Swooping always blocked his ears, like swimming underwater. He could hear his pulse thumping and the rush of his own blood. He swallowed hard until his hearing returned – then wished he hadn't as sound burst back in, piercing the thin veil between the physical world and the Hinterland. Car alarms shrieked in tandem with women, men roared and wept, alternately praying to and cursing a variety of gods and saints. An infant cried out, long and shrill, then fell silent.

Nathanial recovered first, a lifetime of experience kicking in. He took a deep breath. 'Work swiftly and compassionately.' He nodded at Adam. 'I know you'll make me proud.'

He walked away. Luc and Aron grinned at each other, eager to get started. Adam stood still, feeling the ground shifting beneath his feet and a terrible coldness creeping into his muscles in spite of the thick coat. The sounds from the physical world faded and others emerged as his family began to work. Why did *he* always get so confused when he swooped, while his brothers were able to just get on with the job? He stumbled after his father, trying to steel himself for what he had to do.

The woman was kneeling beside her own body, rocking back and forth, sobbing. She was young and pretty, or at least her soul was. Her body must have been beautiful before the concrete had crushed her left side, leaving her face eerily unmarked. She kept reaching out to touch one smooth, unblemished cheek. Adam watched her trying to lie down on her own body, as if she could somehow merge herself back into the broken flesh. It always seemed cruel that the souls could see their own corpses but somehow it helped them to understand that their physical life was over.

When Nathanial appeared beside her the woman started, pulling away from him – until he smiled. His smile was glorious – white-toothed and warm, a smile so uniquely reassuring that Adam watched the young woman melt into it. It was a smile like a lifeboat in a rough sea. When Nathanial took her hand she allowed him to pull her to her feet, graceful and docile.

'Hello, Eva.' His voice was low and kind. 'There's no need to be afraid.'

'How . . . Do I know you?' Her dark eyes crinkled as she looked up at him.

'I'm a friend, Eva, sent to help you.'

'Are you an angel?' When he didn't answer, her eyes widened and so did her smile. '*Madre de Dios!* Thanks be to God!' Her lips trembled a little and the smile faded. 'I am dead?'

Nathanial rested a hand on her shoulder. 'You have a

new life now and a new road to follow. Look! There is a Light ahead of you – your Light! Do you see it?'

Eva followed the direction of his eyes and her mouth dropped open, eyes round with wonder. 'I see it! *Dios*, it is beautiful!'

'This is your road, Eva, your very own road. It's going to lead you somewhere special and I'm going to help you begin your journey.' Nathanial's voice was changing, sending little ripples down Adam's spine. How many Sunday afternoons had he spent throughout his childhood, his own voice becoming a song, reciting under Auntie Jo's stern gaze? He watched Nathanial lean towards the woman and begin chanting in her ear, his voice a low hum. Adam turned away, unable to bear the sight of her starting that long walk onto the Unknown Roads.

He felt numb. He wanted to go home to bed and pull the duvet over his head. He looked around the chaos, at the bodies and their souls beside them. Some of the souls were frightened while others were looking around curiously. He watched Aron help the soul of an old man who blinked at him like a startled tortoise; and he watched Luc bend down and hug the wailing soul of a little girl, her face crumpled with anguish.

Nerves were making him nauseous. He gritted his teeth and jogged forward. People milled all around him in two different worlds but none of the living saw him – only the dead. His eyes darted from soul to soul, desperate to find someone who looked calm. With relief he saw a middle-aged man watching him with a mildly perturbed expression. He glanced away from Adam as if embarrassed, staring at the remains of his own leg protruding from beneath a slab of concrete.

Adam took a deep breath and tried to paste a reassuring smile on his face. His cheek muscles didn't seem to be working very well. 'Erm . . . Hello. Are you OK?' He looked at the man's raised eyebrows and resisted the urge to slap his own forehead. 'No, of course you're not. That was stupid. Sorry.'

The man stared at him, concern crossing his pleasant features. 'Are you well, my friend? I do not know your face. You are here on vacation?'

Adam grimaced. 'Erm, no, not really. More of a flying visit, if you know what I mean.' He gave a nervous laugh, then cleared his throat. What the hell was he *doing*? What had this poor guy done to deserve an imbecile like *him* as a guide into the next world? Adam tried to make his expression neutral. 'Look, the thing is . . . There's been a bit of an accident. Well, an earthquake really. And you see . . . Well, you're dead. I'm very sorry.'

He squinted at the man, expecting anything from violence to hysterics. Instead the man nodded sagely, looking down at his own body or what could be seen of it beneath the concrete. 'I was thinking this did not look so good for me. I was going to have some bad headache, you know what I mean?' He gave a sudden cackle of laughter and slapped Adam's shoulder.

Adam stared at him half suspiciously and forced a ghastly smile. 'I have to say you're taking this well.'

The man glanced over his shoulder and beckoned him closer. 'Let me be honest with you, *amigo*. When I was younger, I . . . was not such a nice guy. So when I saw my body lying there I looked around, expecting all the devils in hell to be coming for me. And instead there *you* are! *Much* better than anything I expected – no pitchfork, you know?' His teeth gleamed and he gave Adam a conspiratorial look. 'So maybe we can keep away from *el Diablo*, eh?'

Adam felt little prickles rise on the back of his neck. 'Well, that sounds great.' He tried to sound casual – nonchalant even. 'You know, I think I can help you. Maybe I can send you on a journey somewhere really nice.'

The man shrugged. 'Why not? There is nothing for me here now. My house is gone, my dog is gone, my mistress is gone – even my wife is gone. I have nothing. Where are you sending me?'

'I don't really know,' Adam confessed. 'But you should be able to see it. Just ahead of you there is a Light. There's a road on the other side and it's going to take you somewhere very special.' He could hear his own voice changing, taking on that magical sing-song quality. 'Can you see it?'

The man swore softly. '*Si!* There, I see it!'

'That's great. No, wait a minute, don't go yet! There are some things I need to tell you first.' The man's eyes narrowed. Adam hurried to reassure him. 'Nothing bad – I just need to give you a few directions.' He took a deep breath and stepped in closer to the soul, placing a hand on his shoulder and his mouth close to the man's ear. He started to chant, slowly at first, worried that he would forget a step in the sequence and send the man wandering blindly along the Unknown Roads. Without directions he could wander for a hundred years on the other side. But as the words tumbled from his mouth Adam's confidence grew and he picked up the pace, almost singing. He could feel the man relaxing, his shoulder loosening beneath Adam's hand, jaw slackening, staring at his Light with a mixture of confusion and longing.

It was done. Adam lifted his hand away from the man's shoulder and took a step back. He could see the soul had forgotten about him already, was already walking forward. There was a brief flare of light and the man was gone.

He breathed in slowly and tried to enjoy the moment. After all, he had done a good thing. He had sent a soul on to the next stage, without fear, onto the Unknown Roads. Mission accomplished. One down . . . He looked around and felt his spirits sink. Lots to go. Some of them were staring at him, faces half pleading and half afraid. One of them reached out towards him, her mouth moving. She might have been praying.

He was going to help her, he really was. Unfortunately, without warning, his stomach lurched and her soul was treated to the sight of Adam vomiting on his own shoes.

Back home several hours later Adam crept up the stairs in his bare feet, his trainers and socks festering in the garden. Other 'fast response' Lumen had arrived from every part of the globe – borders didn't matter when there was a big disaster and lots of sudden deaths. Nobody had said a word to him as he sat weakly beside a rubble pile – but they didn't have to. The weight of his failure felt heavier than the house.

Once upon a time his family had found the nosebleeds

and projectile vomiting fascinating, like a strange illness or a really ugly insect. Most Lumen found the shift from physical world to Hinterland confusing – but in a good way. Their bodies forgot to feel hungry or thirsty. It helped Lumen do their work without discomfort. Adam got confused too – but not in a helpful way. *His* body reacted angrily and lashed out, protesting against the strangeness of it all. And even if he wasn't technically physical in the Hinterland, his body still *thought* it was. The consequences were all too real – and vomit-spattered – when he returned to the normal world . . .

He eased his bedroom door shut and leaned against it with his eyes closed, wishing he could wipe his humiliation away. It was still dark outside. With any luck he could get another hour of sleep before he had to get up and get ready for school.

Clutching the keystone beneath his top helped his mind to quiet down. It was a small, carved, charcoal stone dangling from a fine titanium chain – lightweight but very strong. The smooth, oval edges of the keystone fitted neatly into his palm and a brief flare of energy buzzed up his arm. His own keystone vibrated slightly with the energy of the family Keystones kept in the vault beneath the house. These acted as something between a homing beacon and an energy source, helping Lumen to swoop to a death scene and then find their way home.

The family Keystones were bigger than the personal keystones – some of them were the size of a gold bar and far more valuable. No one really knew where the Keystones came from originally. Luman mythology said that they had come from a power beyond the Unknown Roads, to protect Lumen from disease and help them do their work.

Over the centuries, certain Luman families acquired more and more Keystones and when a Luman died he could take a family Keystone through his Light to 'recharge', before returning it to the Lumen who had guided him, waiting patiently in the Hinterland. A recharged Keystone helped the owners to feel deaths sooner and swoop faster. They were also worth huge amounts of money. The older Luman families like the Mortsons had even sold off Keystones in the past and used the money to invest for future generations. The profits nestled safely in Swiss bank accounts.

Of course nowadays it wasn't the done thing to sell a Keystone – only to chip off a fragment to make personal keystones for women, children and animals. No one knew exactly how many Keystones existed but those not owned by families were carefully guarded by the Curators, the Luman authorities.

After a few minutes holding his keystone, Adam felt tolerably calm. He inched across the dark floor, tripping over his school bag and cursing. The bed felt cold. Closing his eyes, he fought to keep his mind blank and empty. There would be plenty of time to feel crap in the morning. For now, all he had to do was relax and drift off into sleep . . .

His alarm blared into life, a radio jingle making him jump. The excited reporter was shrieking about some breaking news – a devastating earthquake in a minor Mexican city, hundreds feared dead. Adam slammed his hand on the clock radio, stunning it into silence, and stared through the darkness at the ceiling. 'I hate my life,' he muttered.

Chapter 2

dam usually liked walking up the long avenue leading to Bonehill Charitable School. In springtime squirrels and rabbits ran between the trees and the drive was lined with gravel which crunched satisfyingly underfoot. The main school building was an old manor house, made of sandy stone. It always looked warm, even on the wettest, gloomiest January day.

Bonehill had been established as a charity school two hundred years before. It was an eccentric place funded by a Trust. Places were mostly awarded by lottery and pupils travelled there from all over London. Most Luman children went to primary school to learn the basics, then left to be 'home schooled'. Of course the authorities had no idea about the kind of education they were really getting! Aron, Luc and Chloe had liked school OK but they hadn't cared about leaving. They knew the Luman world was waiting for them.

It had taken a lot of begging for Adam to stay on at secondary school. Nathanial and Elise had totally opposed the idea. After all, what was the point of school when your life was already mapped out? As usual it was Auntie Jo who had put up a fight on his behalf. Adam had no idea what she had said to convince his parents – but he didn't care. He felt fortunate to get a place at Bonehill at all.

He didn't feel very fortunate today. It had been tempting just to stay in bed that morning and only a superhuman effort got him on the bus. By the time he had finished his chemistry test first period, Adam was in truly foul form. Even the freezing cold lab couldn't keep him alert and he had to pinch himself under the bench to stay awake. He tried to concentrate on the questions but the numbers and letters kept swimming about on the page like lazy tadpoles.

Afterwards he stumbled along the corridor in a daze, weaving between the laughing, jostling crowds. He really hoped they were going to do something interesting in biology – maybe it would help him stay awake. Failing that he wouldn't mind just lurking in a corner and dozing . . .

His hopes were dashed when he reached the lab. Their tiny but terrifying teacher, Mrs Buzzard, was lining the class up along the wall.

'Because this is a mock practical I'm going to put you into pairs alphabetically.' She ignored their groans and muttered protests and began distributing them round the room. Adam leaned against the wall with his eyes closed until he heard, 'Melissa Morgan and Adam Mortson, over here.'

Adam mooched over to a bench near the back and joined his partner. They took a second to stare at each other in silence, then they both looked away, busying themselves with other things. Adam sneaked a sidelong glance at Melissa. He knew who she was but they had never really talked. They were in the same form but she always sat with her friends. He had a vague idea that she was good at art. She was pretty with long dark hair, pulled back into a ponytail, and very blue eyes. He suddenly realised they were fixed on him, one eyebrow arched into a question.

'Are you all right? Only you look a bit . . . spacey.'

Adam felt his cheeks flame. 'Huh? Oh yeah. I mean, yeah, I'm fine.'

She nodded and started reading their method sheet. Adam breathed an inward sigh of relief. He hated it when girls started asking a million questions. His sister Chloe could ask him one thing – 'Just one thing!' – and suddenly, thirty minutes later, Adam would realise that she was *still* grilling him.

They worked in silence, gathering equipment. Adam didn't really hang around with girls and he never knew what to say to them, especially when they looked like Melissa. He couldn't stop watching her as she weighed out crisps and bits of bread. Eventually she turned and glared at him. '*What?* What is it?'

'Nothing,' Adam said. 'I was just making sure you were doing it righ— I mean, I was just checking you're OK.' He gave her a smile so fake he might as well have been wearing a clown mask. 'You know, I don't want you having to do all the work.'

She rolled her eyes and didn't answer, concentrating on setting up a Bunsen burner. Her silence was starting to unnerve him. 'I need an A in this, especially after how crap

I just did in that chemistry test.' He stopped and blinked, startled at his outburst of honesty.

When he looked at her she was smiling, just a little. 'Yeah, don't we all?'

'I want to do all the sciences in sixth form, if I get the grades. I think I want to be a doctor. First one in the family.' Adam froze. Where were all these *words* coming from? He didn't even know this girl! 'What about you?'

For just a second a shadow passed across her face. Then she shrugged. 'Dunno. Don't know if I'll be coming back here. Haven't really thought that far ahead.'

Something about her tone made it clear their brief conversation was over. They didn't exchange a word for the rest of the experiment. Adam was glad to start clearing things up at the end. What was her problem? Why was she so huffy?

Just as he was congratulating himself on escaping from her the Buzzard spoke. 'You will be staying in your current pair for the next few weeks, until just before February half-term. You'll be devising a project for your coursework. I'll give you the details next lesson.' Adam threw a horrified glance at Melissa. To his outrage she was mirroring his expression. 'It won't be *that* bad,' he blurted out and she flushed and looked away.

The bell rang, saving him from any further mortification. As he stomped down the corridor he surprised himself. For just a fleeting second, he wished he was at home.

Adam's friends were already in the library, at the best table, hidden behind the stacks. Spike was totally focused on his laptop, his head weighed down beneath enormous head-phones. Archie was sketching something, forehead grooved with concentration. From here the 'something' seemed to be a girl with manga eyes and a very short skirt. Dan was leaning back in his chair and throwing peanuts up in the air so he could catch them in his mouth.

Adam pulled out a chair, grunted a greeting and got a grunt back. Clearly nobody was feeling talkative, which suited Adam fine. He pulled out his maths textbook, trying to skim through his homework. He was interrupted by a peanut ricocheting off his simultaneous equations.

He glared at the culprit, who grinned back. 'Sorry, Adam. Trajectory was all wrong on that one.'

'Yeah, just a bit, Dan.'

'Call me Frodo.'

'I'm not calling you Frodo.'

'You don't mind calling me it when we're gaming.'

Adam thunked his textbook closed. 'I would call you Princess Tallulah as long as I'm shooting you in the head at the same time.'

Dan scowled and jabbed a finger sideways. 'You call *him* Spike. Why does *he* get a nickname and I don't?'

'Because he has spiky hair. Hence Spike. You, on the other hand, may be a hairy-footed midget but your *dad* is the only Dark Lord *you* have to worry about.'

Archie sniggered and dropped his pen on the table. 'Yeah, how is the Dark Lord these days, Dan?' He turned his picture round so they could admire it. 'What do you think?'

Adam pretended to study it. 'Never seen those propor-tions in real life.'

Archie grinned and winked. 'You're looking at the wrong websites, mate.'

Dan was still muttering to himself. 'If *he* gets a nickname I should get one too.' He glared at Spike and unleashed a handful of peanuts. They pelted off the laptop, taking Spike by surprise. He tore his headphones off and cursed them. The other three laughed, although their mirth was tinged with awe. Spike could turn swearing into a kind of poetry.

'Morons,' he muttered to conclude his rant. 'I shouldn't tell you what I just found.' He held them in suspense for a minute then grinned at each of them in turn. 'But if I didn't tell you then you wouldn't see how clever I am.'

'What is it?' Dan was almost drooling.

Spike's grin was truly shark-like now. He turned the laptop towards them and spoke in hushed tones. 'Only The Bulb's emails.'

A howl of amazement and disbelief rang out and Spike hissed and flapped his hands frantically until they shut up. Even Adam was impressed. The Bulb, aka Mr Bulber, was their head teacher. He was a short, powerfully built man with massive hands, cold, snake-like eyes and a shiny, bald head. At one time he had been a wrestler and rumour had it that he had retrained as a teacher after paralysing an opponent in a dirty fight.

The Bulb's son Michael was a pupil at the school, a sixth-former, two years older than Adam. His nickname was the Beast, which summed him up pretty well. Like his father (who had obviously pulled strings to get him in) he had a face like a spade and a reputation for solving disagreements in dark corners. The Bulb preferred boys who weren't *too* bright. He didn't like computers, manga, science or *Lord of the Rings* freaks, which put Adam's friends in particular jeopardy.

All of this made the head an irresistible target. Adam joined the goggle-eyed group around the screen. 'OK, let's have a look,' Spike muttered, fingers skimming over the keyboard. He ran a practised eye down the list of emails, scanning the subject lines. 'Boring . . . boring . . . budgets . . . boring . . . Ah-ha!' He clicked on something, eyebrows drawing together. 'Interesting.' He zoomed in on the screen so they could see.

A collective groan broke out. 'You've got to be kidding me,' Archie whispered.

Dan gaped at the screen. 'Compulsory after-school *wrestling?* With that . . . *psycho* as a coach?' His face was pale. 'But I have my orcs and elves role-play after school on a Wednesday!'

Spike looked gloomy. 'Apparently we spend too much time playing online games and he "wants to make men of us all".'

Adam had finished reading The Bulb's rant. His eye ran down the other subject lines and froze. He poked Spike's shoulder. 'Tell me I'm hallucinating.' He pointed a trembling finger at an email near the bottom of the screen. There was a stunned silence.

Spike swore but it lacked his usual gusto. 'He can't be serious!'

Four pairs of eyes locked onto the subject line, written in capitals, shouting across the screen. 'JAPAN TRIP

CANCELLED BY ORDER OF PRINCIPAL'. Adam felt weak with horror. In a long and awful year their planned trip to Tokyo had been the one bright spot on the horizon. It had been organised and funded by a Japanese former pupil who now ran several major businesses in Tokyo. As the words sank in a chorus of outraged voices broke out at once.

Spike slammed his fist on the table. 'I was supposed to be going to the supercomputer convention!'

Dan's face had gone from pale to bloodless. 'Never mind your computers! It's the World Role-playing Game Exhibition!'

Archie picked up his picture of the manga chick and waved it round like a madman. 'How can I meet someone like *her* if I don't go to *Japan?*' His voice rose to a kind of shriek at the end.

Adam didn't say anything. He couldn't. He'd been abroad lots of times but it always involved a war or a disaster or an epidemic . . . It was going to be his first real holiday abroad. First holiday full stop! His family didn't do holidays. Day trips, yes – but even then they were almost always on call, unless some of the northern Lumen could help out. Death was a 24/7 kind of business. 'He can't cancel the Japan trip.' His voice was grim.

Spike was drumming his fingers on the table top. 'No, you're right – he can't. We're not going to let him. We need a plan.' His face brightened. 'But in the meantime . . .'

Adam frowned. 'What are you doing?'

'Just sending an email.' Spike returned to the first email – 'Compulsory wrestling after school for boys' – and pointed at the subject line. 'In this age of equality a wrestling club shouldn't be for boys only, should it?'

Archie glanced at his manga girl. 'I'd give it a go myself if *she* was involved.'

Spike smirked. 'Exactly. Of course boys are usually stronger than girls but girls have excellent balance from all those high heels. So maybe we need to level the playing field.' He added another word in the subject line. 'I think we'll send this to all staff, not just the teachers. The office ladies will enjoy it. And capitals will make sure everyone reads it.'

He hit *send*. Adam stared at the new subject line. 'COMPULSORY AFTER-SCHOOL MUD WRESTLING FOR BOYS AND GIRLS'. Dan gave a great bray of laughter, earning himself a swipe. By the time they had stopped laughing and closed the laptop the bell for the end of break was ringing.

They took their time heading for the exit. Mrs Nostel, the school librarian, had been stacking books, dressed in one of her long, hippy skirts. Her herbal tea was brewing peacefully in a clear glass pot. Adam could see what looked like dead weeds unfurling inside. Now she returned to her desk and poured herself a cup. She unlocked her computer and raised the cup to her mouth, clicking the mouse. They could tell the moment she saw the email. Her eyes popped open, and she choked and spat a great spatter of tea onto her computer screen.

They fled, whooping and cackling along the corridor.

It turned out to be the highlight in an otherwise tiring day. By the time Adam fought his way onto the bus home he was grateful just to grab the last window seat and let his head loll against the cold glass, eyes closed, tuning out the noise. He had almost swooped home, even though he wasn't allowed, just so he could crawl into bed. Of course it was always risky stepping into the Hinterland from the physical world. As far as normal people were concerned the physical world was all there was and Adam didn't fancy explaining to his classmates how he had disappeared into thin air. In the end he decided against it – the nosebleeds always gave him away.

It was a short walk from the bus stop until he reached the house. He paused at the wrought-iron gates leading into the driveway. Iron railings ran along the pavement, with dense shrubbery and old trees hiding the house from view. Something in the very foundations of the place made onlookers pass by quickly, forgetting it was even there. The only new thing visible was the high-tech security system. Adam placed his palm on an electronic pad and the gates swung open, closing as soon as he was through.

He dragged his feet up the gravel driveway to the front of the house. It was old and graceful, grey stone with elegant leaded windows, surrounded by a neat lawn and lots of trees – rowan, oak, pine and yew. All trees had their meaning; rowan for protection, oak for strength, pine for eternity and of course yew – for transformation and rebirth. Some of the Irish Lumen still gave their souls a sprig of yew to take into their Light.

Round the back of the house was a tumbledown shed where Nathanial parked his battered Volvo. The dogs had a pen here and a large paddock to run free in. Of course what could be seen above ground was only a fraction of what lay underneath. Adam doubted that his friends had vaults, crypts or ballrooms beneath *their* houses. His keystone vibrated gently, registering the family Keystones deep beneath the earth, happy to be back on Mortson ground.

He paused and breathed deeply, feeling unsettled. Home was a sanctuary from the world outside – but home was also a curse, a place where he felt like a misfit. Like a failure.

He put his shoulder to the front door, swinging the heavy wood and stained glass aside, trying to close it quietly so he could sneak up to his room. But before he even had a foot on the bottom stair his father's voice called from his open study door, 'Adam? Come in here for a moment.'

Adam almost cursed – then gave a sigh of resignation. He accepted his fate and stepped into the study.

Chapter 3

dam shuffled inside. His father was sitting at his long mahogany desk, staring out into the garden. Adam had always liked this room – the creamy walls, the long bookshelves, books standing neat and alert like soldiers. It smelled like beeswax polish, old paper and his father's aftershave. His favourite thing when he was a child was spinning the globe on the end of the desk, stumbling over the names of countries and capital cities.

Nathanial made a courteous gesture and Adam sat on a low reading chair. It was old and the bottom was sagging, making him sink beyond the point of comfort. He could feel the front edge of the chair digging into the backs of his thighs.

When his father stood up he towered over Adam but ambled around the room, putting some distance between them. 'So, how was school?'

Adam shrugged. 'All right.'

'Good. I was worried you would be tired today. Blow yourself up in chemistry or something.' Nathanial chuckled and Adam struggled to make his mouth respond. The struggle must have shown because Nathanial's face drooped. He cleared his throat and made his expression carefully neutral. 'So . . . How do you think last night went?'

Adam blinked at him. 'Not very well really. I mean, there was a giant earthquake. I'd say that made it a pretty bad night for most of the people there.'

Nathanial smiled faintly. 'Sarcasm is the lowest form of wit, Adam.'

Adam felt a brief, surprising flare of something between frustration and shame. Just once he would have liked his father to yell and curse and rage; in short, to lose his temper. Maybe it would have made Nathanial seem more human. He sighed. 'I'm really tired. I just want to go and sleep for a couple of hours. I've got loads of homework tonight.'

Nathanial tapped the ends of his long fingers together. 'I see.' His face was thoughtful. 'You won't have to worry about that kind of thing for much longer.'

Adam's heart kicked inside his chest. He tried to keep his voice even. 'Well, I have a few years left. By the time I get through sixth form an—'

'Adam.' Nathanial cut him off and now his face wasn't quite so calm. 'Son, I'm not sure where you got this idea from but you know it's quite impossible. Your Auntie Jo convinced me to let you stay on until you finish your CGEs but after that . . .' He spread his hands in a helpless gesture.

Adam scowled. 'They're GCSEs. For, like, the millionth time. And I can't be a doctor if I haven't gone through sixth form.'

Nathanial studied him, half amused and half exasperated. 'Where on earth did you get this doctor idea? It certainly didn't come from your mother or me.' He shook his head, baffled.

Adam wanted to say something dazzling, something that would penetrate his father's one-track mind and make him understand that there was more to life than death. Unfortunately he couldn't say anything because a familiar feeling was prickling around the edges of his vision, turning his stomach and beading his forehead with sweat. He took a deep breath and tried to push the feeling away.

It was a struggle. Usually he could do it without even thinking about it. But now, when he felt so tired, he was weak. It took a lot of effort and he didn't want Nathanial to notice. His family thought he had grown out of *this* little peculiarity.

The Mortsons, like all Lumen, had a death sense. It was what told them when a person had died and how they had died. It helped them to track the soul so they could swoop and send the soul into the afterlife. This was a Luman's job – to guide the dead, show them their special Light and send them safely onwards. Some, like the Mortsons, were specialists in particular areas; others would help anyone and everyone, regardless of how they had died. The death sense was essential for the job.

Adam however had something extra – what might have been called a 'doom sense'. He could sometimes feel the death *before* it happened. In their world someone like him was called a Seer. When Adam was a child Nathanial had been quite excited about this ability – after all, Seers were rare. A talent like that would make his son the fastest

Luman in the land, ready to guide a soul before the person in question had even died.

Adam had other ideas. He hated the sick, twisting sensation he got inside. He hated the knowledge that someone's life was about to end. Death didn't frighten him – he had seen how the souls relaxed in the Hinterland, once they saw their Light and their own special road. But those souls had been people with lives and plans and dreams. *He* didn't want to know that their dreams were about to end before they knew themselves. Another wave of nausea gripped him and he forced his mind to slam an invisible door closed, locking the premonition out.

Nathanial hadn't noticed. He strode along to the last bookcase, pulling out a heavy leather-bound book. When he sat down his face was reverent and melancholy in equal measure. The cover was embossed with the two golden symbols of the Luman world, the lantern and the key. A Luman had to light the way for the soul in his care, revealing the doorway into the next world. He lifted the cover and ran the back of his hand over the thick paper inside. 'I never thought I would become the Keeper of this book.'

Adam shivered, trying not to look away. He felt both attracted to and repelled by the book. The pages were heavy cream, the soft grain of the paper at odds with the sharp blackness of the ink inside. As Nathanial turned the pages Adam could see the writing changing – spidery on some pages, neat and precise on others. *The Book of the Unknown Roads* held all the collected knowledge, wisdom and law of the Luman world. It had been handed down through generations and only High Lumen could own such a book.

The Mortson copy was ancient and his father was only its most recent Keeper.

Maybe Nathanial was thinking along the same lines. His voice was soft. 'Sometimes I think of those who have gone before me. Of what they learned before they finally walked the Unknown Roads themselves.' When he looked at Adam his eyes were bright and hard. 'Do you think *they* chose the life they had? Did it occur to you that maybe they had dreams of their own, just as you have? We have a job to do.'

Adam shifted in his seat. He risked a peek at Nathanial, seeing the shadows under his eyes and the grey sprinkling his dark hair. His father was starting to look old. Being High Luman – overseeing all the Lumen and souls in the Kingdom of Britain – wasn't exactly a walk in the park. He felt a curious stab of pride, mingled with his usual resentment.

Nathanial cleared his throat. 'It might surprise you to know that I wasn't always so keen to be a Luman myself, Adam.' He grinned, suddenly looking much younger. 'I wanted to be a racing driver.' The grin faded. 'Sometimes it's better to accept your fate gracefully. Dreams are just that. We are what we are.'

Adam tried to keep his voice even. 'You don't need all four of us to follow in your footsteps. Aron and Luc can be Lumen and Chloe will marry Ciaron. You really don't need me to be a Luman. I'm no good at it anyway.' He hated how whiny and pleading he sounded.

Nathanial frowned. 'You need to do your bit, Adam. Populations change. There are more people in this part of the Kingdom than ever before. And there's no guarantee that Ciaron will come here. He may wish to remain in Ireland and follow in his father's footsteps. If we could have had more children perhaps things would have been different but . . .' He stopped, leaving the rest unsaid.

'I can't do it.' Adam stared at the floor. He could feel his cheeks burning. 'I get a nosebleed every time I swoop. I *always* say the wrong thing. I can't even guide souls without throwing up.'

'It's all in your mind, Adam,' Nathanial said patiently. 'Of course your mind feels attached to the physical world; you spend more time here than in the Hinterland. Just keep remembering that no one world is more real than the other. Everything is energy. Use your keystone for help – that's what it's there for. A little piece of both worlds.' He saw Adam's sceptical expression and sighed. 'Maybe things will get easier when you come of age and get Marked. Until then some confusion is normal.'

Adam snorted. Getting Marked meant taking the oath and becoming a full Luman, bound by all the laws of their world. A Marked Luman like Nathanial didn't need a keystone any more. Of course at this rate Adam was *never* going to be good enough to come of age. 'Yeah, but nobody else gets as confused as *me*.' It was true. Even Chloe could swoop with ease – and she hardly ever got to practise.

Nathanial cleared his throat. 'Well . . . you're still learning. Not everyone's a natural.' He paused, obviously torn between his desire to be honest and his desire to be encouraging. 'Adam, what we do . . . Not everyone can do it.'

Adam almost rolled his eyes. 'Yeah, I gathered that. I

don't think the people in my class have to worry about dispatching souls into the afterlife.'

'I don't mean that.' Nathanial sounded almost snappish – which by his standards meant he was really angry. 'There are plenty of psychopomps and lower Lumen able to assist those who die quietly in their beds. To do *our* work requires a special kind of skill. To deal with souls taken before their time . . . *Finding* them fast and guiding them, explaining what has happened to them before they get lost on the Unknown Roads. There have been many High Lumen in the Mortson line. *You* could be next.'

Adam glared at him. 'I don't *want* to be next! I don't want to be a Luman at *all*, never mind High Luman! I keep telling you – I *can't do it!*'

Nathanial stared at him and the tight disappointment around his eyes was somehow worse than seeing him smash things or shout. 'It's time for you to grow up, Adam. You need to accept who you are. Become the man you're meant to be.'

'And do I get any say in that?'

Nathanial sighed and turned away. 'I have work to do, Adam. You'll have to excuse me. Just . . . give it some thought.'

Adam closed his eyes and shook his head. He knew when he'd been dismissed.

He left his father's study and staggered towards the stairs. As he passed the music room he could hear Chloe murdering Chopin on the old piano, his mother an unappreciative audience. '*Non!* How many times must I tell you?

36

Comme *ça!*' The keys thudded out a recognisable tune, albeit played as though the piano had personally insulted Elise. Adam might have felt sorry for Chloe but he had no room in his heart for compassion. At least *she* didn't have to grow up to be a Luman. *She* just had to *marry* one.

He hauled himself towards his bedroom on the top floor, clinging to the ornate banister, seething inside. He didn't want this – any of this! He couldn't even remember the moment he had first realised he was different; it was so long ago now. All he had ever wanted was to be normal, to blend in with the crowd. Everything about his family made that impossible.

He tried to ignore the portraits weaving up the walls beside him but he could feel the occupants sneering at him. All those Mortsons, a long unbroken line of Lumen. According to the history books they were always the fastest, the wisest, the most charming. The vault below the house was crammed with the Keystones these Lumen had gathered. There had been more High Lumen with the surname Mortson than any other. They were guardians of the dead, shepherding souls into the afterlife. Not just any souls either but the most tricky souls, those who had died suddenly or violently. The Mortsons had always specialised in this kind of work – fast-response Lumen, needed all over the world at times, not just in their own Kingdom.

The thought of it, the weight of all that history and expectation, exhausted him. Adam slipped into the coolness of his room and pitched headfirst onto the bed.

When he woke it was dark outside. Adam lay in bed, blinking and stretching. There had been a period when he was younger when he used to wake up and pretend his life was all a dream. All he had to do was find his way out of it, into his *real* life in the real world. He didn't waste time daydreaming any more.

He crept downstairs, hoping to find the kitchen empty. Only one lamp glowed and for a second he thought the coast was clear but Elise was standing at the back door, smoking one of her long, thin French cigarettes. When she turned towards him Adam started. His mother's face was always pale but tonight she looked ghostly. She nodded her head but didn't speak, blowing smoke into the cold night air.

Adam tried to smile. 'Those things will kill you.'

She arched an eyebrow but didn't answer. He could feel her building up to something; probably another lecture. He couldn't face it. Hoping to distract her he asked if there was anything for dinner.

It worked. Her face filled with outrage. 'Of course there is dinner! Tell me one night in your life when you have not had dinner?' She stubbed her cigarette out and dropped it into an Oriental vase, slamming the back door closed. Adam watched her dish up casserole and vegetables and muttered his thanks, hoping she would go away and leave him to eat in peace. Instead she poured a glass of wine and sat down opposite him. 'So. How was *l'école?*'

It always irritated Adam when she used the French word for school, although he couldn't say why. 'It was OK.'

'Mmmm.' The noise she made could have meant anything. 'Your brothers never cared for it. They were happy to leave when they finished the junior school. I ask you every day how it was and every day you tell me it is "OK". I wonder why you fight so hard to go there if it is only "OK".'

Adam glanced at her. 'Because that's what people my age do. They go to school.'

'Not people like us, Adam.'

He watched her sipping her wine. His mother was beautiful. She had brown eyes and long blonde hair, falling gracefully around her pale, heart-shaped face. He didn't think he had ever seen her without make-up. At primary school he had watched other mothers come to collect their children and been fascinated by their trainers and ponytails, their short nails and bare faces. Elise would appear, somehow looking like a queen beside everyone else. She was always charming but never friendly, deflecting questions by asking them instead of answering.

Adam had listened to his friends talking about their mums. He had even tried the word on her once – 'Mum!' – but she had looked at him so sharply he never tried again. She sometimes let Chloe call her *Maman* if she was in a really good mood.

Neither of them spoke. Adam chewed and swallowed mechanically while Elise brought him some fruit salad. It was only as she left the kitchen that she turned to him again. 'Adam. What I said last night . . . that I was ashamed of you. It was unkind.' Just as he thought she might apologise she added, 'It was also the truth. Your father works too hard. He needs you all to assist him. Make me proud of you, like your brothers do.'

Adam listened to her heels click a retreat and pushed away his fruit salad without appetite.

He thought about going straight to bed, then decided to face the music. He hadn't seen his brothers since the night before. When he peered into the tiny TV den there was no sign of Aron but Luc, Chloe and Auntie Jo were all squeezed onto the sagging sofa watching some people running around and screaming. They were being chased by a man who had chainsaws instead of hands. When he caught up with one guy and lopped his head off they roared their contempt at the pitiful spray of blood that came out of the corpse's neck. Even Chloe looked disgusted. 'There'd be, like, ten times more than that!'

Sure enough, when Adam entered the room Luc paused and twitched his nose delicately. 'Does anyone else smell sick . . . ?' he muttered. Then Luc winked and Adam slid inside, feeling sheepish but hoping the worst was over. The film came to a satisfactorily gory conclusion, screen awash with blood and body parts. The others seemed to enjoy it but a few scenes reminded Adam of the earthquake victims. He tried to take a detached interest in it all – after all, he was going to be a pretty useless doctor if he couldn't look at a bit of blood.

When it was over, Auntie Jo flicked off the TV. She was wearing another one of her collection of vast, brightly patterned kaftans. Adam was pretty sure there was a whole mountain village somewhere being kept afloat by her insatiable kaftan demands. She pulled out her laptop and her doughy fingers danced across the keys so she could perform the nightly ritual of reading them their horoscopes. She loved horoscopes, even though she scoffed at them. 'As if the Fates are going to paint their intentions on the sky for some sweaty little mortal to write about!' When she got to Adam's she put on her thrilling 'horoscope voice' to read it to him. 'A fateful pairing will soon show you your destiny. Seize it boldly – nothing ventured, nothing gained!'

Luc snorted. 'Best pair him with a sick bucket then.' He stretched luxuriously and nudged Chloe with his toe. 'Bring me a cup of tea, wench!' When Chloe retaliated with a string of four-letter words Luc just laughed. 'I'm only training you for when you get betrothed.'

Chloe scowled at him. 'I'm not getting married. I'm going to be a Luman.'

Luc sniggered. 'Yeah of course you are. That's why Mother keeps giving you piano lessons and cookery classes.' He changed his voice, doing a faultless impression of Elise's accent. 'A Luman's wife must be an excellent hostess.'

Auntie Jo frowned. 'Times are changing, Luc. Chloe might be High Luman one day – and then she'll be your boss. You'd better be nice to her.' She turned to Chloe and grinned. 'Anyway, she doesn't have to get married. I never married and it didn't do me any harm, eh?'

Chloe glanced at her and looked away, affronted. Adam felt a surge of annoyance. All right, Auntie Jo looked a bit of a mess at times but they saw a lot more of her than they did of their mother. Elise was usually too busy cleaning something or perfecting some new recipe. Chloe sighed and heaved herself to her feet. 'I suppose I *could* do a bit of piano practice before bed . . .'

41

Luc bounced up beside her. 'Yeah, I better go myself.'

Auntie Jo's eyebrows drew together. 'Go where?'

'Just for a little walk. Exercise helps you to sleep better. You should try it.'

She snorted. 'That's what we have whisky for. One hour, Luc. No parties, no girls, no trouble. And make sure you have your keystone. Nathanial might need you later on.'

Luc's face fell. 'It's Aron's night on duty. Anyway, they're already on a call-out.' He saw Adam's unspoken question and made an impatient gesture. 'Two cars on a motorway.' He smacked his hands together and shrugged. 'Racing your mates plus fog equals stupid dead people.' He followed Chloe out into the hall, poking her until she yelled at him.

Adam sat with Auntie Jo in companionable silence. The fire was dying down and Morty and Sam lay sprawled in front of it, dozing. They were Irish wolfhounds, a gift from 'Uncle' Paddy and they took up most of the available floor space. They were supposed to be working dogs – trained in Ireland and wearing Mortson keystones on their collars – but Nathanial rarely went on a job big enough to need them. They were underused and getting lazy. Adam felt lazy himself.

Auntie Jo sighed deeply, absorbed by something on her laptop. Adam glanced at her sidelong. She was warm and shabby and occasionally vulgar – the polar opposite of his mother. Elise tolerated her rather than liked her and it was very clear to all of them that Auntie Jo was the black sheep of the family and a 'bad example', especially for Chloe. It was hard to believe that she was Nathanial's sister – and yet in spite of her bolshie nature and barbed remarks she was fiercely loyal to her brother and he to her.

Adam still didn't really know why she was living with them. Once he had overheard Elise talking about a betrothal that had ended. Auntie Jo always wore a silver locket round her neck and occasionally when she fidgeted with it the catch would open. On one side was her keystone; on the other an old photo of a man. Adam had always wondered who he was – maybe the man she had planned to marry? Certainly for all her bravado sometimes Auntie Jo seemed a little bit . . . lost.

Adam didn't like thinking about it. He didn't care what she had done or why she was living with them – he was just glad she was there. Elise was an excellent hostess but a less enthusiastic mother. She was better at talking to guests at her Luman dinner parties than she was at talking to Adam. In a funny sort of way it was Jo who was the heart of their home. 'Do you like living here?' he blurted out, without really meaning to.

Auntie Jo answered without looking up. 'Of course I do. I have toast, whisky and fast broadband. I even see you lot when it suits you. What's not to like?'

Adam paused, not sure how to put his thoughts into words. 'Well . . . I suppose I was thinking . . . didn't you ever want to go and *do* something?'

Auntie Jo *did* look at him now, one eyebrow arched. 'What do you mean, *do something*?'

Adam was already regretting the direction this conversation was taking. 'Well, I know you didn't get married and all but . . . Couldn't you have gone and done something else?'

Jo pulled a face and set her laptop down. 'I wasn't really brought up for anything else. Anyway, what would I do? Where would I go?'

Adam stared at her. 'You could go *anywhere*. Anywhere in the whole world.'

Jo frowned. 'But why would I want to do that?'

Adam chewed his lip. 'There's a whole world out there. I mean, that's why it's good to go to school and pass your exams and get a good job and be able to go and see everything.'

Jo muttered something that sounded suspiciously like, 'Lot of bloody nonsense.' But Adam wasn't letting her get away so easily. 'No, but seriously. You could have gone off travelling. Backpacked round Australia! Hung out in Thailand!'

Jo sniggered and waggled her ample torso beneath the kaftan. 'I'm not sure Thailand's ready to see this booty in a bikini. Anyway, what's the point?'

'Well, I guess the point is to live your life. You're going to die some day, you see.' Adam's throat was clenched. What was wrong with his voice? It sounded broken – odd and breathless.

Auntie Jo clutched her hands to her heart. 'I'm going to *die*?!' She started laughing at the look on his face but her expression softened. 'Adam, you think too much about things. We are what we are. We're not like other people. The only job I ever wanted was to be a Luman and women have never been allowed to be Lumen. So that's that.'

'Would you be one now if you could?'

She shrugged. 'Probably. But it's too late for me. I doubt it will even happen in Chloe's lifetime. Maybe she'll marry that Irish Luman and her daughters will be able to work.'

'It's so old-fashioned, all of it. Girls can do everything now!' Adam shook his head at the madness of it all. After all, his father was stretched to the limit, desperate for more Lumen.

If Chloe, Auntie Jo and all the other women could be Lumen – problem solved! It was only stupid tradition stopping them.

Auntie Jo snorted. 'Change takes a long time. Look at your mother. That woman could rule the world if she wasn't stuck here making casseroles all day.'

'She hates me.' The words came out before Adam could stop them. He froze, feeling small and stupid, wishing he hadn't said anything.

Auntie Jo frowned. 'She doesn't hate you, Adam. Elise loves you. She just doesn't want you to fail.' She hesitated. 'Failure isn't the done thing in our world. Elise wants you to be a good Luman, not feel ashamed about being a bad one. She nags you because she cares.' She laughed, a little bitterly. 'Trust me, I've seen what happens when a Luman doesn't fit in to our world and there's no happy ending. So . . . just keep practising. You'll get better at things.'

The clock struck midnight. Adam stood up and stretched. He still had an hour of homework to do before he crawled into bed. He paused at the door and looked back at Auntie Jo. She was staring at the dying glow of the fire, face blank. Suddenly she reached down the side of the sofa and pulled out her ever-present hip flask. Adam watched her and felt an odd mixture of love and anger. 'I'm sorry you can't be a Luman.' His voice sounded small. 'I don't even *want* to be one. I wish we could swap places.'

Auntie Jo took a swig of whisky and sighed. 'I know. Those balls are wasted on you, boy.' She gave a sudden cackle of mirth.

Adam scowled and went upstairs.

Chapter 4

ver the next two weeks Adam was left in relative peace. There were no call-outs big enough to need him, which meant he could get through the day at school without falling asleep. Aron still snorted contemptuously every time Adam entered a room and neither of his parents had much to say to him. He should have felt grateful but occasionally he felt them watching him and exchanging significant looks. At times like that he gritted his teeth and pretended not to notice.

School had become his real refuge. At break times he would sit in the library and listen to Dan and Archie and Spike moan about being there, desperate for the weekend to arrive. He would nod and agree but sometimes he felt like leaping to his feet and telling them they were idiots! They had no idea how much of a *fight* it was for him to be here.

They were still obsessed with The Bulb's plan to cancel the Japan trip. The after-school wrestling had been deferred, thanks to the outrage caused by the mud-wrestling email – but it was a hollow victory compared to the horror of losing the Japan trip. Spike had snooped around further and found that it didn't suit The Bulb to go because he wanted to take them to a wrestling camp that week, in the hope of unearthing a hidden passion for the sport. Spike ranted and Archie clung misty-eyed to his tattered manga chick picture – but in the end it was Dan who gave them the brainwave they needed.

He was in his usual seat, munching through a small mountain of pistachios. Archie was sketching a new manga strip and Spike was scowling and muttering as he checked The Bulb's latest emails. 'He wants to take our whole year group to some place in Scotland. They've built this giant wrestling school in an old army camp. We have to eat badger steaks and egg yolks for a week and sleep on camping mats. It's supposed to make us more aggressive.' He sat back and gave a despairing groan. 'He always ruins *everything*! All those lovely supercomputers in Tokyo! And that mad git wants us to spend a week in a shack strangling each other!'

Archie stared bleakly at his manga strip. 'I'll never meet a ninja chick in Scotland.'

Adam squinted at the pictures. 'Do ninjas usually wear bikinis?'

Archie gave him a withering look. 'It's not just any bikini. It's an *armoured* bikini. She can shoot poisoned darts out of it.' He made vague hand movements somewhere around his chest. 'Pow pow!'

Dan was crunching his way through his pistachios, a dreamy expression on his face. 'If only there was a big wrestling tournament in Japan at the same time.'

Spike froze. 'What did you say?'

Dan continued to stare into space. 'You know, a wrestling thing in Japan. Something that would make The Bulb *want* to go there.'

Spike stared at him. 'You are a bloody genius.'

Dan nodded, an agreeable expression on his face. 'Yeah, I am sometimes.' He hesitated. 'And just remind me, why am I a genius today?'

Spike grinned around the table. 'Because that's what we'll do. We'll say there's this amazing wrestling tournament in Japan the week we're supposed to be there – and then The Bulb will want to go!'

Archie looked up from his drawing. 'Yeah, but there isn't any tournament.'

Spike drew a long, shuddering breath. 'I *know* there isn't. We're going to make one up!'

Adam frowned. 'But their wrestling is different – it's sumo. You know The Bulb isn't interested in sumo. He told us before – it's just fat men in nappies running around cuddling each other. He thinks it's for wimps.'

Spike rolled his eyes. 'So we'll pretend it's a different type. A special kind of wrestling that hardly anyone knows.' He gave them all a fiendish grin. 'He's going to lap it up!'

Archie glanced at his bikini-clad ninja, expression torn between hope and scepticism. 'But how are you going to do all this?'

Spike raised his hands skywards, as if asking heaven for strength. 'Oh ye of little faith! It's easy. We'll set up a fake email account and a fake website. Keep it simple. Then we'll send him a few emails as bait and reel him in!'

Archie's face fell. 'Oh. I thought you actually had a real

plan.' He shook his head sorrowfully. 'I mean, I know The Bulb is stupid – but even *he's* not *that* stupid.'

Spike was grinning again. 'You only think that. Trust me, when it comes to computers The Bulb is even dumber than you can imagine.' He leaned forward and lowered his voice. 'Remember I had to go to his office back before Christmas? He was blaming me for something –'

'– which you did,' Dan interjected.

'Which is entirely beside the point,' Spike continued, glaring at Dan. 'Anyway, it was really early in the morning and his secretary was sick. She'd turned his computer off and he couldn't even figure out how to turn it on. He kept stabbing at it with his giant fingers. It was getting embarrassing so I turned it on and showed him how to give me a detention slip. I even printed it for him. Trust me, he won't believe it's possible for someone to set up a fake email account. He's a moron.'

Adam tapped the tabletop. 'It might work,' he admitted. 'But don't make it *too* easy for him or he'll get suspicious.'

Archie nodded. 'Yeah, make it sound like some secret society of ninja wrestlers or something.'

Dan sat with a Zen-like smile. 'This is the best idea I ever had.'

Spike snorted. 'Right, I need to think . . . Has to come out of Japan . . . proxy server, that's what I need . . . bounce it through Russia.' He descended into unintelligible muttering, fingers pattering across the keyboard. Two minutes later he sat back with a look of satisfaction. 'I'll have to do the website later but that's the account created. Now all we have to do is send the first email.' He frowned and suddenly shoved the laptop towards Adam. 'Here, you write it.'

Adam stared. 'Why me?'

Spike shrugged. 'Team effort. Archie can help you.'

Adam stared at the screen for a few moments. He did know a bit about sumo because Nathanial had once sent a sumo wrestler's soul into the afterlife. The man was a 'stable master' – a sumo trainer who ran his own school. He had been visiting London and had choked on a piece of toffee.

Adam shuddered at the memory. He chewed his lip, waiting for inspiration to strike. Slowly he began to type, the others chipping in occasional suggestions, until at last all four of them were staring at the finished email.

Dear Bulber-san,

It has come to our attention that you were once a great professional wrestler and that you will be visiting our country. As you know Japan is the home of real wrestling. We do enjoy watching your fake wrestling on the TV (it is very entertaining) but here in Japan it is considered a suitable hobby only for little girls and old women in retirement.

If you would like to learn more about real men's wrestling we might be willing to consider admitting you to one of our dojos. Our mystical art form combines some movements from sumo and Western wrestling but the rest is a great secret, revealed only to a chosen few. However, there would be certain conditions. Only those who are worthy can cross our sacred threshold of learning.

The Sensei

Adam looked around the table. 'Are we really doing this?' Three heads nodded in unison. He hit the 'Send' button.

Spike took the laptop back just as the bell rang and clicked into The Bulb's inbox. After thirty seconds there was a subdued ping and their email appeared. He looked around the table, face carefully nonchalant. 'It's amazing how much you can achieve with one laptop and one break time.'

Adam shook his head in wonder. 'You're going to end up in one of those high-security prisons.'

Spike smirked. 'Nah, mate. I'm going to be too busy ruling the world.' He stood up and winked. 'Catch you later.'

Adam was still grinning as he walked into biology a few minutes later. Melissa was already at the bench, gathering together the equipment they would need. She smiled when she saw him. 'Somebody's in a good mood.'

Adam shrugged. 'Yeah, not bad.' He threw his bag under the bench and helped her gather test tubes and pipettes. It was getting easier, working together. Melissa had been cautious for the first couple of lessons but now she was starting to relax. They had even chatted a bit this week. It probably helped that Adam could speak in full sentences around her now.

She poked him in the ribs. 'Oi, space cadet. Hand me the method sheet, will you?'

He watched her reading. Melissa always seemed to give whatever she was doing her total concentration. He liked that. Sometimes his thoughts ran madly around his head – like right now, for example. He *should* have been thinking about the work but instead he was noticing that Melissa had cut her hair shorter. It made her look different. She looked . . . good.

Once their experiment was started all they could do was sit and wait. Melissa hopped onto her stool. 'So, what bus do you get?' When Adam told her she raised her eyebrows. 'Nice area round there.'

Adam shrugged. 'I guess so. What about you?'

The bus number didn't mean anything to him but the name did. 'The 704. To Lime Hill.'

Adam looked away. 'Oh right.' He hesitated. 'Isn't that where –'

She sighed and interrupted, 'Yes, where the riots were. But that was *years* ago. It's a lot better now.'

Adam felt embarrassed, without knowing why. 'I've never been round there.'

'You should come down sometime. There are some really cool vintage shops there now, and an art gallery. Little cafes. It's getting nice.' Her face changed as she spoke, brightening, eyes shining. She used her hands a lot when she was talking. She looked different.

Adam wished he could get that excited about where he lived. 'There's nothing much where I live. Just houses.'

Melissa gave him an ironic look. 'Really big houses.'

Adam paused. He'd never really thought about it before. 'I have a big family. My mum and dad, two brothers, one sister. And my Auntie Jo. And two really massive dogs.'

She smiled. 'I always wished I had a big family. You're lucky.'

Adam snorted. 'You think?'

Her smile wavered. 'Yeah. I only have my mum. But my aunt lives nearby so that's not too bad.' She swore suddenly and leaped up. The water in their beaker was boiling and now it was streaming down the outside. On instinct Adam lunged for the beaker, forgetting the heat.

'No!' Melissa seized his hand. Her fingers were cool but a wave of something like fire sped up Adam's arm. For a second he thought he was touching the hot glass but a second later Melissa let go and the electric feeling faded a little.

Adam stared at his fingers. They were tingling. He swallowed hard and looked at Melissa. 'Thanks. I forgot it was hot.'

She shrugged. With the Bunsen burner turned down they sat again but somehow Adam felt on edge. What was *wrong* with him today? Melissa was chatting about their experiment and he nodded at intervals – but he couldn't stop looking at his fingers. The tingling was gone but the memory of it was still there, a ghost sensation.

'Are you OK?' Melissa was staring at him.

He realised his mouth was hanging open stupidly and snapped it closed. 'Yeah, of course.'

'You looked a bit like those guys.' Melissa grinned and nodded at the shelves on the wall beside them. They were lined with glass jars, full of murky formaldehyde. The ghostly remains of fish, reptiles and small animals stared out wide-eyed, mouths gaping.

Adam shuddered. 'Those jars are so creepy.'

Melissa tilted her head to one side and looked at them. 'I don't think they're creepy. They're just . . . sad.'

'They're dead. They don't care.'

Melissa's face was thoughtful. 'But they *were* alive. They had a little life and one day someone came along and killed them and stuck them in a jar.'

Adam shrugged. 'That's what happens. Everything dies.'

'But if they had *known* . . .' Melissa tailed off. 'If they had *known* they were going to die they would have done something different. If that mouse had just run a different direction maybe it wouldn't be in that jar right now. It just had to do one thing differently and it wouldn't be there.' She shook her head and shivered. 'It's freaky, you know?'

'Yeah, well, they wouldn't know what to do differently. Nobody knows when they're going to die so –' he began – then froze. The fine hairs on the back of his neck lifted. Time seemed to stand still. He stared at the jars, heart thudding. Of course the animals inside didn't know they were going to die. People were a lot smarter than animals and even *they* didn't know when they were going to die. But *he* knew.

He closed his eyes, feeling dizzy at the simplicity and brilliance of the idea. He didn't want to be a Luman but Nathanial needed all his sons to assist him. But if some of those who should have died survived . . . Just maybe Nathanial wouldn't need him. Adam would be able to stay on at school.

All I have to do is save them, he thought. *If fewer people die suddenly then no one will need me to be a Luman! I can be a doctor and see the whole world. Go anywhere I want!* His head swam a little. The world had suddenly expanded into something full of possibilities. He could have his own life, free of swooping and guiding and the Hinterland. Nobody would be disappointed in him. He wouldn't have to face nosebleeds or throwing up. He would be *free*!

A delicate cough interrupted his earth-shattering revelation. Melissa was staring at him, hands on her hips, head cocked to one side. Clearly she thought he had lost his marbles. 'I hate to interrupt your little meditation there, Buddha, but we have about two minutes to pack everything up.'

He nodded without speaking. She moved so that the window was behind her. Chilly winter sunlight illuminated her. She was a genius, an angel, a *goddess*. She had given him a plan, a way out. He stared at her silhouette, mesmerised.

She stepped back until he could see her face again and smiled. His stomach turned to warm water. She leaned in towards him and her lips parted slightly. She was saying something and probably it was something genius. He held his breath.

Melissa arched her eyebrows. 'You know, sometimes you seem OK. And then other times . . . you're really weird.' She shook her head and walked away.

Adam stared at her retreating back. 'You have no idea,' he muttered.

For once he couldn't wait to get home. The house was silent – or almost silent. Loud snores were emanating from the den and when he peered round the door Auntie Jo was sprawled on the sofa, head back, mouth hanging open. Her hip flask was lying on the dark wooden floor beside her. After a quick peek he found all the other rooms empty. Elise and Chloe had probably gone shopping and Nathanial and Adam's brothers were obviously on a call-out.

The Fates were on his side. There would never be a better time. His plan was fluttering round inside his head, fragile, like moth wings beating against a windowpane. He would be crossing a line. Better not to get *too* excited until he checked a few things out. Stealthily he crept along the hall, hesitating outside Nathanial's study, one hand resting on the door handle. None of them were allowed into the study unless Nathanial was there. The rule was so sacrosanct that Nathanial had never even considered putting a lock on the door – he simply trusted that he would be obeyed. If Adam got caught in here Nathanial would strangle him . . . Wincing as the door creaked, he took a deep breath, and slipped inside.

The room was cool and dim. The day had turned cold and grey and without the afternoon sunlight the study looked less inviting than usual. The bookcases seemed to tower over him threateningly, almost as if they knew what he was up to.

Adam didn't give himself time to think about what he was doing but walked along the row of books until he saw his prize. *The Book of the Unknown Roads* nestled at the far end of the room, the leather cover worn smooth in places. As he slid the huge tome from the shelf, his hands tingled, as if a tiny electric charge had passed through them. He sat down on the floor cross-legged, touched his keystone to the cover and eased the book open.

There was no contents page or index but Adam was relying on his Mortson blood and keystone to guide him. He didn't really understand how the book worked but just as Lumen could move between the physical world and the Hinterland, so the writing in the book could appear and disappear, depending on what the Luman reading it needed. He could sit for hours and never get any closer to what he was looking for. Only the blood bond, his keystone or years of training could teach a Luman how to navigate the book and use its secrets.

Luckily the book had spent more time in the hands of the Mortsons than any other family and it responded like a well-trained dog, knowing what he was seeking better than he did himself. Even as he sat, the leather cover resting in his lap, the pages rippled and lifted of their own accord until the book lay open around the middle.

The writing here was a spidery scrawl, the ink faded to a dark brown. It looked disconcertingly like old blood. Adam squinted at the bottom of the page. Sure enough, the emblem was old but definitely the Mortson seal, a flaming torch in a black circle. One of his ancestors had written these pages. He breathed out, relieved. Without the blood bond he might have spent hours searching for answers with no success.

This section was called simply, *On the Fate of Men*. He bent his head closer to the page, trying to make sense of the spiky letters.

All men have a season, a time ordained to them by the Fates and powers above. At a time decreed they

shall find themselves at the borderland between worlds,
where Lumen will guide them onto the Unknown
Roads.

That time shall be chosen by no man. It is not the
place of the Luman to be Saviour or Executioner.
Neither may any Luman play Judge. The Curators
will uphold the law in these matters.

Adam shivered at the mention of the Curators. As High
Luman Nathanial was in charge of all the other Lumen in
his Kingdom – but even High Lumen were only a link in
the chain. The Curators were former Lumen who governed
all the Lumen across the globe. Lumen were generally a
civilised bunch. They tended to avoid violence so the
Curators' roles were mainly honorary – but occasionally
they would have to take action against a rogue or incompetent Luman.

Adam gulped. He was thinking about becoming *both*. He
was already an incompetent Luman but the book was quite
clear – a Luman didn't have the authority to save a soul
from death any more than they had the authority to condemn
a soul. He'd be breaking Luman law if he interfered with
the Fates and saved any human soul who should have died.

He chewed his lip, feeling a hard knot of defiance twisting
in his stomach, reluctant to give up his master plan. After
all, maybe he had been given this idea *by* the Fates. No
one else had ever done it – at least no one he knew of.
Maybe the Fates had *chosen* him to do this. All right, it was
pretty unlikely but still . . .

He froze, hearing a noise. It sounded like the distant

thud of a door. Someone was home. He muttered a curse, feeling only slight relief when he heard Chloe laughing and chattering. Nathanial wasn't home yet but that didn't mean Elise wouldn't come in, finding out what time they should have dinner. He needed to get out of there.

As he closed the book it seemed to shudder in his hands. He stuffed it back into its place on the bookcase, full of guilt. What he was planning to do . . . If he got caught he was going to be in so much trouble. More trouble than he could even imagine. His father might be the High Luman but it wouldn't be enough to save him. The Curators' Concilium would be called to session. He might be an embarrassment to his family now but if he went through with this and got caught he would drag the Mortsons into total disgrace.

He peered round the edge of the doorway. The hall was still empty. Adam took his chance and darted upstairs to his bedroom. Lying on his bed, head pillowed in his hands, his mind raced – but he couldn't shake the certainty that he was *supposed* to do this. He lay daydreaming, imagining himself still at school in sixth form. He was taller and better looking, smart in the special sixth form blazer and tie. He was sitting in the study area with his friends, drinking tea and laughing. Melissa came over and slid into the seat beside him, one cool hand slipping into his, sending those little prickles up his arm and down through his body . . .

There was a discreet knock at the door and Elise appeared. 'Your father is just home. Dinner in thirty minutes.'

Adam muttered his thanks and lay on, staring at the

ceiling. He imagined his life unrolling before him, an unending path of swooping and souls and the Hinterland. He imagined marrying someone like his mother and having children who would become Lumen and the long days and nights dealing with death after death after death. His chest felt tight, like a heavy stone was lying on top of him. His whole life would be death, until the moment his own Light appeared and he stepped wearily onto the Unknown Roads.

He hopped upright and hurried to the mirror by the door, mind turning over. He saw himself in a white coat, striding round a hospital, shaking hands. 'Doctor Adam Mortson, how do you do?' He imagined a house – an *ordinary* house – full of ordinary children doing ordinary things like homework and playing computer games. He would have a dog – a *normal* dog – not one who could step into the Hinterland and nudge souls towards the Light waiting for them.

Adam stared at his reflection. 'My name is Adam Mortson,' he whispered. 'And I'm going to *live* before I die.'

Chapter 5

dam sat on the edge of his bed and waited, feet tapping on the floor. He had put on a uniform of sorts – black jeans, black boots, black hoodie and a black beanie. Now he felt ridiculous, like a kid wearing his underpants over his trousers and pretending to be a superhero. To save someone he would have to change something in the physical world. If the next death scene was anywhere light and bright he was going to stand out like a sore thumb.

It had taken him three days to find the courage to put his plan into action. Two long days of weighing up the pros and cons. Then, just the night before, he'd been forced to go on a call-out after a landslide in an Italian town. He'd managed two souls before he threw up four times. Even Aron and Luc had been stunned into silence, too flabbergasted to dish out their usual abuse. When he got home Nathanial had made a hearty attempt to encourage him but his mother had simply stared at him, as if wondering whether he was some kind of changeling. That look had somehow decided things for him. They all knew he shouldn't be a Luman. Now he was going to do something about it.

His stomach twitched and he leaped up. Was this it? The doom sense? Or just one sausage too many at dinner? He paced around the room, palms sweaty, and stopped in front of the mirror. He looked pale in the black hat. He suddenly imagined Melissa looking at him and struggled to make her expression admiring . . . but even in his daydream her mouth was hanging open and her eyebrows were in mid-air. He scowled. She was the one who had started all this.

He'd been thinking about Melissa a lot in the last few days. He was supposed to have seen her earlier that day but she had been missing from registration and missing from biology. He'd struggled through the experiment on his own, thoughts wandering, until Mrs Buzzard told him off and made him pack up early. It wasn't *his* fault he'd set the bench on fire . . .

His guts lurched and rolled and now there was no doubt – this was a premonition. Somebody somewhere was about to die unexpectedly. Maybe even violently. Sweat beaded on his forehead and another wave of nausea gripped him. He was so used to blocking the premonitions out that he'd forgotten how awful they felt. No point prolonging the agony. He took a last look at his reflection, surprised at how calm he looked. He could do this. It wasn't a typical Friday night – but then he didn't exactly come from a long line of normal people.

Time to go. He crept downstairs into the night. In the garden, hidden behind the shed, he closed his eyes, clutched

62

his keystone and swooped, letting the feeling in his stomach lead him as everything else fell away.

Adam's first thought was that swooping was much harder on his own. There was one awful moment when he almost lost the doom sense and could have ended up anywhere. He fought to tune into his body and a second later his feet hit the ground, sending him stumbling face first into a hedge. It would have really hurt if he had been landing in the physical world.

Even here in the Hinterland he blinked, wondering if he had gone blind. Blood was pouring from his nose and he cursed, realising that as usual he didn't have a tissue. This time there was no Nathanial to come to the rescue. He pinched it with the sleeve of his hoodie, hoping he would be able to get home. 'Focus, Einstein,' he muttered. He was hardly superhero material but that didn't mean he had to be Blunderboy. Somebody somewhere very nearby was about to die unless he got his act together.

In the Hinterland he was detached from the physical world, which had its advantages. He was at the bottom of a hill, standing in a narrow road, a high hedge on one side and black fields on the other. Rain lashed down around him but he couldn't feel it. He *could* feel a little of the night breeze – somehow a little of it always managed to cross over from one world to the other. His eyes were starting to adjust in the darkness. On the horizon there was a dim orange glow but there were no street lights here. Ahead of him the road stretched away into the distance, rising and falling in dips and humps, but behind him it curved sharply, disappearing behind the hedges.

His doom sense twitched again, stronger now, and another wave of nausea swept through him. The death would be happening soon. If he messed up and someone died his family would be here within minutes. He was going to have some explaining to do. He imagined Aron's meaty arm around his neck and Nathanial's tight, disappointed face . . .

It spurred Adam into action. He jogged along the road, searching for clues. Maybe someone was lying here unconscious in the dark. They might have been hit by a car or charged by a bull or dropped there by aliens . . . He stopped, frustrated. It all sounded so weak and unconvincing. There was no one here and he could feel himself sweating, even in the coolness of the Hinterland. Somebody was going to die. Where the hell *were* they?

He turned and faced the bend behind him and his doom sense stabbed him sharply in the guts. He took a few cautious steps in that direction – and froze. Adam closed his eyes and retched because quite suddenly he *knew* what was going to happen. For just a second a brief vision blazed behind his eyelids – two cars on the same side of the road in the driving rain, the collision and the red car spinning off the road and bursting into flames. He could hear screaming. His eyes popped open – and saw only the darkness of a country lane at night.

Was he hallucinating? Dreaming? He didn't think so. Adam turned away from the bend and faced the long, straight stretch of black road. The blue sports car was the one that caused the accident, coming from this direction, straying into the path of the red car as it rounded the bend, unable to see because of the hedge. He squinted into the darkness. Was that a light glowing in the distance? It was so dark here the car could have been a couple of miles away but he *knew* it was coming. Every cell in his body knew it was coming.

He looked wildly around. He'd been so busy figuring out how to get here and save the day he hadn't stopped to think about how exactly how he was going to do the saving. He didn't even have his mobile with him to call the police – and even if he had what was he going to tell them? *Hi, I'm Adam, phoning to tell you about the crash that's going to happen in about two minutes. How do I know? Where am I? Both good questions, officer . . .*

Feeling desperate, he started running up the road. At the same time two white points of light crested the hill ahead of him and his heart gave a crazy little hop. This was real. This was actually happening. He had the chance to stop someone dying if he could only reach the blue car in time.

Adam's body felt strangely light and silent, feet pattering rather than pounding on the wet tarmac. The rain poured down around him relentlessly and the wind howled but nothing slowed him down. The road climbed steeply and his breath began to come in quick gasps as the lights grew closer and brighter. Even as he ran he could see they were veering from side to side, the car following some weaving path of its own in the centre of the road. What was the driver playing at? Were they sick? Drunk? There wasn't time to think because he had to make it stop while he still could.

He began to wave his arms as he ran, hoping that the

bright halogen lights would pick out his shadowy form. He wished he wasn't wearing black from head to foot – next time he would bring something fluorescent to wear. Assuming of course he didn't make a total mess of things *this* time . . .

The car was roaring towards him and he frowned, wondering when the driver would see him. The lights were rising and falling with the dips in the road, occasionally shining on hedges and fences and trees, but there was no sign of the car slowing down. Maybe in the darkness he would have to be a lot closer. The wind gave an especially vicious gust and the rain turned horizontal, lashing straight into his face. Of course it didn't bother him but . . .

Adam stopped dead and groaned, understanding hitting him like a freight train. Of course the car wasn't slowing down – the driver couldn't see him. He was still in the Hinterland! *I am an idiot!* If he wanted to be seen he was going to have to shift back into the physical world. Push through into the wind and rain and into the path of the speeding car.

His heart was beating faster. He wanted to keep running but he had to stop and focus. He had never done this on his own before. When his family worked together they created a kind of group energy that made it easier to move from one world to the other. He took a deep breath, clutching his keystone and steadying himself. He could do this. He just had to tune into his body and everything around him; let his senses lead him.

The car was much closer now, making it hard to concentrate. He tried to ignore it and sent his attention into his body – his feet on the road, his face pointing into the storm, waiting until he could almost *feel* it. Then he stepped forward.

The shock of the sound and cold and stinging rain left him paralysed for a few precious seconds. He gasped, feeling like he was drowning. The world was a blur of water and wind, battering him like an ant beneath a drainpipe. He tried to shield his eyes from the driving rain and the lights (so close!), squinting, feeling the road beneath his feet. He started to run because there was nothing else he could do, staggering half blind towards the car, waving an arm feebly, trying to call out to the driver, 'Stop!' but his voice was swallowed up in the storm. The lights were so bright it was like staring at the sun. They came closer and closer, turning him into something supernatural, all light and stark shadow.

And then, at the last possible second, just when he realised that the car *had* to hit him, he saw a white face and startled eyes behind the wheel, a mouth dropping open into a perfect 'O' and the lights veered left, the car soaring a little and ploughing straight through the hedge into the field beside him.

It took Adam a few seconds to realise that he was still alive. He stood in the road, blinking stupidly, clutching his arms and waiting for his Light to appear before him. The only light he could see was in the field beside him, where the blue sports car had come to an inglorious halt.

He stumbled towards it, pausing at the gap in the hedge. His head was swimming but the broken branches and wheel tracks in the grass verge were enough to convince him that it had all really happened. As he stood car lights suddenly swept towards him from the opposite direction and he shrank back into the field, confused. A second later they slid past. In the glow of the tail lights he could see the red bumper. For one horrifying second his mind replayed the premonition – the red car swerving off the road, the bright fire in the darkness. The car disappeared safely along the road, its driver blissfully unaware of what had almost happened. Adam had just cheated the Fates out of a soul.

His legs were like jelly as he walked towards the blue car. It seemed to be intact but what if this driver was injured instead? What if they were dead? He was only going to have a few seconds to escape before his family showed up . . .

As he reached it he took a cautious peek inside – only to find a very pretty young woman looking up at him. It was amazing – she didn't seem to have a scratch on her.

When he opened the door she squinted up at him. 'What happened?' She didn't look frightened, simply baffled.

Adam glared at her. She had just breathed pure alcohol over him. It didn't take any superpowers to figure out why she had just almost killed someone. It was amazing she'd managed to get *into* the car, never mind drive out into the middle of nowhere. 'You don't remember?' When she shook her head he closed his eyes and tried to take a deep, calming breath. 'Well . . . I'm guessing you raided an off-licence, drank everything you could get your hands on and then decided it would be a really smart idea to drive home.'

She blinked in the light above her head. 'I don't understand. Who . . . who are you?'

Superman, Adam thought sourly. *I'm the guy who just saved a total stranger from dying horribly. Dying horribly because of you!* His relief was morphing into anger. 'It doesn't matter who I am. Just be happy I was here to help you.' He glared at her but she was staring into space. Great. What the hell was he going to do with her now? He didn't even know where they were!

The woman's face screwed up with concentration – then outrage flashed across her pretty features. 'I was just driving home but you jumped in front of me!'

Adam gritted his teeth. 'No, I didn't. Well . . . actually . . . well yeah, OK, I did. But believe me, it was better that way.' He thought again about the flames bright in the darkness, the awful screaming – and shuddered. 'How could you be so stupid?'

The woman slumped back in her seat, struggling to understand. 'We just had a few drinks after work.' Her words were slurred. 'It's Wally's birthday . . .'

Adam felt his jaw drop. Of course she didn't *know* she'd almost *killed* someone. 'Didn't anybody ever tell you not to drink and drive?' That was all they ever heard about in school and *they* couldn't even get a licence yet!

'Only had a coupla drinks,' she muttered, pouting. She looked sulky and self-pitying.

Adam scowled at her. Somehow she wasn't as attractive any more. 'Yeah? Well, the party's over.' He chewed his lip, looking around the field and trying to come up with some kind of a plan. The rain was relentless. How was he going to get the woman out of here? She could sit here all night in the dark and no one would even know she was there.

There was only one thing he could do. 'Do you have your mobile?'

She grinned suddenly, batting her eyelashes. 'Bit young aren't ya? Giving me your number!' She giggled and her head lolled to one side.

Adam clenched his teeth and tried to smile, wondering if she might actually be the dumbest person he had ever met. 'Yeah, that's it. I'm going to put my number in, OK?' Her eyes were rolling all over the place but she managed to hand him the phone, then slumped back into her seat, humming tunelessly.

Adam dialled for the emergency services, squinting at the GPS miraculously still glowing on the dashboard. When the call went through he cleared his throat and tried to put on a high-pitched voice, feeling ridiculous. He sounded like a cartoon character. 'Hello, police? No, I don't know my number. I . . . erm . . . I hit my head. And I've had a few drinks. I'm in a field.' He rattled off the GPS location and shrilled a goodbye.

The woman was staring up at him bleary-eyed. Adam sighed, not sure whether he'd done the right thing calling the police. Then he replayed the scene in his mind – the red car sliding off the road, the flames and the screams. Suddenly he was quite sure he'd done *exactly* the right thing. He felt a hot crest of anger. 'Listen. You're a total idiot.' He ignored her outraged expression. 'You nearly killed someone tonight. Not really worth it just to impress some guy. I mean seriously, *WALLY*? What sort of a name is *that*?' He paused and tried to get back on track. 'Anyway, just stay here until people find you, OK? And *don't drive*!'

She blinked at him as he used the edge of his hoodie to wipe his fingerprints off the phone. 'Did you put your number in?'

Adam glared and dropped the phone beside her. He could still hear her giggling and making kissing noises as he scurried away.

He waited at the edge of the field until he saw the blue lights approaching. The woman in the car was a moron but annoyingly he felt responsible for her now. The police found the field and as their powerful torches swept through the darkness Adam remembered that he was still in the physical world. He clutched his keystone and quickly tried to push himself back into safety. For one panicked second he couldn't move but suddenly the relentless drizzle disappeared. He was standing in the Hinterland, cold and dripping wet. The air around him felt almost warm compared to the physical world.

He risked walking closer now that he couldn't be seen, watching a policewoman mutter something into a radio. A minute later more blue lights came along the road and an ambulance drew up at the great tear in the hedge. He sighed, suddenly tired, feeling his shoulders relax. They could take care of her from here.

Now came the real test. If he couldn't get home he would have to somehow appear on the road and beg the police for a lift. There would be millions of questions and lots of unsatisfactory answers. He closed his eyes and gripped his keystone tight, letting the energy buzz and flow through his body. Somewhere behind his heart he felt a kind of snag and he thought the word clearly – *Home*. There was a sharp pain and a second later the field was gone.

Back at the house Adam lurked in the garden, pinching his nose, wiping his face clean with his hoodie sleeve. It wasn't raining here so it was going to be hard explaining why he was soaked through. For once luck was on his side. When he slipped inside the kitchen door he found the room in darkness. He sneaked upstairs, wincing at every creaky step.

In the shower a few minutes later he started to shake. He was standing under the hot flow of water, letting it run through his hair and down his neck, across his shoulders and chest. At first he thought it was just the cold. Then a series of images flashed through his mind – the wet field, lights cresting the top of the hill, the woman's face in the car, the red car passing safely by, its driver oblivious.

The enormity of what he had done hit him. He had just saved someone's life. Someone was driving home tonight, maybe to a family. They were going to open the door and take their coat off and make a cup of tea. They weren't going to meet Nathanial and step into their Light and walk the Unknown Roads. He had saved someone's life.

Finally, Adam allowed himself to smile.

Chapter 6

or the rest of the weekend Adam felt ten feet tall. Aron still greeted him with his usual contempt and his parents didn't seem to notice anything strange but Auntie Jo seemed bemused by his sudden good humour. 'Are you feeling OK?'

Adam grinned. 'Walking on air.'

Auntie Jo snorted. 'Hmmmph. Long way to fall from up there.'

Adam frowned. He toned things down after that, feeling his aunt's beady stare following him around the house. It was a relief to return to school on Monday. After sending their email to The Bulb, Adam and his friends had gathered eagerly in the library every breaktime and lunchtime, hoping for a reply. For a few days nothing had happened. Today however, Adam could tell something was different. When he arrived at the start of break, the other three were already huddled round Spike's laptop.

Dan looked up first and grinned through a mouthful of cashews. 'The eagle has landed, I repeat, the eagle has landed.'

Spike's face was triumphant. 'I'll admit it – I was starting to worry. But it looks like he's taken the bait.'

They shifted over so Adam could peer at The Bulb's reply:

Dear Sensei,

I am flattered but not surprised that you have contacted me. Like you I am a sensei, teaching the uneducated. As you rightly say I am well known in wrestling circles (the allegations against me were due to jealousy, nothing more).

Perhaps you have never seen our Western wrestling done properly by a real professional. I am willing to give a demonstration. You will find me more than worthy of instruction.

Bulber

Adam felt a slow smile spread across his face. He shook his head in wonder. 'How can he not realise that *anyone* can set up an email account? He's even dumber than I thought.'

Spike grinned. 'I know. The fish is on the hook. So we'll mess with his mind a bit first and then we'll reel him in.'

They fell silent, looking at each other, slightly overawed by their new-found power. Dan was biting his lip. 'When you say mess with his mind . . . what were you thinking?'

Spike frowned. 'Well, we can't make it *too* easy for him.'

Adam nodded. 'The last email. We said he had to *prove*

he was worthy. So we need to give him something to do.'

Archie scowled. 'Give him something really painful.' He pulled out his notebook and began to sketch an eerily life-like picture of The Bulb being tied in knots by a hideous, scaly monster. He was in a rage because The Bulb had banned the new after-school manga club, claiming that manga was 'unsuitable' for teenagers.

Spike shook his head. 'We have to be smart about this. First rule of war: never let emotions dictate what you do.'

Dan piped up. 'You can't just tell him to bang his head on the wall or stuff like that. He's such a psycho he'd probably *enjoy* that. So we have to make it hard for him. Like, maybe he has to be nice to people or something.'

Spike nodded thoughtfully. 'I think what The Bulb needs is to get in touch with his softer side.'

'Haiku!' Adam blurted out.

They stared at him. 'Haiku to you too,' Dan said politely.

Adam rolled his eyes. 'Japanese people love all that arty stuff like poetry. We wrote some before in English. Haiku – little three-line poems. We'll tell him he has to write some poems.'

'Yes!' They all jumped. Archie was leering around the table, face alight with fiendish glee. 'And make him *read them out* to people!'

There was a murmur of admiration. Dan's eyes were shining. 'I could die happy after seeing that!'

Spike's fingers were already flying over the keys. 'Hmmmmm . . . Haiku . . . oh yeah, I remember these. "A

75

short poem consisting of three lines, with a syllable ratio of five-seven-five".'

Archie's eyebrows drew together. 'What does that even mean?'

Spike spoke in slow and patient tones. 'Well, *your* haiku would be something like, "My name is Archie / I draw ninjas in knickers / Because I'm a perv."'

Adam laughed. 'We'll make him write some love haiku. Everyone knows he fancies Miss Lumpton.' There was a collective shudder. Miss Lumpton was a solid, bosomy woman of indeterminate age, who taught both woodwork and PE. She was very tall – so tall that The Bulb was able to look straight at her chest every time he talked to her. He wasn't very subtle about it.

Once again the laptop was pushed towards Adam. It didn't take as long to produce the email this time.

Dear Bulber-san,

We have considered your words and have decided to give you the chance to prove your worth. The true warrior is in touch with his deepest feelings. It is time for you to share your love with the world. Our beautiful Japanese poetic form Haiku should prove perfect for this job. Perhaps you could inspire your students with your poetic words.

Opening the gates
Of learning to the worthy,
I am, The Sensei.

Dan reread the message and nodded sagely. 'Good idea giving him a clue how to do it. We don't want his head exploding before he gets us to Japan.'

Adam frowned. 'We don't want his head exploding full stop.' He'd seen it before and it wasn't pretty. He ignored the odd looks the others were giving him and hit *send*.

They weren't expecting instant results so it came as a shock to hear the subdued ping of an email arriving in the sensei's inbox just a few minutes later. Spike scrambled to open the latest offering.

Dear Sensei,

I am honoured by your faith in me. Here in England I am famous as a man of profound emotion. My students can tell you what a caring man I am. My ex-wife even told me I was a man who loved too much (she was talking about wrestling but I think this shows my passionate nature).

By happy coincidence I am considered something of a poet amongst my close acquaintances. I can't promise to write a hayki but I have several long poems written about the sport I love and a very special woman in my life. My students will be thrilled to hear me speak from the heart in our next assembly.

Bulber

PS: Should I video my speech to prove it took place? Or will that not be necessary as one man of honour to another?

There was a stunned silence as they digested the content of the email. Then, slowly, Archie began punching the air, an expression of the most profound happiness on his face. 'This is un-be-*lievable*!'

Adam had to clear his throat before he could speak. 'Is he . . . He's actually going to read them out? Like, in *assembly*? *And* he's offering to *video* it?'

Dan whipped out his inhaler. 'I'm not sure I can take this.' He took a quick puff and breathed deeply. 'I mean, this is going to be like watching a car crash in slow motion.'

Not exactly, Adam thought but didn't say anything. 'He *is* going to totally humiliate himself.'

Even Archie shifted uncomfortably in his chair. 'He'll never live it down.'

Spike stared around at them, face aghast. 'What is the *matter* with you lot?!' He stood up to better make his point. 'Why are you feeling sorry for that nutter? He wants to cancel the Japan trip and make us spend a week gouging each other's eyes out!' He shook his head, disgusted at their lack of spine. 'He deserves it!'

The plan might have fallen apart at that point when another ping signalled a new message in the sensei's inbox. There was a lot of pushing and shoving to read it.

PPS: Just wanted to tell you how excited I am about this. I've been meaning to share my words of wisdom with the pupils for some time now and this has given me the push I needed. I look forward to

sending you the video so you can see the profound and
powerful effect of my message.

B

They stared at the screen, mouths gaping. 'He's as mad as a badger,' whispered Archie, shaking his head in awe.

Spike grinned. 'Gentlemen, this is what is called a win-win situation. No reason to hold back now. He *wants* to do it!'

Dan took another hit from his inhaler. 'I'm going to see if I can borrow my dad's camcorder. It's one of those tiny spy ones that looks like a pen. I want to be able to watch it over and over and over . . .'

Spike turned to Adam and raised an eyebrow. 'You're not chickening out, are you?'

'Of course not!' Adam scowled. 'He's signed his own death warrant as far as I'm concerned!' He wasn't a saint. If The Bulb was *that* stupid all Adam could do was stand back and enjoy the show.

'Excellent!' Spike clasped his hands almost as if in prayer. 'Gentlemen, remember this day. On Thursday in assembly The Bulb will make school history. It's a day that will never be forgotten – but we're the only ones who'll ever know that it started right here, right now.'

Dan stood up, totally overexcited. 'Who's with me?!'

They stared at him in silence. Spike sighed. 'There are some things you just can't teach . . .'

*

It was biology after break. Adam took his time walking there. He was so busy pretending that he didn't care if Melissa was there that he almost knocked her over in the doorway. When she turned and glared, he started, flushed and tittered all at the same time. 'Sorry. Didn't see you.' *That laugh made me sound like a little girl . . .* Inside his mind he watched his mirror image slap his own forehead.

'Earth to Adam,' she muttered, waving her hand in front of his eyes.

Adam gave her a toothy grin. 'That's what my name means actually.' His smile wavered in the face of her look of honest confusion. 'You know, "Adam". It means earth. Or man. Something like that.'

She made that face he was coming to recognise – the one that said she thought he was a bit mental but probably harmless. Shrugging, she flung her bag under the bench and sank onto her stool. Her cheeks were pale and she had dark circles under her eyes. She was quiet again today, setting up equipment without her usual chat.

Adam studied her while he pretended to read through their method sheet. He obviously wasn't as subtle as he thought because without even turning towards him she said, 'You're doing the staring thing again.'

'What? Staring? Not staring . . .' he mumbled and retreated behind his notebook.

Melissa sighed and turned her laser eyes on him. 'You *were* staring. But it's OK. I know I look like crap.'

'Were you sick last week or something?' Belatedly, he wished he had told her that she didn't look crap. She looked very not-crap. *As always*. That last thought made him feel uneasy.

Something haunted crossed her face. '*I* wasn't.' She saw his unspoken question and sighed. 'My mum wasn't well. She gets sick sometimes.'

'Oh right.' Adam stared at the bench, wishing he knew what he was supposed to say. He didn't want to sound nosy and he didn't want to seem like he wasn't interested. Caught between those twin impulses he decided to play it safe and say nothing at all.

Oddly enough this seemed to be the invitation she needed to talk. 'She's been sick a lot recently. I keep telling her to go to the doctor but she's scared to miss work.'

'What does she do?'

'She works in a shop. It's pretty near where we live.' Melissa chewed her lip. 'She was walking home last week with her friend and she just fell down. Right on the street.' Her hand made a soft thud on the bench. 'She said she was just tired.'

Adam frowned. 'She should go to the doctor. Her boss has to give her time off work for that.'

'Oh, does he *really*?' Melissa gave him a look somewhere between pity and contempt. 'He doesn't *have* to do anything. Where *we* live there aren't that many jobs around. If you're the boss you make the rules.' She shook her head, clearly regretting the whole conversation. 'What do your parents do?'

Adam hated the question but he had a well-rehearsed answer. 'My dad's a businessman. He travels a lot. And my mum doesn't do anything.' *Except make me feel useless*. He felt an unexpected twinge of guilt, thinking about his neatly folded clothes and tidy bedroom. 'You know, she stays at home. Looks after us. Makes big dinners.'

She gave him an odd, tight smile. 'Must be nice.'

Something clenched in Adam's stomach and stung him into answering. 'Not really. It must be boring as hell. Anyway she couldn't have worked.'

Melissa looked at him curiously. 'Why not?'

Adam silently cursed himself. For about a millisecond he imagined telling her the truth. *Excellent question, Melissa. We're actually weirdos with supernatural powers, who send dead people into the afterlife. We're also real chauvinists who think women should stay at home having little Luman babies and cooking, whether they want to or not.* It was a sweet thought but he settled for saying, 'It's against her beliefs.'

He regretted it as soon as he saw her eyes widen. 'Is she some weird religion?'

'You *are* a girl after all,' he muttered. Where he'd gone wrong was answering the first question. That was how they got you. You thought there was only going to be one but it was like a snowball rolling down a hill and turning into an avalanche. After surviving Auntie Jo's grilling technique he should have been prepared but somehow Melissa had sneaked below his radar.

She was smiling a little, as if she'd read his mind. 'Am I asking too many questions?'

He shrugged. 'Kind of. But it's OK. It's just that we need to finish up.'

She arched one eyebrow. 'I'll have to get you on your own some time.'

It was like everything stopped. Adam froze on the spot. What did she mean, get him on his own? Was that a threat or a promise? And where would she ever get him on his own? Did she want to meet up with him outside school? He suddenly realised he was hoping that was exactly what she meant.

He could just *ask* her if she wanted to go out. After all, they'd been talking for the last couple of weeks. Occasionally he caught her looking at him. He'd always assumed she was just checking he wasn't doing anything mad. But maybe she was looking at him because she liked him? And if she did he *had* to ask her out because the hint was all he was going to get. Could he actually just ask her out there and then? All these thoughts flew through his head at the speed of light. They made him reel.

He got a grip on himself. There would never be a better time. 'We could go out some night.' His words fell out in a blurt, stumbling over each other, becoming one long, garbled sound. Half of him prayed that she hadn't heard and the other half prayed that she had – because he would never find the courage to ask her again.

Her head was tilted to one side and she was giving him one of those cool, appraising looks that she specialised in. 'Go out where?'

His heart was thumping. This was worse than sending a soul onto the Unknown Roads! *Please don't let me bleed or throw up! It will not be cool!* He cleared his throat. 'Anywhere really. We could go to the cinema?'

Her face grew thoughtful. 'I know someone who works in the Arts Cinema. I can get free tickets when it's quiet. I was going to go on Wednesday night.'

'Yeah, sounds good.' He sounded so casual. How was that even possible? He had just asked a girl out!!! Inside his chest a choir was singing, something loud and triumphant. There were trombones and fireworks.

'OK. So I'll get Ben to get us some tickets, will I?'

The choir faltered. One guy struggled on in a cracked falsetto. 'Erm . . . yeah.' Adam tried to find a way to ask the next question without sounding pathetic. 'Is Ben your friend? Or . . . you know . . .'

Melissa shrugged. 'Oh, just a friend.' She paused and gave him a mischievous look. 'Let's just say that you're more his type than I am.'

'Oh right.' Adam coughed but the choir was back in business. 'That's great. For me, I mean.' He stopped and tried to let his brain catch up with his mouth. 'For me with you that is, not Ben.' *What?!* He was saved, literally, by the bell.

Melissa was grinning and not quite meeting his eye. 'You're pretty smooth, Adam.'

He smiled weakly. 'I try.'

She scribbled something down on a piece of paper. 'Here's my mobile number, OK?' She hesitated. 'So . . . just text me, yeah?'

'Will do.' Adam watched her walking away, resisting the temptation to wave at her back. As he made his way to his next class, he reflected that life was something of a yo-yo. One minute it was rubbish and the next it was great. The last seventy-two hours had been pretty amazing. He had saved someone's life, set The Bulb up *and* got himself a date with Melissa.

His heart sang. 'I love my life,' he whispered.

Chapter 7

dam spent the next forty-eight hours in an agony of suspense. He had fought the temptation to text Melissa the second she left the biology lab. He sat on his hands through most of lunchtime, earning some odd looks from his friends but by the time he got home he couldn't resist any longer. 'Hi this is my number Adam.'

Her reply was short and sweet. 'OK.' Adam had frowned and pondered every possible meaning of the word 'OK'. Luc would have been ashamed of him. But OK what? OK, she had the number and she would be in touch? OK, whatever? OK, sucker, you didn't actually think I was going to go out with you-OK? His heart quailed at the thought of having to face her in class if she didn't get back to him.

His fears proved unfounded. She texted the following day to tell him that Ben had saved them tickets and was very much looking forward to meeting Adam . . . Adam sent a suitably casual reply and prayed that she was joking.

In registration she sat on the far side of the room from him. Adam tried not to stare but he couldn't help himself. The more he looked at her the prettier she became. She wasn't one of those girls that every boy in the school drooled over but there was something about her . . . He liked the way she walked, straight down the middle of the corridor, bag slung over one shoulder. She had a laugh with her friends but she wasn't *too* giggly. She didn't pretend to be dumb the way some girls did. And he liked the way, just occasionally, she would look up and see him watching and then she would smile.

He spent Wednesday lunchtime on his own, lurking in a quiet corridor, trying to do his homework so he would be free that night. It was there that Dan found him, scurrying along with frequent glances over his shoulder. Adam frowned, wondering what the problem was.

Dan came straight to the point. 'OK, don't freak out but Michael Bulber wants a word with you.'

Adam looked at him, mystified. The Bulb's son enjoyed torturing people but Adam had never been on his radar. 'Why would he want to talk to me?'

Dan gulped. 'He . . . erm, he's not very happy with you.'

Adam shrugged. 'That's tragic but somehow I'll have to find a way to carry on.' He could tell from Dan's wide-eyed reaction that this wasn't what he'd expected. Adam sighed. 'OK, go on then, what's his problem?'

Dan shifted from foot to foot. 'Well, there's kind of a rumour that you're going out on a date with Melissa Morgan.'

Adam felt his heart swell with pride. People knew! 'Yeah, so?'

Dan stared at him. 'But the Beast used to go out with her.'

Adam shrugged, although inside his heart bled a little. After all, he'd thought Melissa had good taste in men . . . He sighed. 'Well, she's obviously seen the light. So she *used to* go out with him. Big deal! She's not going out with him any more.'

Dan's forehead creased. 'But just because *he's* not going out with her doesn't mean he's going to allow *you* to.'

Adam glared at him. 'I don't need his *permission* to go out with Melissa.' He knew people were a bit scared of Michael Bulber but he found it hard to be scared of anyone who was only a couple of years older than him. There were so many things in the world to be scared of, things you couldn't do anything about. Earthquakes, tornadoes, plane crashes, nuclear bombs. The worst thing the Beast could do was whack him or shove his head down a toilet.

Dan was gaping at him. 'Well . . . OK. I just thought I had better warn you.'

'Cheers,' Adam mumbled. Before Dan had disappeared from view Adam was already immersed once again in his maths homework.

Hours later Adam had discovered something worth being scared about – deciding what to wear on your first date with a girl you really wanted to impress. He didn't exactly have many choices but he laid out what he had. Black tie was probably a no-no. Idly he wondered how many guys in his year had a tuxedo tucked away in their wardrobe. He doubted too many of them were dragged along to matchmaking dinners and Luman balls.

His jeans and boots were a given but he had three

different shirts he could wear. He picked the most casual one and pulled a leather jacket on over it. Standing in front of the mirror he teased his hair into a variety of shapes and styles, before squashing it back to the way he normally wore it. He would only keep playing with it all night.

He had worked out all the details – which buses to get, what time he needed to leave and how he was going to get back. He didn't go out much at night, so he had decided to use the whole 'doing his coursework' thing as an excuse. Nobody else in the house even knew what coursework *was* so he should be able to blag it. It was only six now. He would nip downstairs, have a bite of dinner and then casually say that he was heading out for a while . . .

His stomach fluttered but for once it was in a good way. He was going to take a really nice girl to the cinema. They would talk and laugh and he would do everything in his power to look *normal*. He would even answer a million questions if that was what she wanted. He spent an idle moment wondering if she would want to kiss him, then put it out of his head. He had enough to panic about in the meantime . . .

There was a sudden cacophony downstairs. Morty and Sam were barking – barking in a way that made Adam's stomach lurch. 'Oh crap, no way,' he muttered, frozen with disbelief. At the same time there was a sudden pounding of feet on the stairs and Luc burst into Adam's room.

'Yo! You're up. Big one, we're all going, even the dogs.'

Adam stared at him in horror. 'But . . . I mean . . . what's happened?'

Luc shrugged but his voice was quivering with

excitement. 'There's been a coup. Some country in West Africa, *loads* of people dead. All the fast-response Lumen are going – from *everywhere*!' For once, he looked nervous. 'This is the real deal, bro. We've never done anything like this. It's going to be . . . serious.'

Adam's heart sank through his feet and into the floorboards. 'But I can't! I have to go out.'

Luc gawked at him, then slowly shook his head. 'You know, normally it's kind of funny when you're so crap at everything. But this is something major. This is what we *do*.'

Adam's guts were in freefall but he made one last desperate stab at escape. 'But you know I can't do it! What's the point in making me go when I'm so rubbish at the whole thing? Would *you* want me guiding you? I'm a liability!'

Luc opened his mouth to retort but before he could say anything Nathanial roared up the stairs. 'Luc! Adam! Get down here!'

Adam groaned but Luc was already racing down the stairs two at a time. Adam stared at his reflection and tried to bring his thoughts under control. *Maybe it won't take long. If it's a big job there'll be loads of Lumen there. I just have to go, guide a few souls and not throw up on myself. I can still get to the cinema, if we're back quickly . . .*

'ADAM!' Nathanial was actually bellowing now. The dogs began to howl in chorus.

'Coming!' Adam squawked back and dragged his feet down the stairs. Sometimes you just had to accept that the Fates had you backed into a corner . . .

*

In the Hinterland Adam landed badly, staggering into Luc and Aron and almost falling over one of the dogs. For once he had brought a tissue and got it to his nose before his shirt could get too badly stained, still thinking about his date. But this job . . . this was something different. Only Nathanial had ever seen anything like it and even he stood frozen. Adam stared around the Hinterland, seeing the physical world beyond, and wished he could gouge his own eyes out, rather than see anything like this ever again. Beside him Morty and Sam whimpered, keystones gleaming on their collars.

There weren't enough words in the world to describe the scene around them. They were standing in a narrow roadway, with dusty earth stretching away on either side. The earth was stained red as blood poured and dribbled from an endless mass of corpses. The sun was setting but even here in the Hinterland Adam could still hear the persistent crackle of gunfire. Hundreds – maybe even thousands – of souls stood shell-shocked over the wrecks of their own bodies while Lumen of every nationality began guiding them. Some souls were clinging together for comfort while others tried to scrabble through cloth-wrapped bundles of belongings, unable to grasp the fact that they didn't need them any more.

Nathanial's face might have been carved from marble as he surveyed the scene. A tall, handsome, black Luman saw them and strode over to embrace Nathanial. 'Brother, I thank you.'

Nathanial grasped the man's shoulders. 'We're glad to help, Zahir. But what happened?' Luc and Adam exchanged glances. Zahir was High Luman of the West African Kingdom. Luman Kingdoms didn't always follow political borders, especially when those borders had changed frequently over the centuries. The vast African continent was divided into seven separate Kingdoms, each with its own High Luman.

Zahir's face was calm but a small muscle pulsed in his jaw as he spoke. 'These people were refugees. Many of them were leaving the towns and villages, trying to cross the border. There was a battle between government soldiers and their rivals. Those fleeing were caught in the middle.' There was no anger in his expression, only a kind of weary sorrow.

Nathanial swallowed hard. 'That's why so many are women and children, yes?'

Zahir nodded. 'There are many hundreds dead and more still dying.' As if to emphasise his words there was a loud explosion further down the road and a chorus of screams. He nodded at Adam and his brothers. 'I am glad you brought your sons. We will all be needed tonight. May the Light speed you, brothers.'

As he walked away, Adam grabbed Nathanial's arm. 'We have to do something.'

Nathanial looked startled but pleased. 'We're about to. I'm glad you're so eager tonight. Let's get to wo—'

'No!' Adam interrupted. 'I mean do something about the *soldiers*. They're still killing people! We have to make them stop!'

Nathanial recoiled and Aron and Luc muttered something. Two nearby Lumen had come to greet Nathanial.

They heard Adam's words and exchanged horrified glances, before hurrying away as if embarrassed. 'I'll pretend you didn't say that,' Nathanial said softly.

Aron was less tactful. 'You are such a moron.'

Adam turned on him. 'You're the moron!' His heart was beating too fast. He turned back to Nathanial. 'We could stop them killing all those people. We could just . . . appear in front of them or something. Scare them! We could pretend to be journalists! Make them think everyone knows what they're doing!'

Two spots of colour had appeared on Nathanial's pale cheeks. 'Have I taught you nothing? You know we cannot intervene! It is for the Fates to determine whether these people live or die. Our job is to help those who have perished.' He turned away, ready to start work.

'It's evil!' Adam hissed. His anger felt dangerous, like it might boil over into violence. He tried to take a deep breath but his lungs were too tight and his heart was thudding too hard. 'It's evil watching all these people die and not doing anything to stop it. If we don't do anything then we're as evil as those soldiers!'

Nathanial wheeled around and gripped Adam's shoulder hard. His eyes glittered. 'If you want to help these people then do the job you were born to do and don't try to change what cannot be changed.' He whistled for the dogs and stalked away without another word. Aron shot him a disgusted look and followed his father.

Luc stared at him with a kind of wary respect. He started to say something, then broke off. A disturbance of some kind had broken out amongst the souls. Those Lumen who weren't already guiding began sprinting towards the scene from all directions.

Adam felt drawn towards what was happening along with everyone else. He followed Luc towards the commotion. Female voices were shouting and the only women there were the dead. As he got closer he saw what was happening and his heart jolted.

The souls of two dead soldiers were cowering together in the centre of a large group of furious women. One of them was screaming, her face twisted with hate. 'I know you! You killed my husband and my son, two days ago! You burned our house and left us with nothing! That's why we had to run!' She began to sob.

Another woman pushed through. She dragged forward the soul of a small girl, who stood chewing her thumbnail, terrified. 'You shot my daughter!' Her face was etched with horror and disbelief. 'I screamed at you! I begged you, please don't hurt her. She is a child! You shot her there in front of me! And then you shot me!' She broke down and wept, while her child clung to her. There was an angry murmur of sympathy and disgust.

The soldiers' eyes darted from side to side. They made Adam think of cornered animals. Both of them were young and fit, but one had a stupid, brutish look about him. The other one had a certain wily cunning in his expression. He tried to take control of the situation, even here in the Hinterland. 'I did not kill you, woman. You are mistaken. Get away from us!'

There was a roar of fury from the women and they surged in. The man screamed in sudden terror, understanding at last that his gun wouldn't save him here and that these women would tear him limb from limb if they could. Suddenly Lumen burst through the crowd and gathered around the men. They joined hands and a great ripple of light passed between them, forming a circle of golden flames. The women fell back, unable to breach it.

Zahir stood in front of them. His sorrow was so naked and painful that Adam almost looked away. It quietened most of the women, apart from the one still holding her child. 'Why are you protecting them? They murdered us in cold blood!'

Zahir bowed his head. 'My heart is bleeding,' he said softly, so softly that it made the fine hairs on the back of Adam's neck rise. 'We are not the judges, only the guides. Each of you has a road to walk now but I believe . . .' His voice faltered for a second, then grew stronger. 'I believe that we will all make account for what we do. I send these men to answer for their actions.'

There was murmur through the crowd, a mixture of satisfaction and disgust. The brutish soldier was looking all around, frantic to escape. He seemed relieved when one of the African Lumen stepped forward and quietly began reciting the Unknown Roads.

The cunning soldier wasn't convinced. 'What do you mean, called to account? I was just following orders!' His voice was high and cracked. 'I won't go! You can't make me go!'

Zahir stared at him and for just a second his eyes glittered. 'No, I cannot make you go. I will simply tell you the way, as is my duty. But if you choose to stay – there is nothing for you here. Only the Hinterland.' He waved around them. 'Your Light will remain but only you can choose to walk through it.' He began to murmur in the soldier's ear but the young man shrugged his hand away and cursed him.

Adam didn't watch any more. There were souls everywhere – he had never seen so many in such a small area. More Lumen were arriving but the sound of shots, explosions and screams still pierced the veil between the physical world and the Hinterland. New souls kept appearing, faster than the Lumen could guide them. He was going to have to do his bit.

And he did, for once without complaint. His resentment seemed small and petty, in the face of so much sorrow and misery. He watched Nathanial ask the mother and her child if they wanted to walk the Unknown Roads together and send them gently into their Light. Aron and Luc worked alongside some Lumen he recognised and many others he didn't. Sam and Morty wove in and out of the souls, gently herding them together with a nudge of their noses. The soul of a little boy clung to Sam's fur, resting his forehead on the wolfhound's shoulder, and the big dog turned and licked his face tenderly.

Adam sent four souls onto the Unknown Roads and when he was sick, he simply wiped his mouth and carried on, losing all track of time. Night had fallen swiftly and at last the sounds of gunfire were petering out. Some of the souls had been waiting for hours. They seemed shell-shocked by everything that had happened, grateful to give themselves into a Luman's care.

Finally the crowd had thinned. The Lumen from other parts of the world were clasping hands and saying their parting words while the African Lumen wearily finished guiding the last few souls. Nathanial came and stood with his sons, giving Adam a neutral look. Zahir approached them. 'Thank you, brothers, as ever.'

Nathanial nodded and said the traditional words between Lumen. 'Our Light is your Light, brother.'

Adam glanced at the young soldier, still standing by his Light, refusing to step through it. Zahir followed the direction of his eyes and his mouth set into a hard line. 'He will go through. Sometimes they wait for a long time but in the end they will all go through.' He shrugged. 'I hope for his sake he will listen to the directions he is given.'

The soldier saw Adam staring and glared at him. 'What are you looking at?' he spat. There was a sheen of sweat on his soul's smooth, dark skin. His mind was still clinging to his physical memories, unwilling to accept that his life was over.

Adam shook his head and turned away, feeling sick to his stomach. The soldier made his skin crawl. All he wanted to do was get out of here. And a moment later he gathered with his family and swooped for home.

Fine drizzle was falling when they arrived back in the garden. They made a subdued group; even the dogs slunk towards their beds with their tails between their legs. It was the middle of the night, the darkest hours before dawn. Elise had left the kitchen light on and a flask of hot chocolate but none of them felt like drinking it. Nathanial shrugged off his camel-hair coat and gestured to his sons to follow him into the study.

He switched on the lamp and perched on the edge of his desk while they stood silently in front of the bookcases. Adam could see that his father's face was almost grey in the dim light, etched with exhaustion and something else. Nathanial looked at them each in turn for a long moment before he finally spoke. 'I'm sorry you had to see that tonight.'

They shifted from foot to foot, Adam and Luc exchanging uneasy glances. Nathanial never apologised for taking them on jobs. As far as he was concerned death was a part of life and as Lumen their lives were not really their own. They were only doing their duty.

Nathanial cleared his throat. 'I always knew that eventually I would have to take you on that kind of job.' He gave a ghost smile. 'Somehow an earthquake or a landslide just seems unfortunate. It's nobody's fault – there's nothing personal in it. But tonight . . . A job like that is the very worst kind. I understand the temptation to intervene but that is not our role. All we can do is help the dead as best we can.' He was careful not to look at Adam as he said this.

Adam stared at the floor, feeling his cheeks burn. He could almost feel *The Book of the Unknown Roads* reproaching him. He tried to remember exactly what he had said to his father earlier that evening, gripped by a strange mixture of guilt and defiance. He had accused Nathanial of being evil, of ignoring the suffering of those being slaughtered; of being as bad as the soldier. He knew that wasn't fair – but somehow it seemed almost as bad to stand back and *watch* an evil thing happening as it was to do it. Even thinking about the woman and her child sent a brief, hot flare of rage through him.

Nathanial sighed. 'It's getting late. You should go to bed and get some sleep. You made me proud tonight, all of you. If there's any justice there won't be another call-out before the morning.'

Aron and Luc shuffled towards the door, with Adam bringing up the rear. Just as Adam was about to leave the room he felt a hand on his shoulder and turned. Nathanial's expression was more raw and unguarded than Adam had ever seen before. 'I know how difficult it is to make sense of what happened tonight. This is something that all of us have to struggle with. There is nothing I can say that will make it any easier but I hope that in time you'll learn that our laws are there for a *reason*. Sometimes there is a bigger picture that we can't see.'

Adam stared at him bleakly. He wanted to say something generous and sympathetic but no words came to mind. There was just a dark space there, full of the sound of women sobbing. His body felt different, as if a great weight was resting upon his shoulders, pressing him down into the floor.

The worst thing was he knew it wasn't just witnessing the massacre. Part of it was knowing that tonight he had lost some of his respect for his father – and he wasn't sure if it would ever come back.

Upstairs Adam flicked on the light and stared around his room as if he had never seen it before. There was his bed, with the faded blue duvet. There were the curtains, closed above the desk where his mobile lay. He had a sudden, brutal flashback and gasped at the force of it. Dusty road, dark green leaves, blood soaking into the ground and eyes staring at him, empty and dead in the physical world, stunned in the Hinterland.

He was sweating, a cold film of it all over his body, and it made him feel dirty. In the mirror, he could see his shirt had reddish-brown bloodstains on the collar and front. A small crust of sick had dried in one corner of his mouth. His hair was stuck to his head and his eyes were like blue marbles in a saucer of milk. Nine hours earlier he had been planning to meet Melissa for his date.

He dragged his feet over to the desk and stared at his mobile like it might explode at any second. Had she phoned him? Texted him? He didn't think she was the kind of girl who would forgive and forget being stood up. Why the hell hadn't he brought his mobile? Maybe he could have slipped away somewhere, into the undergrowth and sent a quick message . . . *'Sorry, can't make it, taking care of dead people in Africa . . .'* Yeah, of course he could have.

He touched the screen and saw a new message waiting. There was only one. 'Where are you?' Then nothing. He imagined her tapping her phone, looking up and down the street on tiptoe, biting her lip a little. He imagined her puzzlement and disbelief and finally anger when she realised that he wasn't coming. He had blown it.

He crawled into bed and pulled the cover over his head, willing himself to sleep; keeping his life at bay for a few precious hours.

100

Chapter 8

hen Adam woke up the next morning the whole world looked grey. He lay blinking for several seconds and realised he was still under the duvet. Worse, he realised that his alarm hadn't gone off – he hadn't set it the night before. He flung back the cover and gave a despairing groan at the time. He should have been in school half an hour before.

Normally he would have sprung into action but instead he lay back in bed and pulled the duvet up to his chin. He should have been cosy but something was wrong. He felt flat and depressed. He couldn't be bothered getting up. What was the point? Either he would have to go into school and face Melissa's wrath or he would have to stay here and get sent on call-outs. It was, as Spike would say, a lose-lose situation.

What could he say to Melissa to make her understand? He ground the heels of his hands into his eyes and tried to find some inspiration. The problem with his life was that he could never be totally honest with anyone. He was trying to live in two worlds without ever belonging fully in either.

Sometimes he longed to tell his friends the truth about his family. He was tired of never inviting them round, telling constant lies. The trouble was it would be too easy to make a mistake – say the wrong thing, swoop in front of a visitor . . . and then the Luman world would be exposed. It was impossible for Adam to bring his two worlds together – but there were only so many times you could pretend your sister had measles or that workmen were wrecking the place.

And what about Melissa – or any other girl for that matter? If he wanted to have a girlfriend he was going to have to bring them back eventually – except he couldn't. How was he going to get round that? Never date anyone until he had left home? Pretend his whole family was dead? Tell lies for the rest of his life?

In the end, this was why Lumen stuck together. They grew up together and married each other and had children together – because who else could possibly understand what they did? They were human beings but not the same as everyone else. Something about them was different.

The scientist in Adam was always curious about what made him special. Why could he swoop and see the Hinterland when his friends couldn't? Obviously the keystones were part of it but there was more to it. Was it genetic – something in his DNA? Or was it just that he had been taught from childhood to see the world differently? After all, his friends didn't even know the Hinterland was *there*. Maybe the truth lay somewhere in between.

He sighed. Whatever his problems were, lying in bed

wasn't going to solve any of them. It was time to get up and face the world – or rather both his worlds.

When he walked into the kitchen Luc was already there, munching on a pile of French toast. He appeared to have upended an entire bowl of sugar over the top slice and was crunching his way through it with relish. He raised an eyebrow when he saw Adam. 'Thought you'd have been away to playschool by now.'

'Slept in,' Adam mumbled. He threw some bread in the toaster and squinted into the fridge for inspiration. In the end he settled for a banana and chocolate spread.

Luc set his knife and fork down with a sigh, obviously needing a break. 'Ahhhh, breakfast of champions. *You* could do this every day if you stopped messing around pretending to be normal. As if anyone wants to be *normal*.'

Adam snorted. 'Yeah, imagine getting to make French toast all day every day. What a brilliant way to spend your life.'

Luc grinned. 'I don't make it actually. Chloe's best at it. She makes it and I eat it.'

Adam rolled his eyes. 'Don't you ever get bored?'

Luc paused and frowned. He'd clearly never thought about it before. 'Of course I don't get bored. I haven't got time to be bored.'

'But what do you *do* all day?' Adam persisted. Suddenly he really wanted to know. After all, maybe *he* was the idiot. Maybe Luc got to spend all day doing really cool things in between call-outs while Adam slogged through English and history.

A shifty expression came over Luc's face. 'This and that. Places to go, people to see – you know?'

Adam didn't know but he wasn't going to admit that to Luc. It was something of an enigma, how Luc managed to seem so at ease in his Luman life *and* the 'normal' world. Certainly he spent most of his free time out and about, but no one ever knew what he was up to. Knowing Luc, whatever he was doing he was having a good time. 'Don't you ever feel like you're just wasting your life?'

For the first time Luc looked stung – not to mention incredulous. 'We're Lumen! We're doing what we're born to do! Do you reckon the dead think we're wasting our time when they're standing there lost, wondering what the hell's going on?' He shook his head, looking disgusted. 'The rest of us do fine. *You're* the one spending your life with your face in a pile of books. If anyone is wasting their life it's *you*.'

Adam felt his fists clench. 'Those books are going to help me save people's lives.'

Luc laughed without malice. 'Everybody dies, Adam. You're just delaying the inevitable. And that's why we'll never be out of business. Best job in the world.'

Adam gave up trying to talk to him. The problem with his family was that they all thought life revolved around death. He smeared chocolate spread on his toast and tried to plan what he was going to say to Melissa. How angry was she going to be on a scale of one to ten . . . ?

Luc interrupted his thoughts. 'Oh, Mother said don't make any plans for Saturday night – not that *you* ever have any. She's having a dinner party and we all have to be there.' He adopted hushed, dramatic tones. 'The Concilium are honouring us with their presence!'

Adam's heart sank. Brilliant. Just as he had started breaking Luman law, the Luman law-enforcement authority had decided to pay a visit. Of course there was no reason why they should know anything about what he had been doing. Nathanial was High Luman so the Concilium visited at least once a year, as a courtesy. Elise always got in a flap but it gave her an excuse to buy a new dress and show off some fiendishly difficult recipe.

Luc was still talking. 'They'll probably start fishing to see who Chloe's going to be betrothed to.'

Adam nodded without speaking. The whole betrothal thing freaked him out. There was something so medieval about it all – and yet he could understand the logic behind it. It kept the Luman families united, especially the most powerful and prosperous. It stopped turf wars over souls and Keystones and meant that Luman children grew up knowing they were part of a global network of Lumen. It gave them a place in the world.

Everyone had a place in the world – apart from him. He chewed through the last bite of banana, throwing a surreptitious glance at Luc, who was still happily devouring his French toast. Why couldn't he be happy with what he had, just like Luc? He could stay here all day, playing computer games or watching TV or taking the dogs out. Maybe he would even find out how Luc whiled away the hours.

As if Luc was reading his mind he spoke. 'Look, if you want to stay home today, I suppose you could come out with me. Just going to meet a few friends but they probably wouldn't mind if you tagged along.' He rubbed his hands together. 'Got a few things lined up for this afternoon if there aren't any call-outs.'

Adam wavered for a second, tempted. He was curious about how Luc spent a typical day – who he hung out with, how he knew them, what they got up to . . . It had to be more interesting than geography! But at last his conscience won and he stood up with a sigh. 'No thanks. I'm going to go and stick my face in some books. And then some day, when you come off the motorbike you're not supposed to have, I'll sew your leg back on. You can thank me then.'

Adam arrived at school just in time for the start of break. To his mingled disappointment and relief there was no sign of Melissa. She was probably with her friends, telling them all what a loser he was . . .

As he jogged along the corridors he noticed the atmosphere in school was different. There was a kind of near-hysteria in the air. People were cackling and talking too loudly. He noticed two boys in his year pretending to declaim something, while the crowd around them collapsed with laughter. It was only when he reached the library and found his friends that he realised what had happened.

Dan stood up so fast that his chair fell over and thunked onto the carpet. 'You missed it! How could you *miss it?*'

Adam stared at their disapproving faces in bewilderment. 'Miss what?'

Archie shook his head in disbelief. 'You missed *assembly!*'

'Oh . . . right,' he mumbled, trying to sound disappointed. 'Yeah, you know, dentist.'

Spike gave him a suspicious look. 'You missed the chance to see The Bulb's humiliation so you could go to the *dentist*?'

Adam's eyes widened. 'I forgot,' he said, knowing they wouldn't believe him. Only something serious could make you forget that your psycho head teacher was going to humiliate himself in front of the whole school. Something major, like a bloody massacre in West Africa . . .

Dan cut in. 'It was amazing. No other word.' He slumped back in his now upright chair, expression blissful. 'It was kind of like . . . spiritual.'

They fell silent, faces rapt. After a moment Adam cleared his throat. 'So he actually *did it* then?'

Spike grinned. 'Oh yes. And luckily for you, we recorded it for posterity.'

Dan produced what looked like a fancy pen. 'I brought my dad's spy camera. We were just about to hook it up.'

Adam almost asked why anyone's dad would want a spy camera but decided now wasn't the time. They didn't call Dan's dad the Dark Lord for nothing . . . He watched Spike attach a cable to the pen and connect it to his laptop. A moment later a wobbly image appeared on the screen – a sea of heads, a stage and The Bulb striding to his lectern. The camera swivelled wildly from side to side, making Adam feel seasick.

Dan shifted in his chair. 'Takes a bit of getting used to.'

The figure on the screen suddenly jumped closer – Dan had obviously discovered the zoom button. The Bulb stared down at the teachers and pupils below with an unusually benign expression. Something that might have been a smile crept across his lips. For some reason it made him *more* terrifying, rather than less so and a swift silence fell in the hall.

The Bulb cleared his throat. 'All of you know that before I became a teacher I was a professional sportsman. A wrestler!' The word rolled off his tongue with such relish that Adam shivered. 'However, this doesn't mean that I don't have a sensitive side. *Au contraire*, I consider myself something of a poet! And today I have decided to share some of my musings with you all.'

Adam held his breath, not quite sure what he was going to see. The Bulb stared around the hall and then in a fit of daring pulled his tie down and tore it over his head. He rolled up his sleeves and undid his top button. And then The Bulb began.

The next few minutes passed in a blur, literally. Tears were pouring down Adam's cheeks. He could barely see. Somehow Dan ended up on the floor in a ball, convulsed with laughter. Archie clutched onto the nearest bookshelf, doubled over, hiccupping weakly. Only Spike watched the whole thing with a tight little smile, but his eyes blazed with triumph.

On screen The Bulb finally came to a stop. His expression was one of benevolent pride. Clearly he was delighted with his performance. Adam wasn't quite sure how. Even from the tinny laptop speakers it was clear that every pupil in the Hall was laughing hysterically. Off screen he could hear the sound of someone retching. Maybe from where The Bulb was standing it sounded like cheering.

Dan managed to crawl onto his knees. 'I think my favourite one was the Ode to Lumpton.' He held one hand up in the air and stared at the ceiling, rapt. 'The great wedge of your beautiful bosoms! Your luscious lips! Your succulent smile!'

Archie was still gasping, having run out of oxygen for anything more. 'Nah, the wrestling one was better. Especially that bit about "the sweaty grapple of your naked flesh".'

Adam shook his head. 'I can't believe he did it. He *actually did it*!' His spirits lifted just a little.

Archie grinned. 'He didn't just do it, he loved doing it! He emailed the sensei straight afterwards to brag about it.'

'So we set him another little job.' Dan gloated.

Adam felt a momentary twinge of guilt. 'Isn't the poem enough? I mean, he's made a tit of himself, even if he doesn't realise it.'

Spike rolled his eyes. 'Oh, don't worry, your Holiness, we made it easy. We told him to show love to an enemy. And since *we're* his enemies it might work to our advantage.'

Adam grinned. He was glad now that he had come into school. It was a symbol of everything he wanted – the chance to have a normal life, just like everyone else. Luc didn't know what he was missing!

Spike kept his expression neutral. 'So . . . Heard you had a date last night. How did it go?'

Adam sighed, the good feelings abandoning him. 'It didn't. Well, *I* didn't. I couldn't go.'

Archie winced. 'Ah. That explains a lot.'

Adam's heart skittered. 'What do you mean?'

Archie pasted on a very fake smile. 'Oh, nothing to worry

about. I just heard Melissa's friends slagging you off this morning but I'm sure once you've explained . . .' He tailed off, looking at the others for help.

It was Dan who piped up, with his own particular talent for saying the wrong thing at the wrong time. He turned to Spike. 'You fancied Melissa for ages, didn't you?'

Spike drew back and something unreadable crossed his face. 'No I didn't!'

Dan persisted, as only Dan could. 'You did so! You kept searching for her online! And you used to hang around outside the art room when she was in there at lunch – ouch!' He glared at Spike and rubbed his arm. 'I'm only saying!'

The bell rang, cutting through the awkward silence that had suddenly fallen. Adam glanced at Spike, who was apparently absorbed in packing up his laptop. He wasn't quite sure what to say. Spike had never said anything about Melissa but then he *wouldn't*. He liked to pretend that he was above normal human emotions. Adam struggled to think of something to ease the tension. 'Well, cheer up. I've pretty much blown it.'

Spike shot him a cool glance. 'You do whatever you want, mate. I'm not interested. Never have been, never will be.' He tucked his laptop under his arm, walking away before anyone could follow him.

Dan grinned. 'What did I tell you? He *totally* fancies her!'

Adam kept his eyes peeled for Melissa all day, even though the cowardly part of him felt like hiding under a table rather than having to explain himself. Dan's revelation about Spike was worrying him too. He didn't want to fall out with Spike – he was one of his best friends – but why hadn't he said anything before? What were the rules in this situation? Was he supposed to back off – or did he get the girl because he had made the first move? It was frustrating.

It was after lunch before he saw her. He was still fretting about things when he saw Melissa walking along the corridor ahead of him. His heart skipped a beat but he knew it was probably better to get the conversation over with. He called her name quickly, before he could chicken out. 'Melissa!'

She turned round but her face became a mask when she saw him. 'Oh. Hello.'

'Can I talk to you for a minute?' Adam saw she was about to make an excuse so he cut in quickly before she could walk away. 'Look, I'm really, really sorry about last night. I would never have done that if I didn't have to do. I was really looking forward to seeing you.'

She shrugged but her expression thawed a little. 'So what happened?'

Adam had considered a variety of explanations, ranging from the heroic ('I saved an old lady from robbers!') to the pathetic ('My mum wouldn't let me go out!'). In the end he had decided to go with something half-truthful. 'We had kind of a family thing. Like, an emergency.'

She raised an eyebrow. 'You could have texted.'

'I got home really late *and* I ran out of credit,' he mumbled. It sounded weak but plausible.

Maybe it was his hangdog expression that convinced her in the end. She sighed. 'OK, whatever.'

She was turning and walking away. Adam felt a moment of panic and cursed his own stupidity. He hadn't really planned this far ahead. All right, she hadn't punched him in the nose but she hadn't exactly thrown herself into his arms either – not that he would have known what to do with her if she had. He cleared his throat. 'We could do it another night!'

She seemed to rotate on the spot until she was staring at him incredulously. 'What, I could hang about waiting for you? We never "did it" the first time.'

Adam resisted the urge to bang his forehead on the corridor wall. 'I know. But I did really want to. It was just . . . something came up. I couldn't get out of it.' He wished he could fall on his knees and pour out the whole sorry tale. Maybe then she would take pity on him, instead of looking at him like he was a slug.

Melissa shrugged. 'Well, it would have been nice but don't worry about it.'

'But we could go out another time. Maybe tonight?'

'I've got loads of homework tonight,' Melissa said. She didn't look too upset about it.

'Well, what about Saturday?' Adam stopped, stupefied by his own daring.

Melissa shook her head. 'I work Saturdays.'

'Tomorrow then,' he blurted out, past caring if he sounded like some desperate stalker type. 'Tomorrow night, if you haven't got anything planned.'

Melissa stared at him. Her expression was unreadable. 'I don't usually go out on Friday night. I have to be up early on Saturday for work.'

'Well, maybe something quick. You know, just . . .' He tailed off and froze. What *did* you do with a girl on a Friday night? His brain rewarded him with several images, all of which would have earned him a slap. He felt his cheeks flaming.

She looked at him curiously. 'You're pretty keen for someone who stood me up. If you were me, would *you* go out with you tomorrow night?'

Adam had to take a moment to translate what she was saying. 'Probably not,' he muttered. 'But maybe I'd look at me and realise how much I wanted to go out and how sorry I was for messing things up.'

Her eyes widened, a little startled at his honesty but she *did* smile. 'Well . . . I guess we *could* get a quick coffee. I mean, you like coffee, don't you?'

'Yeah! I love it!' Adam grinned at her, ignoring the voice in his head reminding him that coffee, like guiding souls, made him puke every time. He would have said he liked drinking cat sick if it meant she would give him another chance. 'I can call at your house for you if you want?'

'No,' she said, too quickly. 'I'll meet you in Flip Street. There are some good places around there.' She paused. 'So I'll see you about eight?'

'Yeah, sure,' Adam said, trying to look casual, humble and pleased all at the same time.

'OK. And Adam . . .' She narrowed her eyes but smiled a little. 'If you're not there tomorrow . . . Don't bother asking a third time.'

Adam grinned and watched her walking away. Yes! He was still in with a chance! He headed towards his next class with just a hint of a swagger in his step. He was almost there when something seized his shoulder, twisted him and propelled him backwards. His head thwacked painfully into the wall and for a moment Adam saw stars. After his vision had cleared he found himself blinking up at Michael Bulber.

'You're Adam Mortson, aren't you?' The corridor appeared to have mysteriously emptied behind the Beast. He was taller than his father but equally broad. His eyes were the same eerie, pale blue but unlike The Bulb he had dark hair, cut close to his head. His hands were enormous and one of them was now twisting the front of Adam's shirt.

Adam cleared his throat. 'Pleased to meet you.'

Bulber smirked. 'Likewise. I hear you know a friend of mine. Melissa Morgan?'

Adam shrugged, or rather tried to. It was hard because the Beast was still clutching his shirt. 'She's in my class.'

'But you're not in hers. She's out of your league.' Bulber leaned closer to Adam. His breath smelled like tuna sandwiches. Adam resisted the urge to turn his head away. 'She used to be my girlfriend. Maybe I'll hook up with her again sometime – or maybe not. Either way, *you* keep away from her.'

He gave Adam a little push, then let him go. He was already turning away, having delivered his warning. It had never occurred to him that Adam might have more to say on the subject. It had never occurred to Adam either but somehow he found his mouth open and words spilling out. 'Why would I do that?'

Michael Bulber paused mid-step and blinked, clearly

wondering if he had imagined the small voice beside him. He swivelled sideways and stared at Adam. 'Did you say something?'

Adam tried to dig deep and find some courage. The Beast hadn't sounded that scary before but now he was up close . . . 'You heard me. Why would I stay away from Melissa? She's not your girlfriend any more – if she ever was. I heard you just went out a couple of times.'

Bulber laughed suddenly. For such a big guy he had oddly small, pointy teeth. 'Do yourself a favour and stop talking.'

Adam shrugged. 'I'm just saying, you do—' His words were cut off by Bulber's hand grabbing his throat and pressing him back against the wall. Adam coughed and choked as the Beast glared into his eyes. Was the guy nuts? They were in the middle of a corridor! Someone could come along at any moment! Of course, Adam reflected with a sinking heart, it probably helped if your dad was the man who handed out the punishments . . .

'Michael, why aren't you in class?' They both jumped at the same time, two heads snapping sideways to find The Bulb frowning at them. He didn't seem at all perturbed that his son was holding a younger pupil pinned against a wall.

'This little tit was trying to take something of mine!' Adam did a double take. He couldn't believe the whiny voice Michael Bulber had just put on. 'I was just giving him a little warning not to do it again.' He took his time releasing Adam's throat. Adam coughed and glared at him balefully.

The Bulb sighed. 'Michael, we've had this conversation

115

before. That's why I'm here. I'm the man to come to if you have a problem.' For the first time he looked at Adam and his face tightened with dislike. 'Why are you not in class, Mortson?'

Adam gave him an incredulous look. How was he supposed to answer that? *Well, sir, I was just on my way when your psycho son decided to strangle me* . . . Somehow he didn't think that would go down too well. 'I'm just going there now, sir.'

'I'll escort him there if you want,' Bulber said. His odd, fishy eyes glinted.

Adam swallowed hard and thought quickly. 'I don't want to be Michael's enemy, sir. We just had a bit of a misunderstanding but it's important to show love and kindness to our enemies, you know? I hope he can forgive me.'

The Beast was staring at Adam as if he had lost his marbles but The Bulb had a thoughtful expression, just as Adam had hoped. He could almost hear the cogs grinding inside The Bulb's head. Was this a good opportunity to put the sensei's teaching into action? Would it be enough? There was a stand-off while The Bulb made up his mind.

At last he sighed and turned to his son. 'Meeting people like Mortson is just one of the many crosses we have to bear in this life. As my son you're my representative amongst the students and I need you to lead by example. So, I want you two to shake hands like gentlemen.'

Michael Bulber's mouth had dropped open. He stared from Adam to his father as if he were hallucinating. Adam took advantage of his confusion by holding out his hand with a suitably humble expression on his face. He even murmured, 'Sorry about the misunderstanding, mate.'

Bulber gave him a hate-filled look but with his father standing beside him he was trapped. He reached for Adam's hand but Adam was smart enough to only just touch it before he pulled his fingers to safety. No point having his hand crushed along with his throat.

The Bulb had a look of profound satisfaction on his face. He nodded, pleased. 'Right, Mortson, you can go.' He put his hand on his son's shoulder and began walking in the other direction.

Adam couldn't resist. 'Michael!' He waited for Bulber to twist towards him and tried to make his expression sincere. 'That thing you were talking about. You know, the woman problems. You should do what your dad did. Try writing her a love poem. Works every time.'

And as the Beast's face darkened with rage, Adam reflected how quickly a bad day could turn itself around.

Chapter 9

y 7:30 the following evening, Adam was pacing up and down the pavement outside a cafe called Milky Moo. Melissa had texted to say that she would meet him there at eight o'clock. Tonight he was taking no chances. He had come home from school, showered and put on a non-bloodstained shirt. He had even skipped dinner in case he somehow got caught up in a call-out.

He tried to look as if he came here all the time but secretly he was thrilled to be in Flip Street. He knew Luc liked to hang out round here but Adam had tried in vain to get invited along. Now it was Friday night and he was here, in the coolest part of the city, waiting for a girl. *An actual, real-life girl!* Admittedly as he looked into Milky Moo his heart faltered. It seemed to be full of Japanese exchange students, girls with shiny black hair and very short skirts. They were screaming a lot, in a happy kind of way. He should probably bring Archie here, especially if the Japan trip didn't go ahead . . .

He felt nervous and tried not to. He had been working with Melissa in biology for weeks now and after their awkward beginning it was easy talking to her. She was funny without being bitchy and she liked to tease him without being nasty. There were so many things he wanted to ask her. Unfortunately, he had to find a way of doing this without answering any questions in return. That was going to be the tricky bit.

He looked up and down the street, starting to enjoy the vibe. The pavements were filling up. Everyone was dressed to impress and ready for a good night. He felt so *normal* being here with everyone else, just waiting to meet a girl and hang out together. Why couldn't his life be like this all the time? *Someday it will be*, he thought. Something touched his shoulder and he spun round. Melissa was there, grinning. Her hair was pulled back off her face and tied up with some kind of clip and her eyes had dark stuff round them, making them even more like lasers. She looked amazing! 'You look really nice,' he blurted out, then stopped horrified. He hadn't even said hello yet! *Don't look desperate*, he commanded himself.

Melissa didn't seem to think he had said anything strange. 'Thanks. I guess you weren't taking any chances this time.' Her eyes glinted.

'Yeah,' Adam mumbled, rubbing his hair and feeling sheepish. 'So where would you like to go?' A chorus of shrieking and giggling rang out inside Milky Moo and he winced but tried to look enthusiastic. 'Do you want to go in here?'

Melissa looked horrified. 'God, no! I mean . . . Do *you* want to go in here?'

Adam felt weak with relief. 'No! But I don't really know what's round here.'

Melissa snorted. 'Trust me, we can do better than this.' She started walking and he followed, dazed at the number of people still pouring into Flip Street. It was too busy to talk but after a few minutes Melissa seized his hand for just a second and dragged him into one of the side streets. There was a battered sign on the wall, written in Cyrillic script, with a hammer and sickle beside it. He followed her through a steel door and down a flight of steep steps, trying to pretend his hand wasn't still tingling.

They emerged into what might have been an underground bunker. There were no windows and dim lights lit the corners. The walls were covered with old maps, mostly of Eastern Bloc states that no longer existed. The tables were low stone slabs, as were the benches, although they were at least covered with colourful, scruffy cushions.

Already the first room was buzzing with people, some their age, some older. Music beat low in the background and Adam could see two further doorways off the main room. Directly ahead of them was a long, scratched bar. A tall guy behind it spotted Melissa, jerked his head in greeting and mimed drinking a coffee. She grinned and nodded. He turned to Adam and raised an eyebrow enquiringly, holding up two fingers. Adam shook his head violently, panic-stricken at the thought of having to drink a coffee and pretend to like it. 'Just lemonade thanks,' he bellowed, far too loud. People turned and stared for a second, then returned to their conversations.

Melissa was looking at him oddly. 'Don't feel like coffee,' he said and paid for the drinks.

They wove through the crowd until Melissa somehow located a tiny space on the stone bench. They sat down but it was a tight squeeze. Adam could feel her thigh curving against his and tried to ignore it so he could still breathe.

Melissa didn't seem to notice. She was looking around with bright eyes. 'I love this place. It's called Petrograd. They make the best coffee.'

'It's nice.' Adam smiled, suddenly aware of a powerful happiness nestling in his chest. He was in Flip Street in a cool cafe with a really cool girl. He couldn't exactly say this was normal for him but at least for once it was abnormal in a good way.

Melissa recognised someone in the far corner and waved at them. 'I come here a lot. I work just round the corner. In Alter-Eden.' She said it like he should recognise the name and when he didn't her face fell a little. 'It's this brilliant shop! Really massive. Loads of vintage stuff and new designers. Not really expensive stuff, just quirky.'

They chatted for a while and Adam began to let his guard down. They swapped stories about primary school and argued over favourite films and foods. He eventually confessed his dislike of coffee and Melissa admitted that she couldn't drink milky tea without retching. They talked about everything and nothing. She was easy to talk to.

Too easy to talk to, he realised after a while. He had started telling her a story about Auntie Jo visiting another Luman's house . . . and then realised he couldn't tell her the funny bit at the end where Auntie Jo set the toaster on fire and swooped to safety . . . The problem was he

121

couldn't relax *too much*. The easier it was talking the more likely he was to let something slip – and so he fell into an uneasy silence.

As if things weren't awkward enough a couple squeezed in beside them. The boy was a couple of years older than Adam, tall and muscular with a goatee. The girl had pink hair and lots of piercings. Clearly this was an irresistible combination for Goatee Guy because as soon as they sat down he leaped on Pink Hair and proceeded to devour her alive. Adam tried not to stare, fascinated. Surely snogging her with all that metal in her face was a hazard. He didn't want to have to interrupt his evening to guide Goatee Guy into the afterlife . . .

Melissa drank the last of her coffee and made a face. It must have been freezing – they had been there for well over an hour. It was probably time for her to go. He wondered if she felt left out looking at the couple beside them. Maybe she expected Adam to start eating *her* alive. He looked at her appraisingly, trying to work out what Dan would have called his trajectory. He could angle his head left and go in, under the nose . . .

Melissa turned suddenly and drew back a little when she saw his face. He realised he was staring at her with an almost hungry expression and tried to smile. 'Do you want another disgusting coffee?'

She laughed and relaxed. 'Nah, I need to go soon. But we could grab a pizza slice if you want? There's a little Italian place round the corner . . .'

At the precise moment she said the word 'corner' Adam felt something stab him in the guts. He almost doubled

over in his chair but managed to stay upright. 'Yeah, that
. . . sounds good.'

'OK, I'll be back in a minute.' Melissa smiled at him and
disappeared into the crowd.

Adam watched her go through dull eyes, unable to
believe his bad luck. He had waited a week for another
premonition – without success. Why did he have to get
one *now* when everything was going so well? Another
pain racked him and he groaned, folding in half, his head
resting on the stone table. It was so strong! Goatee Guy
was staring at him. 'You all right, mate?' Adam couldn't
answer but managed to nod and turn away. He was quite
touched that Goatee Guy had interrupted his meal to
ask.

Why was this happening? He hadn't tuned into the
premonitions tonight. Typically, on the nights he had sat
at home feeling bored there hadn't been a single twinge!
Now his intestines seemed to be dancing some kind of
mad jig. He felt as if he had swallowed lots of sharp
wriggly things.

'Are you ready?' Melissa was standing over him, looking
concerned.

'Yeah, just tying my shoelace.' He managed to stand,
although the pain made him want to curl up in a ball on
the floor and rock backwards and forwards. He followed
her up the stairs, pushing past the crowds trying to get
down into the bunker.

Above ground once again, Adam walked beside Melissa,
trying not to stumble. People were walking towards them
from every direction. He could feel sweat in his hair,

threatening to spill into his eyes and sting them. Melissa was chattering and Adam tried to listen but the feeling in his stomach was getting stronger.

Why was the premonition so powerful? Gritting his teeth he tried to tune into the sensations in his body. He couldn't explain why but he felt sure that only one person was in danger. So for the premonition to be so strong maybe the person was somewhere nearby . . . He stretched onto tiptoe and looked up and down the length of Flip Street, eyes darting over the crowd, past pubs and clubs, past side streets and alleyways.

His eyes snagged suddenly on one particular lane, on the far side of the road. The stabbing sensation in his gut returned with full force and he knew he was in the right area. Someone in that alleyway was about to die – and by a quirk of the Fates the one person who could know that was standing across the street.

Melissa had turned and was staring at him, face concerned. 'Are you sure you're OK?'

Adam tried to nod. 'I'm fine, just hungry.'

Melissa pointed up the road to the right. 'The pizza place is just up here, the next little side street.' She grinned at him. 'I promise it will be worth it when we get there.'

Adam tried to smile back. 'Listen, I just need to go and get some money out, OK? Why don't you go on round and get a table? I'll be there in a few minutes.'

She gave him a suspicious look. 'OK . . . But it's all right if you need to go home.'

Adam shook his head. It took more effort than he had expected and fresh sweat broke out on the back of his neck. 'No, honestly, I'm fine. I'd really like some pizza. I'll be there in five minutes, I promise.'

Melissa shrugged and nodded. 'Whatever you want. I'll see you there.'

He watched her walk up the road and slumped back against the building behind him, feeling the cold stone through his hair. He tried to turn down his doom sense. When it was too intense he couldn't think straight. He was sure that the next victim was in the alleyway. Feeling a little stronger, he ducked and wove through the crowds and crossed the road, scurrying along in the gutter for speed.

At the end of the narrow alley he paused and bit his lip. There were no obvious doorways – only large, industrial dustbins. Past them the alleyway stretched away into darkness. It was impossible to tell what was at the other end. The icy weather was keeping the worst of the smell at bay but there was definitely a hint of rotten food in the air.

He stood for a moment, puzzled. There was no sign of anyone so where was the next victim? The feeling in his stomach was still there. Had they not arrived yet? He took a cautious step forward, then reeled sideways with shock. Just like the time in the country road a clear vision appeared in front of his eyes. He could see a young man lying on the ground, tangled in a sleeping bag. The sleeping bag was stopping him from escaping the gang gathered round kicking and punching him.

Adam staggered into the wall and retched weakly. People behind him laughed and hooted and a stranger thumped his back. 'Go home to your mammy, son!' Adam felt his cheeks flush and he groaned aloud. They thought he was drunk. *If only*, he thought. Instead he was about to go down a dark alley and try to convince a total stranger that he was about to die.

Still holding onto the wall for support, Adam crept into the alleyway. Within a few feet the walls seemed to close in around him. It was amazing how much quieter it was so close to the main road. He squinted into the gloom, letting his eyes adjust. It would be so much easier to go into the Hinterland but that would mean appearing out of thin air which would probably give the homeless guy a heart attack. Which, as Adam reflected, kind of defeated the object.

He could almost see now. The walls on both sides were lined with industrial bins. A few black bags had overflowed and were strewn in his path. The smell here was overwhelming – fetid, something like rotten apples and cheesy socks. It made him feel like retching all over again.

'All right, mate,' a voice called out. Adam leaped a foot in the air and swung left, startled. A lighter flicked and a face appeared out of the darkness, pale skin and bright brown eyes beneath a black beanie. The man was young, perhaps a couple of years older than Aron but not nearly as muscular. Stubble peppered his cheeks and jaw. He seemed friendly but his eyes were wary. 'You lost?'

'Erm . . . Hi.' Adam's relief was short-lived. All right, he had found the next victim but now he was going to have to think fast. The premonition gave him a fresh stab in the guts. 'How are you?'

'Oh, I'm good thanks,' the man said cheerfully with no apparent trace of irony. 'Not the warmest of nights but what can you do?' He had a hint of an accent, something soft and lilting. He was curled up on the ground. It still came as a shock seeing the sleeping bag from his vision. This guy was going to die very soon unless Adam could convince him to make a run for it.

'It is cold,' Adam agreed. 'Still, if you had a nice cup of tea that would warm you up.'

The man raised one eyebrow into a perfect arch. 'Oh aye, I'll just put the kettle on, will I?'

Adam gave a silent groan at his own stupidity. The poor guy was just trying to bed down for the night and now he thought some moron had come to torment him. He tried to smile. 'Well, there's a really nice cafe around the corner. It's called Petrograd . . . Great coffee!'

The homeless man was gaping at Adam. 'Do you really think I'd be lying here if I had the money to go and get a nice latte?'

'But I could give you money,' Adam said, scrabbling in his jeans pocket. He had a fifty pence coin and a £20 note. He thrust them at the young man, who blinked, looking from the money to Adam's face and back to the money.

To Adam's horror he shook his head. 'I don't need your charity, mate.' His voice had become gruff. 'I'm trying to sleep here. Now, no offence but sod off, will you?'

Adam felt a rising sense of panic. 'But you can't stay here!'

The man stared at him and something steely came into his expression. 'I sleep here every night. Don't tell me what I can and can't do.'

'But it's dangerous!' Adam stalled, trying to sound convincing. 'I mean it's *really* cold tonight! You could freeze!'

'Yeah well, at least here I've got plenty of cardboard. The bins keep most of the wind out anyway. It's a good spot. Just leave me to it!'

'I can't,' Adam said miserably. 'You have to go!'

He had finally broken the young man's patience. He leaped to his feet with startling speed, wriggling clear of his sleeping bag and Adam braced himself, half expecting a punch. 'Get the hell out of here! Telling me I can't stay here! You're worse than the pigs!'

Adam stared at him in desperation. He was making a mess of everything! The sharp stabbing pain pierced him again and he groaned and doubled over. He was running out of time.

The homeless man dipped his head and peered at Adam. 'Are you all right?' His face was concerned. It touched Adam that in spite of everything the man in front of him still cared about other people, even if the whole world seemed to have abandoned him.

He straightened up painfully. All he could do was try telling the truth. 'I'm all right.' He hesitated. 'But you're not going to be. Some men are going to come down here and hurt you. They're going to kill you. That's why I want you to go. Please – just *go*!'

The young man's eyes widened. To Adam's amazement he swore and bent to grab his sleeping bag and rucksack. 'Well, why the hell didn't you just tell me that in the first place?!'

Adam stared at him dumbfounded. It hadn't occurred to him that it could be so simple. 'I . . . I didn't think you'd believe me.'

The homeless man scowled. 'There are plenty of nutters about. They got me once before.' He turned to walk away and paused when Adam called him back. He looked at the money in Adam's hand. 'I told you, I don't need your charity.'

'It's not charity,' Adam muttered, thinking about his bedroom, his house, Elise's dinners . . . 'Just take it, will you?'

The young man gave him a long, hard look, then shrugged and took the money. 'Cheers.'

Adam watched him disappear and slumped back against a bin, weak with relief. He kept thinking that saving people was going to get easier but people were so *unpredictable*! It was much easier working with souls. They were frightened and disorientated. They trusted Lumen enough to do what they were told. But while they were still alive . . . that was a different story.

There was a sudden cacophony at the end of the alleyway. Girls shrieked out on Flip Street and a chorus of male voices jeered and mocked them. Adam cursed himself. The homeless man had gone but the gang didn't know that. They were going to arrive and find him missing. Then they were going to find Adam. Somehow he didn't think they were going to be happy to see him . . . Shuddering, he scuttled down towards the far end of the alley. It stank. What the hell was he going to tell Melissa? That he had fallen into a sewage pit on his way to get some money out?

He only made it halfway down the alley. He had just crouched down behind some black bags when a group of men walked into the alleyway. Adam froze, wondering if they had seen him. They strode straight to the gap where the young man had been lying. The first one there cursed and kicked the big industrial bin. 'He's not there!' The others muttered and swore. There were six of them in total and the smallest one spoke up. 'I saw him earlier.' He wandered down towards Adam's hiding place but it was a half-hearted effort.

The first man, obviously their leader, cursed again. 'Yeah, well, he's not there now.' He hawked and spat on the cardboard bed the young man had so carefully assembled. 'It's his lucky night.'

Adam breathed out slowly. If they left soon he wouldn't stink *too* badly by the time he got back to Melissa . . . But to his dismay, instead of disappearing their leader produced a bottle of something and lit a cigarette.

They stood talking in low voices, obviously not in any hurry. Adam sighed and settled back against the wall, still on his haunches. It felt like he had left Melissa an age ago but it couldn't have been more than a few minutes earlier. If they would just *go* he could get back to her before he blew it for good . . .

At last, after what felt like a lifetime, they threw their cigarette butts down and swaggered back onto Flip Street. Adam made himself count to fifty before he dared to stand up. The alleyway was empty now and he breathed slowly through his mouth. Another save. One more would make a perfect hat trick. Sooner or later he was going to get better at this hero stuff. He couldn't get any worse.

He picked his way over the rubbish. It was harder to see now with the lights of Flip Street ahead of him. The homeless man's cardboard bed gave him a pang. It was covered with spittle and cigarette butts. Somebody seemed to have used it as a toilet as well.

He felt a weary, pointless kind of anger and tried to feel happy again. He was going to go back to Melissa and eat some pizza. Maybe if he got brave enough he would even try and kiss her. He wished he'd brought some chewing gum . . . His foot struck something hard and it fell over and smashed on the ground.

Adam winced and bent down. It was a vodka bottle and judging by the puddle on the ground it had been almost full. He frowned. The gang had forgotten to take it with them. They were going to miss it and when they came back they weren't going to be very happy to find it broken. Definitely time to get out of there.

He straightened up and hurried towards the street – just as a large, broad-shouldered silhouette ran round the corner, almost ploughing straight into him. Adam's heart skipped a beat. It was one of the gang. He peered closer at the figure. There was something familiar about him . . . He stared and felt his mouth drop with shock – just as the other guy recognised him.

He was looking at Michael Bulber.

Chapter 10

n any other circumstances, the Beast's expression would have been comical. '*You!*' He stared at Adam. 'What the hell are *you* doing here?'

Adam stood frozen for a moment, stunned at his bad luck. He realised his mouth was still hanging open and snapped it closed. 'I . . . erm . . . I was here earlier. I dropped my wallet. Well, I thought I had but I found it! Lucky me, eh?'

Michael Bulber stared at him. 'Yeah, lucky you,' he said slowly. 'You know, I think you're telling me lies.' He looked down and noticed the broken bottle. '*And* you knocked over Baz's vodka.'

Adam put his hands in his jeans pockets and kept his voice casual. He tried to peer past Bulber but this close he seemed massive; big enough to block out most of the light from the street behind. In spite of himself he took a step back. 'Yeah, sorry about the vodka. Look, I need to go.' He moved his arm in a gesture of invitation and tried to smile. 'It's all yours.'

The Beast's eyes narrowed. 'What are *you* doing in Flip Street? Didn't think it was your kind of place.' His face grew thoughtful. 'Unless you're not here on your own.'

Adam resisted the urge to squirm. 'Yeah I was supposed to be meeting a friend but . . . Well, something came up.' He faked an enormous yawn. 'Pretty crap but I think I'll just go home now. You know, have an early night.'

Bulber gave him a look of such total contempt that for a moment Adam thought he was home and dry. Unfortunately he had obviously inherited his brains from his mum rather than his dad and he held out one enormous paw, blocking Adam. His eyes narrowed still further, becoming slits. 'Melissa used to like coming to Flip Street. But then you wouldn't have been stupid enough to bring her out when I told you not to, would you?'

Suddenly a red-hot rage filled Adam's stomach. It was startling, like something had caught fire inside him. Who the hell did Michael Bulber think he was? What made him think he had the right to tell Adam who he could and couldn't go out with? He felt a surge of recklessness. 'Yeah, all right. You've solved the mystery, Einstein. I'm out with Melissa, not that it's any of your business. I mean, you went out like – what? Twice? Three times? She was hardly the love of your life.'

For such a big guy the Beast moved fast. His hand shot out, seized the front of Adam's shirt and slammed him into the dustbin behind. Adam felt a terrible pressure on the front of his throat before the button popped off and the pressure eased. The Beast was staring at him with cold hatred. 'You think you're so smart, don't you? You and your little friends, all in the library looking at porn or Bible stories or whatever it is you freaks do. But you're all on your own here and this time nobody is going to save you. Not even my dad.'

Still holding Adam's shirt he reached into his jacket pocket and pulled out his mobile. He made a call, never taking his eyes off Adam's face as he spoke. 'I've got a present for you. Come back to the alley.' Adam could hear a voice on the other end of the line protesting and the Beast's face tightened with frustration but he kept his tone even. Obviously he was talking to the leader of their little gang. 'I promise, you're going to enjoy this.'

He slid the phone back into his pocket and something pleased and vicious came into his expression. 'I didn't want us to get lonely so I thought I'd see if some of my other friends would come and join us. You'll like them, I promise. I'll ask them to play nicely but . . .' He shrugged and grinned. 'Sometimes they get a bit carried away.'

Adam smiled sourly. 'Yeah, I can imagine.' He might have saved the homeless man but he hadn't planned on becoming the target himself. Maybe he could provoke the Beast. Make him angry enough to make a slip-up . . . 'If *you're* the brains behind the operation I doubt you've got beyond playing with building blocks. Or maybe you're not the brains behind it all. Maybe you're just a follower. I didn't have you down as the lapdog type.'

The Beast laughed. 'If I were standing where you're standing I wouldn't be so brave.' His eyes were shining and his voice became tighter, full of intensity. 'This isn't school. There are no teachers. Your mummy and daddy aren't going to come and save you.'

Adam looked at him with a kind of wary disgust. 'Guess it's lucky that homeless guy wasn't here.'

The Beast's eyes widened. 'You heard us, didn't you?

And then you *told* the guy we were coming and he ran away. Fucking hell, they're going to kill you. I mean like *properly* kill you.' He shook his head and started laughing with a mixture of amazement and excitement.

For the first time Adam felt a pang of real, honest fear. He was reminded almost painfully of the young soldier the night before. What was it with some people? It was like they were broken inside; like something was damaged or just missing. They didn't have any brakes.

He tried to make one last appeal. 'You don't have to do this. Just let me go before they get here.'

The Beast stared at him incredulously. 'You still don't get this, you little prick. I'm not doing this for them. I'm doing this for *me*. I'm going to maim you and I'm going to laugh while I do it.' He smiled broadly. 'And then I'm going to tell Melissa what I did and how you cried and pissed yourself.'

Adam laughed suddenly, not really knowing why. He could actually believe that the Beast would be thick enough to do that. 'Yeah, she'll really like that. You certainly know how to impress the ladies.' He leaped back, just avoiding a meaty fist, almost falling over the broken bottle. He had to get out of here. There was no way he was going to take a beating from Michael Bulber. It was bad enough at home being cornered by an enraged Aron but at least he knew Aron wouldn't actually kill him. With the Beast he wasn't so sure.

He darted forward, then leaped back once again, cursing silently as the Beast blocked him. He couldn't escape onto Flip Street, which left him only the far end of the alley.

He was pretty sure it was a dead end but maybe he had missed something – a ladder, some bins he could climb on, a flying carpet . . . He backed away a few paces, then turned and ran into the darkness. His fears were confirmed when the older boy laughed and didn't follow. He obviously knew the layout. Sure enough, when Adam ran past his original hiding place and down to the far end of the alley he found himself facing a blank wall, way too high to climb over.

He turned back towards the street and felt his heart sink. Shadows had appeared behind Michael Bulber. Reinforcements had arrived. He couldn't hear what they were saying but he could tell from the Beast's animated tone that he was telling them about Adam's part in their earlier disappointment. A couple of them swore and started walking towards Adam but Bulber called out, 'He was here tonight with my ex. Give me first go, lads, will you?'

There was a chorus of jeering and catcalls but obviously the Beast had been granted his wish. He swaggered along the narrow alley, the gang following behind. Adam shrank back against the wall, pressing himself into the shadows. There was only one thing he could do to save himself but he knew it was utterly forbidden. On the other hand he also knew he was going to be seeing his own special Light tonight if he didn't get out of here.

His senses were hyper-alert. The Beast slowed, obviously wary that Adam had prepared himself in some way – that maybe he was hiding with a weapon, ready to leap out and do battle. The idea almost made Adam laugh aloud – he didn't deserve that much credit. Bulber was moving closer.

Adam could see his head in silhouette, moving from side to side like a predator's, hunting in the darkness for his prey.

He was running out of time. The Beast was just a couple of metres away and he paused, staring straight at the dark spot where Adam stood frozen. It was now or never. And just as the Beast surged forward Adam took a deep breath, clutched his keystone and stepped from the physical world into the Hinterland.

Adam had a moment of total disorientation when Michael Bulber passed straight through where he had been standing in the physical world and smacked into the alley wall with a yelp. On instinct he leaped sideways, even though he knew Bulber couldn't hurt him here in the Hinterland.

'He's . . . He's not there.' Michael Bulber was clutching his hand. He bent double, squinting into the darkness. 'But he was here!'

Without warning the leader of his gang came up behind him and punched him hard in the face. The Beast staggered backwards and hit his head on the wall, sliding to the ground in a graceless heap. The gang leader stepped towards him, his voice a low growl. 'Do you think you're funny? Are you trying to be funny?'

Michael Bulber looked like a man who had just seen a ghost. He was fighting to get his breath back. 'He was here! I just saw him! I don't know where he we—'

'Shut up!' the gang leader roared. Even in the darkness Adam could see the spittle flecking his chin and the fury in his eyes. 'Thought you would have a bit of a laugh, did you?' He kicked Bulber in the stomach and the Beast doubled up on the ground completely winded.

Adam felt a twinge of fear and guilt. He tried to tell himself that Bulber had been just about to use him as a human punchbag but even so, he didn't especially want to see the idiot being killed.

Still in the Hinterland he ran back to Flip Street and hid behind the first bin in the alley. He took a deep breath and pushed back through into the physical world. As quietly as he could he crept to the corner and when he was almost out of the alley he deepened his voice and shouted, 'Oi, lads, watch it, the pigs are coming!'

As soon as he said it he stepped back into the Hinterland and ran to check Michael Bulber's fate. The gang leader gave him a final kick for good measure and muttered, 'Someone else's lucky night. Don't play little jokes on me, Mikey. Broken my funny bone once too often, know what I mean?'

The gang followed him sheep-like out of the alley leaving the Beast lying on the filthy concrete. He tried to stand and gave a whimper. Clutching his side he pulled himself up the wall and staggered to his feet. Adam felt another twinge of remorse – until he reminded himself that *he* had almost been the one beaten up.

Adam expected the Beast to follow his 'friends' back onto Flip Street but Bulber had other plans. It was very dark but he began to grope his way along the alley walls, searching for Adam. 'Where are you, you little shit? I know you're here!' Adam held his breath, even in the safety of the Hinterland. The Beast was standing right beside him, feeling his way along, his hands passing through Adam's torso; or where his torso would have been if he had been in the physical world. It was disconcerting.

'You were here!' Bulber hissed but now there was an edge of fear in his voice. Finally, he blinked and shook his head, as if trying to clear it. He turned and stumbled after his friends.

Adam breathed a sigh of relief. At last! Now he had to find Melissa and get ready for some serious grovelling. He sped across the road, still in the Hinterland, running through people and cars until he spotted the pizza place. There were too many people around to simply appear so he had to run to the end of the lane and into an empty doorway before he could step back into the physical world.

He resisted the impulse to dash straight into the cafe. Instead he gave his clothes a dubious sniff and scraped something slimy off his shoe. Finally he took a deep breath and walked into the cafe, trying to look cool and apologetic at the same time.

It was a small, shabby kind of place with rickety tables and mismatched chairs – but the smell was out of this world. The air was rich with dough, oregano, and garlic and the three men behind the counter were having a passionate argument in Italian. He was pretty sure they were talking about AC Milan.

Melissa was sitting alone at a table in the back corner. She had an empty plate in front of her and another to one side holding a slice of pepperoni pizza. When she looked up her face was tense and unhappy.

'I'm really sorry,' Adam blurted out, hating himself for

the easy way lies began to trip off his tongue. 'First cash-point was empty, then the second one had a big queue, then I got lost . . .' He tailed off.

Melissa didn't seem to have noticed his absence. She was frowning at her mobile. 'My aunt called me five times when I was in Petrograd but now she's not answering.' Her nose wrinkled. 'What's that smell?'

Adam felt his cheeks burn. 'Erm . . . Probably the drains. Old sewers round here, you know?'

Melissa nodded but she seemed distracted. At that moment her mobile rang and she pounced on it. 'Hello! I've been trying to ring you back!'

Adam could tell straight away that something was wrong. Her face paled and her hand flew to her mouth. When she ended the call she sat staring into space for a moment, shell-shocked. Adam hesitated, wondering if he should put his hand over hers. He settled for poking her arm. 'Is everything OK?'

It was like Melissa came out of some kind of trance. She stood up so fast her chair screeched across the tiled floor and toppled onto the ground. 'I've got to go.'

Adam stared. 'OK. Is . . . everything all right?'

'No,' she said. Her face was still pale but calm. 'My mum isn't well but she's with my aunt. At the hospital. I have to go.'

Adam's thoughts were racing. He tried to think of something helpful. 'Do you want me to go with you? On the bus I mean?'

Melissa looked at him as if he'd gone mad. 'No, of course not! I'll be fine,' she snapped but her face softened. 'Look, I have to go but it was nice, OK?'

'Yeah, it was great,' he said – and the odd thing was he meant it. In spite of having to save a homeless guy and himself from a gang of psychotic thugs, he realised he would do it all again just to spend another hour with Melissa. 'I hope your mum is OK. And maybe we can hang out another time?'

'Yeah, maybe,' she muttered but she wasn't really listening. Her thoughts had already left the building and now her body was following behind. She was walking out of the door, the evening forgotten.

'Bye then,' Adam said to her receding back and stared at his pizza slice. He took a bite and almost spat it out. It was freezing. Melissa must have been sitting here for ages. He sighed and stood up to leave, dragging his heart behind him.

He found the doorway blocked by a hairy Italian giant. The man's stomach strained beneath a grubby white T-shirt and several thick gold necklaces. Adam was engulfed in a wave of cave-manly sweat. 'You pie!'

Adam blinked. A pie? What was the guy talking about? It was only when the giant rubbed his finger and thumb together that Adam realised what the man wanted. 'Oh right, *pay*.' He reached into his pocket – and remembered the £20 note he had given to the homeless guy. Just when he thought the night couldn't get any worse . . . He gave the pizza man his most winning smile. 'I'm sorry, I don't have any money.'

The man grinned, exposing lots of gold teeth, and cracked his knuckles. He gave an expressive shrug. 'One way or another, you payyyyy!'

Adam gulped. Clearly the Fates were not on his side tonight. For just a brief moment he found himself wondering if he was going to make it home alive . . .

Chapter 11

wenty-four hours later Adam was scowling into his bedroom mirror. It was Saturday night and his black bow tie was strangling him. Any minute now the Concilium would be arriving and he would spend the next couple of hours trapped at the dinner table.

Had his date with Melissa really only happened the night before? It felt like a dream. Only the finger-shaped marks on the back of his neck made it real. The pizzeria owner had frogmarched him to the nearest cashpoint, taken a tenner and stormed off, cursing extravagantly in Italian.

Adam could still feel the bruises where his starched shirt collar pressed on them. He didn't care. If he closed his eyes and concentrated hard he could remember the place where Melissa's thigh had touched his . . .

'Adam!' He was jolted back to reality by his mother's bellow. Most of the time Elise was too ladylike to raise her voice but when she did she sounded amazingly like an enraged hippo. He sighed and smoothed his hair one last time.

Down in the hall everything was perfect. The tiled floors

and wooden wall panels had been polished until they gleamed. There were no coats or abandoned trainers lying around and the dogs had been banished to their pen. Candles stood glowing in tall iron stands and the sideboard was covered with fresh flowers. The air was sweet with their scent.

Just as the house had been scrubbed up, so had the occupants. Everyone stood in line in order of importance, Nathanial nearest the door, Chloe and Auntie Jo at the far end. Elise would be allowed to stand beside Nathanial because she was the hostess tonight. The rest of the women in a Luman line-up were usually the least important, especially the unmarried ones like Auntie Jo. Adam tried to imagine explaining his world to his friends – or worse still to Melissa – and cringed at the thought.

'Hurry up!' Elise hissed, eyes glittering. She dragged him into place between Luc and Chloe, tweaked his bow tie and rubbed a microscopic smut off his chin with a licked finger. Adam flinched away protesting and she hurried back to Nathanial's side, muttering imprecations in French.

Luc gave him a sardonic glance. 'We clean up good, don't we, bro?'

Adam snorted but when he turned to Chloe his jaw dropped. She was wearing make-up and a floor-length pink dress. Her hair was swept up in some kind of elaborate bird's nest and she had either swallowed growth hormones or put on high heels. 'You look *nice*,' he said.

Chloe threw him a slit-eyed glare, suddenly looking much more like herself. 'Thanks for sounding so surprised.'

'She's being fattened for the kill,' announced Auntie Jo

cheerfully. 'Lots of the Curators have unmarried sons. Your mother has big plans for you, Chloe!' Chloe rolled her eyes, looking half embarrassed and half pleased.

Elise gave a haughty sniff. 'One spinster in the family is quite enough, Josephine.'

'Elise!' Nathanial frowned and his wife looked away, guilty but unbowed.

Auntie Jo winked at Chloe. 'She thinks you can do better than the Irish.'

Nathanial glared at her and she sighed and held up her hands in surrender. '*Mea culpa*,' she muttered. 'The truth apparently hurts.'

'The Irish are our closest neighbours. I would be proud to see Chloe betrothed to an Irish Luman.' Nathanial spoke quietly but they all knew the conversation was at an end. Even Elise didn't say anything but just wrinkled her nose.

There was a sudden, thunderous bang. Everyone jumped, even though they had been expecting it. Twice more something hit the door ceremonially and then it swung open. The Concilium had arrived.

There were thirteen of them in total, all men of course. The current Chief Curator was Heinrich, a German Luman, grey-bearded but spry and one of Nathanial's oldest friends. He embraced Nathanial warmly. 'Our Light is your Light, brother.' He bent his head and kissed Elise on both cheeks. 'My dear, you grow more beautiful every time we meet!' Elise smiled, demurred and nodded in agreement all at the same time.

As Heinrich moved along the line the other Concilium members followed him. Adam had his hand shaken twelve times but then there was a pause. The last member of the Concilium was still talking to Elise. He was a tall, handsome man with a high forehead, blond hair and sharp green eyes. He spoke in English out of deference to his surroundings but it was clear that, like Adam's mother, he was French. 'It is always a pleasure to see you, Elise.'

Elise gave a cool nod. 'And you, Darian. Congratulations on your appointment to the Concilium.'

Darian inclined his head. 'Your mother and sister send their regards.'

Elise gave him a cold smile. '*Merci*, Darian. I see them from time to time.'

Darian smiled back but it didn't quite reach his eyes. 'You are fortunate to have such an . . . understanding husband.'

Adam frowned. The words were innocent enough but somehow the man's tone made them sound insulting. He glanced at Nathanial and knew immediately that his father had caught the jibe. Nathanial's face was still calm but two high spots of colour had appeared in his pale cheeks. Darian moved along the line, greeting them all courteously, but without warmth. When he reached Auntie Jo his lip curled.

Nathanial stepped forward. 'Please, come into the parlour. We can have a drink before dinner.'

Heinrich's eyes sparkled. 'You always have a marvellous cellar, my friend.'

Luc sniggered and turned it into a cough. He whispered to Adam as they followed the party into the room. 'I want to be in the Concilium some day. What a life! You get to just swoop all over the world eating and drinking every night. It must be brilliant!'

Chloe overheard and gave him a vicious poke in the back. 'Yeah, but what about your family? They get left at home all the time. Men shouldn't get married if they want to be in the Concilium.'

Luc smiled enigmatically. 'Well, maybe you're right. And why buy the cow when you can get the milk for free? Ow!' He glared at Auntie Jo and rubbed his ear. 'That hurt!'

Auntie Jo scowled. 'It was *meant* to hurt! You're not too old for a mouthful of soap . . .'

Adam grinned and gazed around the parlour. It was a large pleasant room, just off the formal dining room. There were few chairs but plenty of space for people to mingle and chat. At one end a large mahogany table was set with bottles of champagne and elegant crystal flutes. Nathanial poured the wine for everyone and raised his glass in a toast.

Adam shuffled from foot to foot, trying to hide his boredom. These evenings were always the same. They would drink and chat for a while, then make their way through to the long table in the formal dining room. It would be beautifully set and Elise would serve tiny, elegant portions of fancy food. The women would clear up while the men went upstairs to the drawing room to talk about Luman politics. Finally, the Concilium would leave and everyone would sneak downstairs and make a sandwich, too kind to tell Elise that her dainty morsels wouldn't fill a mouse.

Adam felt awkward and out of place. Aron was looking very grown-up and sensible, making conversation with a Curator called Rashid, a pleasant Indian Luman who had only joined the Concilium a few years previously. Luc was surreptitiously refilling his champagne glass and ignoring Chloe's remonstrations.

Auntie Jo sidled up beside Adam, clutching an empty glass and looking merry. She was wearing a long, sparkly dress in petrol blue, made for a woman considerably daintier than Auntie Jo. 'So the wives got left at home tonight as usual. I suppose it doesn't matter. They never have much to say for themselves.' She reached into her clutch bag and shovelled something into her mouth.

Adam stared. 'Is that *toast?*'

She nodded and gulped. 'I'm starving! Anyway, you know we're only going to get a mouthful for dinner. Probably something green with sauce over it.' She looked glumly around the room and her eyes narrowed. 'That snake needs watching.'

Adam followed her gaze and found that Darian had tailed Elise over to the table and cornered her there. He was standing just a little bit closer than was strictly polite. Adam threw a nervous glance at his father but Nathanial was far too involved in his conversation with Heinrich to notice.

Auntie Jo's eyes glinted. 'He never gets the message. It would be pathetic if it wasn't so creepy.' She cleared her throat and raised her voice. 'So, Darian, still no bride?'

The room fell silent. Elise's eyes widened and Darian pivoted slowly towards Auntie Jo. He gave her a menacing look and inclined his head. 'I have not yet had that good fortune. My new duties keep me busy.'

'I see. I hope you're not still carrying a torch for Elise!'

She turned to Adam and stage whispered, 'He proposed to your mother you know, years ago. Of course she turned him down – she was already mad about your father.'

Adam's jaw dropped for two reasons. Firstly, because he couldn't imagine Elise being mad about *anyone*. Secondly, because Auntie Jo had made only a token effort to lower her voice. It was the kind of whisper you could hear at the other end of a football pitch. Everyone in the room had heard it, just as she intended – including Darian. He was staring at her with a mixture of revulsion and naked hate.

Even Auntie Jo seemed to realise that she might have gone too far this time. She grinned and tried to lighten the atmosphere. 'Cheer up, Darian. I'm still on the market myself, you know, for the right man.' She made an inviting gesture and waggled her ample behind.

Elise made a kind of choking gasp and forced a smile. 'Josephine, Chloe – perhaps you can come to the kitchen. It is time to serve dinner.'

Auntie Jo winked at Adam and followed Elise out of the room with every appearance of meekness.

'Bon appétit!' said Elise with a flourish. Adam looked up the table and saw his mother smiling broadly, delighted with the murmurs of appreciation. He had to admit the dining room looked amazing. The whole room was lit with candles, the bright flames reflecting in the silver cutlery, the glasses and the huge mirror over the sideboard. The white cloth was immaculate and elegant flower arrangements ran down the centre of the table.

He wasn't quite so excited about the food. Auntie Jo

had been bang on target with her gloomy predictions – something green was about right. He stared into his bowl with some apprehension. 'Erm . . . What is the soup?'

Nathanial spoke up quickly, always conscious of Elise's prickly feelings. 'It is one of your mother's specialities – a secret recipe!' To Adam's surprise, he took her hand for a moment. 'There is no better hostess in the land.' Elise smiled at him, eyes soft. For a moment Adam felt as if he was seeing something he shouldn't be.

'Elise, you have outdone yourself!' said Heinrich. His thin face was full of happiness. 'It is such a joy to be with you all once again. There is no greater pleasure in life than spending time with one's friends.'

Adam tried to follow the conversation but it was hard stuck at the far end of the table, just one place above Auntie Jo and Chloe. He didn't mind; it gave him a chance to think about the night before. He had spent all day wondering if he should text Melissa and ask about her mum but in the end had decided against it. He didn't want to make her feel like he was snooping – and at least they had finally managed to go on an actual date. Still, he felt uneasy without really knowing why.

He thought about Auntie Jo's revelation in the parlour. Luman marriages were usually arranged between families, although always with the consent of both the bride and groom. He hadn't known that Elise had been so much in demand, although it made sense. Her grandfather, Adam's great-grandfather, had been High Luman of France so she came from an important family. She was beautiful and charming and knew how to entertain. She was everything a Luman could want in a wife.

He sneaked a look along the table. Darian was eating his soup with great care, savouring every mouthful. Adam tried to imagine a younger version of Darian sitting in a house somewhere in France, his parents beside him, waiting to meet Elise. What had happened? Why had she turned him down? How had she even met Nathanial?

He shuddered and decided not to think about his parents' courtship. It was too weird – and gross – imagining them as teenagers. He sat and played with his green soup until the table was cleared. He was already bored and they were only on the first course. The Curators were all much older than Nathanial, apart from Rashid and Darian. Aron was talking but Adam could see that Luc wasn't really paying attention. Instead he kept peering at something beneath the table.

Adam's eyes widened. Luc had his mobile phone out and was obviously texting someone. Elise would be prepared to sign his death warrant for less than that. He nudged Luc. 'What are you *doing?*'

Luc didn't even glance up. 'What does it look like I'm doing?' he muttered. 'I'm not on duty tonight and the Concilium never stay for too long. Just making a few plans for later this evening.'

Adam scowled. Luc made things seem so simple. He always managed to have his nights out, even though he was almost a full-time Luman now. His mobile rang non-stop and usually there were girls' voices on the other end. Adam felt a mixture of admiration and irritation when he looked at his brother. Nothing ever seemed to bother him. If Luc had taken Melissa out on a date *he* wouldn't have ended up almost being butchered by a sweaty Italian.

As if reading his mind, Luc slipped his phone back in his pocket and turned to Adam. 'You went out last night. Where'd you go?'

Adam shrugged and tried to look cool. 'I just went out with a friend from school for a coffee.'

Luc's eyes narrowed. 'You don't like coffee so you must have been trying to impress someone. Who is she?'

Adam sighed. He considered lying for a microsecond then realised it was pointless. Luc was such an accomplished liar that he could generally read deceit immediately. 'She's just a friend. She's my biology partner.'

Luc snorted with mirth. 'Biology partner? Spare me the gory details, bro!' He sniggered to himself.

Adam scowled. 'It wasn't like that . . .' he began, then tailed off. What was the point in talking about Melissa? Luc didn't know her, which was probably just as well or no doubt she would have joined his legion of fans. Anyway, so far there was no guarantee he would be seeing her again.

Luc seemed oddly pleased about the whole thing. 'Well, at least you did something you weren't supposed to do. You know, apart from puking up when you should be guiding souls. I thought you were going to be like Aron and just wait for Mummy and Daddy to find you a wife. At least I'm not the only bad guy in the family.'

Adam stared at him baffled. How could Luc see himself that way? Didn't he realise he led a charmed life? Nathanial and Aron respected him, Elise and Chloe adored him and even Auntie Jo was fond of him, even if she *was* the only woman in the world not to fall for his patter. He was an irritatingly good Luman, always knowing exactly what to say to the souls, especially the women. He always looked so . . . *together*. How could he think that *he* was going to be the one to disgrace them all?

Luc seemed oblivious to Adam's thoughts. His phone made a barely audible beep and a satisfied smile appeared on his face as he read the latest message. He grinned at Adam. 'Life is sweet! Guess I better do the political bit.' He started chatting to the Curator beside him, an elderly man with enormously thick glasses.

The evening dragged on. Everyone else seemed to be enjoying themselves. Only Adam and Auntie Jo were bored. He was glad she was sitting beside him. She kept him entertained with scandalous stories about what the men on the Concilium were like when they were younger, while Chloe alternated between giggling and looking outraged. He knew he probably shouldn't be listening to them but they *were* funny. They sniggered together until Adam caught his parents giving him stern looks.

Darian was glaring at them, no doubt convinced that they were still mocking him. Auntie Jo sighed. 'I suppose I better offer an olive branch there . . .' she muttered. She pasted a (slightly scary) smile onto her face and cleared her throat. 'So, Darian, you must be very proud to have joined the Concilium. I heard you were the youngest ever Curator.'

Darian narrowed his eyes, torn between his loathing of

her and pride at his appointment. At last he gave a grudging nod. 'I am honoured to serve.'

Nathanial nodded. 'You obviously have many talents,' he said quietly but sincerely. 'We wish you well.' Darian bowed his head but didn't make any attempt to hide the sneer on his handsome features.

Heinrich was watching his latest Curator as he spoke. A flash of disappointment crossed his face. 'Darian is young but he has a particular gift. He is a Seer.'

There was a murmur around the table. Adam froze, feeling something icy grip his heart. He forced himself to take a deep breath. It didn't mean anything. It was just a coincidence. The Concilium came to visit every year . . .

Only Chloe looked confused. Heinrich smiled at her and explained, 'As you may know a Seer is a Luman who can feel a death before it actually occurs. It is a rather rare gift. It allows a Luman to guide the soul with the greatest possible speed after death.'

Chloe nodded and looked at Adam. 'You used to be able to do that, didn't you?'

The icy grip tightened. Every eye in the room had suddenly turned towards him. He cleared his throat and tried to sound casual. 'Yeah, but only when I was a little kid.'

'We thought he had an illness,' Nathanial said suddenly. 'Then we realised what it was and we got quite excited for a while.' He tried to smile but he couldn't quite hide his disappointment.

Elise was more forthcoming. 'Such a shame he lost his gift! Adam does not have the natural ability of our other sons. It might have helped him.' She gave an expressive shrug.

Adam chewed doggedly through a mouthful of potato and tried to swallow his anger along with the food. His cheeks were burning. When he risked looking up Heinrich was still watching him. His face was kind. 'It is a gift – but a burdensome one. You should rejoice that the Fates chose to remove it from you.'

Nathanial nodded at Darian. 'A burden indeed. Perhaps you have grown accustomed to it.'

Darian's lip curled. 'I have never found it burdensome. It is an honour to be able to serve the Concilium, particularly where there has been wrongdoing.' He smiled at Nathanial but it wasn't a friendly smile. There was something malicious about it.

Heinrich shifted in his chair, looking uncomfortable. 'This is not a suitable conversation for the table. I do not wish to insult our hostess by giving less than my full attention to this delicious meal.' He smiled at Elise.

Elise smiled automatically but her eyes were like daggers when she turned to Darian. 'What can you mean, "wrong-doing"?'

Darian's eyes darted from hers to Nathanial and back again. 'I mean that there are Lumen who walk amongst us who choose to break our laws. It is my privilege to bring these people before the Curators for judgement.'

Nathanial frowned. 'They must be few and far between. I know that we are rarely troubled by rogue Lumen.'

Darian sneered. 'And yet you have such a Luman walking within *your* Kingdom as we speak!'

Nathanial's eyes narrowed. 'There is no "rogue" within our ranks.'

Darian smiled and his eyes glittered with triumph. 'Then perhaps, High Luman, you can explain why someone is interfering with the Fates and saving human lives? And how we might find this Luman and give him his penalty – death!'

Chapter 12

dam choked and spat a mouthful of spinach onto the pristine tablecloth. His eyes streamed tears and he managed to gasp, 'Sorry . . . Wrong hole!' between Auntie Jo's vigorous thumps on his back. He couldn't have looked more guilty if he had tried.

Luckily the action at the other end of the table was keeping people occupied. There was uproar. Luc and Aron were sitting with their mouths hanging open. Nathanial was on his feet, face grim, while Elise – Elise, the perfect hostess! – was actually *shouting* at Darian in French! Adam blinked, wondering if he was hallucinating. The elderly Luman beside Luc was glaring at Darian through his bottle-thick glasses. 'It is for the Chief Curator to raise these matters! Not you – and not here!'

'Enough.' Heinrich's voice was quiet but there was something about him, a kind of force that brought everything to a standstill. 'Darian, you have insulted your hosts. I must demand an apology.'

Darian turned towards him, some of the satisfaction wiped off his face. 'Apologise? I have done nothing wro—'

'You will apologise to your hosts.' There was a steely ring beneath Heinrich's mild voice.

Darian's throat worked. For a moment he looked like he was swallowing glass. At last he composed himself and spoke in a dull tone, completely at odds with his glittering eyes. 'The Chief Curator is of course in the right. If I have caused offence I can only apologise, especially to our hostess.' He bowed his head at Elise. 'These were not matters for the table.' He looked up and Adam saw with surprise that there was something pleading in the way he looked at Elise. Darian seemed to shrink a little when she turned away, face frozen.

Auntie Jo stood up. 'I think we all need some pudding, don't you?' The women cleared the table and conversation slowly resumed but Adam's head was spinning. He couldn't think straight. *Death penalty?* Had he heard that right? He knew interfering with the Fates was forbidden but all he had wanted to do was save some lives. Now he was in danger of losing his own.

Luc was watching him. He nudged Adam in the ribs and spoke softly. 'Are you all right?'

Adam nodded but couldn't speak.

Luc's eyes narrowed and his face grew wary. He was obviously trying to sound casual but struggling. 'You didn't actually . . . do anything, did you? Anything stupid?'

'Of course not!' Adam snapped. 'What do you think I did? I can hardly sort out dead people, never mind the ones who are still alive!'

'Hmmm.' Luc made a noncommittal sound. He seemed sceptical. Only Adam's incompetence was saving him from suspicion. 'No, I suppose not.' He began talking to Aron but kept sneaking occasional glances in Adam's direction.

Adam managed to shovel a spoonful of pudding down his throat and passed the rest to Auntie Jo, who was eyeing it like a starving wolf. She ate it in a single gulp and sighed. 'God, your mother drives me mad but she knows how to cook, I'll give her that! Now if she could just quadruple her portion sizes . . .'

Adam tried to smile but he felt sick. The minutes passed a heartbeat at a time until finally the table was cleared. The men would go upstairs to the drawing room for coffee and brandy while the women started tidying up. Adam could finally leave the table, find a dark corner and try to breathe again.

He muttered an excuse and fled along the hall, slipping through the kitchen door and out into the garden. It was a bitterly cold night, the ground hard and frosty underfoot, air sharp and painful inside his nose. He watched his breath plume and thought fleetingly about the homeless man the night before.

Adam kept walking until he reached the dog pen. Morty and Sam stood up and stretched as he approached, wagging their tails in greeting. He slipped in beside them and hugged them hard. They licked his cheeks and he felt the coldness on his skin once they moved away. The same coldness was creeping inside him – but this was different. This was fear.

He tried to think straight. OK, he knew Lumen weren't allowed to interfere with the Fates and he knew that any Luman who did so would be punished. The Fates weren't exactly famous for their soft hearts. He just hadn't expected the punishment to be the *death penalty*! He could kind of see the justice – a life for a life. By saving the car driver and the homeless guy Adam had robbed the Fates of two lives. It was lucky they could only kill him once.

There was only one place where he could get answers. Part of him knew it was crazy even thinking about it while the Concilium were still there – but he was going to lose his mind if he had to make small talk with his future executioners. Plus he *hated* brandy. Only one book could tell him what tortures awaited him.

Adam avoided the kitchen, knowing that his mother and Auntie Jo would probably be washing up. Slipping round the side of the house was a pain but he was able to sneak into the hall undetected. He pressed his ear to the study door but couldn't hear a sound. Inching inside he was relieved to find the lamp already switched on.

He had the room to himself. Adam scurried straight to the end of the bookcase and grabbed *The Book of the Unknown Roads*. A deep breath settled his stomach a little. Sometimes the book seemed almost alive and it didn't respond well to nerves. He touched his keystone to the cover and closed his eyes, letting the leather covers rest in his palms, filling his mind with what he wanted to know. All he could do was hope that one of his ancestors had written about what happened to rogue Lumen.

It soon became clear that he was going to be disappointed. The book did open at a recent page but the reference was too brief to be helpful. It simply said that the Concilium had the power of life and death over any Luman who broke the law. There was nothing concrete, just dark hints that it wouldn't be pleasant.

Adam tried again to focus his thoughts but again when the pages flickered he found only a short mention. Maybe his noble ancestors hadn't been tempted to break any laws – and so had no interest in the consequences for those who did. Maybe Auntie Jo and he *were* the only black sheep in the family after all . . .

He glanced at the door, torn between frustration and fear of getting caught. He could try flicking through the book but the pages weren't always the same. There were thousands of years' worth of wisdom crammed into a few hundred pages, information appearing and disappearing depending on the skill and need of the Luman reading it. He'd been lucky last time that the book responded to his Mortson blood and keystone – but the book could be capricious. Maybe it *knew* he wasn't supposed to be reading it . . .

There was a sudden clatter of footsteps on the stairs above and to Adam's horror he heard Nathanial's voice in the hall, calling to his mother in the kitchen. 'Elise, I just need to have a quick word with Heinrich. We won't be a moment.'

For one awful second Adam thought he might actually be sick. He was about to get caught reading a book he wasn't supposed to touch in a room he was banned from entering. Worse, he was going to get caught by a High Luman and Chief Curator. They would want to know what could have driven him to such extraordinary lengths and just maybe they would figure it out . . .

He scrambled to his feet so quickly that his head swam but he managed to shove the book roughly back into the bookcase. 'Sorry,' he whispered, then felt faintly ridiculous. His eyes darted around the room, panic-stricken. He could slump on a chair and pretend he felt sick but Nathanial would be livid – and suspicious. They all knew not to come into the study without Nathanial's express permission – which was going to make him even more furious when he caught Adam.

At the last second Adam's brain came out of its paralysis and made itself useful. On the back wall of the study there were two tall cupboards, built in with louvred doors. One of them was shelved and used as storage for extra books but the other was empty, apart from a few old overcoats and ceremonial capes. There wasn't even time to think before Adam found himself scrambling inside – just as the study door swung open. He pulled the cupboard door closed behind him and held his breath.

Heinrich entered first with Nathanial close on his heels. Through the slatted door Adam could just see that the Chief Curator was frowning. Nathanial closed the study door, not quite slamming it but sounding like he would quite like to. He rounded on Heinrich almost immediately. 'Did you come here to ambush me?' His face was pale and set.

Heinrich put a gentle hand on his arm. 'You know me better than that.'

The affection in his voice took the fight out of Nathanial and he slumped into his chair, rubbing a weary hand across his eyes. 'How did Darian end up on the Concilium? You must see that the man hates me!'

Heinrich shifted uncomfortably. 'He has talent but I fear . . . I fear we have made a mistake.' He sighed. 'I had hoped that time might have healed Darian's wounds but perhaps I was too optimistic.'

'But surely he cannot still hold a grudge after all these years?' Nathanial sounded incredulous.

Heinrich shrugged. 'He believed that Elise was intended for him.' Adam could see his father's face change and Heinrich saw it too. 'Do not blame yourself. Elise made her choice and she chose well.'

Nathanial smiled faintly. 'I still don't know what she sees in me.'

Heinrich snorted. 'It is not our place to see inside a woman's mind. There are mysteries which even we Lumen cannot illuminate!'

Nathanial sighed. 'Are Darian's accusations even true? I know he's a Seer but . . .' He tailed off.

'We don't know. I simply hoped to mention our concerns so you could carry out your own investigation.' Heinrich paused, picking his words carefully. 'It is of course a serious allegation. It was not Darian's place to raise the matter – but it would be remiss of me not to make you aware of it.'

Nathanial looked bewildered. 'But I cannot think of a single Luman who would be foolhardy enough to interfere with the Fates! We all took the oath! We all know the consequences of breaking the law!'

'There was a report this week, from Africa. That Adam had been overheard arguing with you about . . .' Heinrich paused and chose his words delicately. 'About intervening in events.'

Nathanial's mouth dropped. 'You aren't suggesting that *Adam* had something to do with this?' Behind the louvred door Adam stopped breathing. His heart was beating so loudly he couldn't believe the men hadn't rushed over and dragged him out.

'Of course not,' said Heinrich, finally showing a hint of impatience. In the cupboard Adam almost choked with relief. 'He hasn't even come of age yet – and frankly, he doesn't seem to have inherited the Mortson talent for our work, if you will forgive me for saying so.' He sighed. 'None of us are saints, Nathanial. You were one of the youngest men ever to be made High Luman. People look at your position, your wife, your home with envy. Adam should have known better than to say what he said. People choose to take it as a sign that you are not keeping order in your own household. How then can you keep order in your Kingdom?' He held up his hand as Nathanial started to protest. 'My friend, I am only telling you what will be said. What has *already* been said.'

Adam felt a great spear of guilt slip in between his ribs. His angry words were still fresh in his mind. He remembered the shock on Nathanial's face and the contempt on Aron's when he told them they had to do something to save the refugees. And now, too late, he remembered the Lumen approaching Nathanial to greet him – and how they had hurried away, embarrassed, when they had heard what Adam had said. He almost groaned.

'I see,' Nathanial said softly. He looked crushed but he stood up and bowed his head. 'I will of course investigate. The Concilium will always have my full support.'

Heinrich smiled and looked relieved. 'Thank you. I know I can count on you.' His smile wavered. 'I'm getting old, Nathanial. Perhaps my judgement has erred but the other Curators voted for Darian. I did not wish to overrule them, especially when . . .' He tailed off and took a deep breath. 'My remaining time on the Concilium is short. My time *here* is short.'

In the cupboard, Adam froze. Had he heard Heinrich correctly? Obviously he had, judging by the look of anguish on Nathanial's face. 'No!'

Heinrich gave him an ironic smile. 'My friend, you can safely assume that I know the signs.' His smile faded and his jaw set. 'So now you must do two things for me. Firstly, when my Light appears I want you to be the one to guide me and to receive my Keystone.'

Nathanial looked like a man standing in the middle of an earthquake or quicksand – as if the world he thought he knew was shifting beneath him far too fast. 'This is too much to take in.' He struggled to compose himself. 'I will of course be honoured to guide you.'

Adam's eyes were wide in the darkness. He wasn't supposed to be here and he definitely wasn't supposed to know that Heinrich was dying. It made him feel weird and queasy. How odd would it be to know you were going to die? Lumen didn't tend to get sick – they just kind of . . . stopped, like their battery had run out. No one knew for sure why but most Lumen thought it was something to do with the keystones and the protection they gave their owners.

Guiding a Luman was a great honour, especially when

they were important like Heinrich. Most of the wisdom in *The Book of the Unknown Roads* had been passed from one Luman to another as the deceased passed through his Light and returned briefly to hand over a freshly 'charged' Keystone. Why hadn't Heinrich chosen one of his own family to do the job? A Keystone like that was worth a fortune; Adam's own keystone was just a fragment of a Mortson stone, a literal chip off the block.

Heinrich smiled. 'And secondly, when I am gone I want you to take my place on the Concilium.'

Nathanial stared at him. 'You know I can't do that.'

Heinrich nodded. 'And it is your very reluctance to join the Concilium that makes me think you must. Some Lumen wish to become Curators because they believe it will bring them power and status. If *you* join I know it will be because you wish to serve. I cannot think of any better reason. My Keystone will act as a bond of my wishes.'

Nathanial shook his head. 'Don't ask me to do this, Heinrich. I have a family. They need me too.'

'You have a chance to make our world a better place for your family. For everyone!' The old man sounded excited. 'It is time for change in our world, Nathanial. Before I go I want to bring a great storm! But when I am no longer here I need someone to continue my work.' He saw the question on Nathanial's face and laughed. 'No, don't ask me anything. I will not tell you. My plans are still brewing. But soon you will see the fruits of my labour and perhaps then you will want to keep my dream alive.'

'I won't sacrifice everything I have worked for to right your mistake, Heinrich.' Nathanial's face was calm but

Adam could see the tension in his father's jaw. 'I don't know why you appointed Darian but what is done is done. In any case, you know he will do everything he can to block my appointment. I can't do this, even for you, old friend.'

'I could command you, you know.' Heinrich said mildly. He sighed and his shoulders slumped. 'But I will not do that. Not to you. All I ask is that you give it some thought.'

Nathanial bowed his head but didn't reply. The two men sat in silence for a few moments. Now that the initial shock was wearing off, Adam was getting bored and uncomfortable. His foot had gone numb and the fur collar on the ceremonial cloak was tickling his nose. He was desperate to move and sneeze but if the two men knew that he had overheard their conversation . . .

Heinrich stood. 'We should not keep the others waiting any longer.'

Nathanial shook his head and answered automatically, 'No of course not.' His face was sad and he rested his hand on Heinrich's shoulder for just a second. 'I'm sorry, my friend.'

Heinrich smiled. 'Don't be sorry. We of all people know there is nothing to fear. I will be ready soon – maybe even impatient.' His voice became lower but as he turned towards Nathanial Adam could see the old man's eyes were bright. 'Don't you wonder sometimes what it must be like? To step through? To see the other side? All these years we have relied on our books and learning but soon . . . Soon we will see the far side of the road.' He grinned. 'I for one am curious!'

Nathanial's eyes were a little too shiny. 'Some day,' he

said softly. 'Not just yet, I hope. Don't leave us too soon, Heinrich.'

Heinrich chuckled and opened the study door. 'You'll be the first to know.' Nathanial smiled and clapped the older man on the back, following him out into the hall, leaving Adam alone with one numb leg and his thoughts in turmoil.

He managed to count to ten, then couldn't wait any longer. He sneezed explosively, hopped out of the cupboard and fell flat on his face, trying to rub the feeling back into his foot. Lying on the floor, blood rushing painfully into his toes, his head whirled with everything he had heard. He tried to imagine Nathanial on the Concilium but it all seemed unreal. It was like your dad being asked to be a king of the world! They would be Luman royalty. The idea of it made Adam squirm with embarrassment.

As he slipped out into the hall he tried to come up with a plan. He needed to go upstairs, drink some brandy and try not to throw up. Then as soon as he could escape he would go up to bed and stay out of trouble. That would be the best thing. Just lie low and avoid attracting any attention to himself . . .

'What are you doing down here?' Adam leaped a foot in the air and glared at Chloe who had appeared from nowhere. She glanced at the closed door behind Adam. 'Father isn't in the study. He's upstairs – where *you* should be.'

'I'm going now,' Adam snapped. His heart was still beating fiercely. 'What are *you* doing down here? I thought they'd have you pouring drinks or something.'

She held up a tray of glasses. 'They all brought different

liqueurs as a present. There's a really disgusting German one Heinrich brought. Luc gave me a sip. Anyway, they ran out of glasses.' She eyed Adam hopefully. 'You could take them up if you wanted. It's bloody hard walking up millions of stairs in a floor-length dress.'

Adam might have taken pity on her but at that moment two enraged female voices began shouting from behind them. He turned round; the hall was empty. Obviously his mother and Auntie Jo were in the kitchen having one of their sporadic arguments. Most of the time they stuck to sniping at one another but occasionally they really let loose.

Chloe rolled her eyes. 'Actually, on second thoughts I'll take them up myself. I'm not going back in there before I have to. They're going to start throwing things in a minute.'

Adam watched her stomp upstairs (no mean feat in high heels), intending to follow – but curiosity was getting the better of him. He was discovering a talent for eavesdropping. Maybe he could be a spy if the whole doctor thing didn't work out . . .

Feeling only a tiny bit guilty he slid towards the kitchen door. Elise was talking heatedly. Her accent always became stronger when she was angry. 'You cannot insult a guest in this house! *Especially* not a *Curator*!'

'Standards must be slipping if that serpent slithered his way onto the Concilium,' Auntie Jo grumbled. 'Anyway, I was rescuing you. He had you backed into a corner! He would have jumped on you like a dog on a bitch if he could have!'

'Pah!' Elise spat. 'I do not need your help, Josephine!

Darian's family is well connected! There are unmarried sons!'

Adam could almost hear Auntie Jo rolling her eyes. 'You wouldn't seriously marry your own daughter off to someone like him, would you?'

Elise didn't answer but Adam could hear pans being slammed into the huge stone sink. Suddenly, worse than that, he heard another sound – a sound he had only ever heard once before. It was the sound of his mother crying.

Auntie Jo sighed. 'There's no point getting upset, Elise.'

Elise gave a choking sob. 'I know! But why did they have to make Darian a Curator? He *hates* Nathanial! There will be no rest! He will be watching for any blunder, however small. And Nathanial is so tired! Always so tired! If only we had more sons.'

Auntie Jo made a comforting noise. 'You're a good wife to Nathanial.' She gave a sudden snort of laughter. 'God knows you drive *me* to distraction but *he* seems quite fond of you.' She sighed. 'You never know, maybe some day they'll get their act together and finally allow women to be Lumen.'

Elise made an outraged sound, somewhere between a squawk and a gulp. 'I do not think things are as desperate as that yet!'

Auntie Jo laughed. 'You're a true product of your upbringing, Elise. Never questioning, never challenging anything.'

'*Our* upbringing, Josephine,' Elise snapped. 'Your family raised you well – *all* of you. Your views are not their views.'

'Let's not talk about my family.' There was a dangerous edge to Auntie Jo's voice, something taut that Adam had never heard before. Maybe she realised it herself. She cleared her throat. 'Look, I think we've had enough arguments tonight, don't you? I'm going to have some toast. Go nuts! Have a slice!'

Elise sighed. 'Not all the problems of the world can be solved by toast, Josephine.'

'No,' agreed Auntie Jo. 'But toast is a *great* place to start!'

Adam managed to gulp down a mouthful of brandy without spluttering and chatted for a few minutes with Rashid. He stood feeling edgy for another hour, listening to people talking, avoiding Darian at all costs. He also avoided Heinrich although he felt guilty doing it. Heinrich was a nice man but Adam wasn't sure what the etiquette was when you had hidden in a cupboard and overheard a Luman cheerfully discussing his own demise.

At last, he made an excuse and muttered his farewells. Up in the safety of his bedroom he tore his bow tie off and flung it in a corner, thankful that no one at school would ever know that this was how he had spent his Saturday night. His date with Melissa felt even more unreal after the evening he'd just had.

He tried to sleep but his mind was packed with thoughts, wriggling around like live sardines in a can. He couldn't stop thinking about what Heinrich had said to Nathanial – that Adam's outburst reflected badly on Nathanial; made it seem like he was losing his grip on things. The intensity of his shame surprised Adam. Lying in bed a great, hot wave of guilt almost scalded him. He thought about his mother's tears and her worries about his father.

It was time for him to step up and be a better Luman. He was getting too old for whining and complaining. If he was sent on a call-out he would go and do what he had to do. But the other part of him – the part that wanted a normal life – was equally sure that he would keep saving people if he got the chance. He would have to take a break for a while, wait for the dust to settle – but as soon as Darian's suspicions had time to wane he would tune into his premonitions once again.

Tucked up in bed, warm and cosy, his fear of the Concilium had shrunk to something manageable. He was only fifteen! They couldn't go round murdering fifteen-year-olds! He would just have to be careful not to get caught . . .

Extremely careful.

Chapter 13

dam was almost excited on Monday morning as he hurried towards the biology lab. He didn't expect any of his friends or family to understand why but the weekend at home had dragged by. Everyone was subdued after the Concilium's departure – and Darian's accusation. It had taken a major effort just to look Nathanial in the eye over breakfast on Sunday morning.

Here in school all of that felt far away and unreal. Adam was just a normal boy in a blazer that was getting too short in the sleeves. He wasn't a potential fugitive with a death warrant hanging over his head. He was just on his way to class to sit beside Melissa and chat and maybe see if she fancied another coffee some time . . .

Except she wasn't there. Adam's good feelings slid down a notch as he sat alone at the bench. After today they only had one more lesson working together and it was the following day. What if she was absent again? He would never get to ask her out!

The stool beside him felt very empty. Was she OK? Was her mum OK? He chewed his lip, wishing he had texted her over the weekend. At least that way she would have known he cared. He sighed and rested his chin in his palm. The problem with dating was that he hadn't a clue what he was doing. In *his* world Nathanial and Elise would arrange everything for him so they hadn't really taught him the basics. It was like trying to play a game without knowing any of the rules. With a blindfold on, in a foreign country, in the dark. Under water.

He managed not to set the bench on fire again but was still glad when break time came round. Scuttling through the corridors, he kept his eyes peeled for Michael Bulber but so far so good. Once through the library doors he gave a sigh of relief. Mrs Nostel was bananas – but happily that meant she wasn't scared of The Bulb *or* his son. If the Beast started causing trouble she would throw him out – which would at least give Adam time to think up a good story.

There was no sign of Archie but the other two were already there. Dan was nibbling Brazil nuts and playing some kind of game on his phone. Spike glanced up from behind his laptop, not looking friendly. 'You didn't by any chance run into The Bulb on Friday afternoon, did you?' When Adam nodded he cursed and glared at him. 'Great. That's why he's been bragging to the sensei about having shown love to an enemy. Or, to be precise, to "a particularly odious specimen of a boy; a slimy, sneaking toad who makes my skin crawl, a weaselly worm who had tormented my own son".'

Dan grinned. 'All that poetry has paid off. He put a lot of effort into that!'

Adam blinked, not sure whether to be flattered or annoyed. Then he shrugged. 'I thought you'd be happy it worked. You saved me.'

Spike didn't look very happy at all. 'I wanted to make him sweat for a while. Now we're going to have to give him something else to do.'

Adam felt a sharp pain in his palms. When he looked down he was surprised to find his fists clenched, nails digging in. 'Yeah, sorry about that. Next time I'll just let the Beast tear my head off, shall I? You know, so you can play your little game a bit longer.'

Dan groaned. 'I told you the Beast would get you. You should forget about Melissa. Plenty more fish in the sea. And you know, Melissa *is* a nice fish. But there's no point having all those fish floating about waiting if a . . . a great white comes and swallows you before you can get your hook into *any* of them. And then it eats the fish you wanted to eat *anyway*.'

Adam struggled to follow Dan's metaphors to their tortured conclusion. 'Melissa's not a fish. And the Beast isn't a great white. He's just a bully.' *Except he's not*, he admitted to himself. *He's more than that. He's a* psycho *bully.*

'So did you go out with her?' Dan demanded, once again timing his question to perfection.

Adam kept his voice casual, trying not to antagonise Spike any more than he already had. Spike was fun to have as a friend but as an enemy he could pretty much hack into your life and turn it upside down . . . 'Yeah, it was OK. She had to go home early. Don't know if we'll go out again.' He turned to Spike. 'You never know what a girl is thinking.'

Spike made a noncommittal sound. 'Who knows what girls think about. Mostly make-up and pop stars. My sister's always bleating on about that guy with the blue hair. She has posters of him everywhere.'

Dan grinned. 'That's the guy who dressed up as a girl in his video. He put on high heels and everything.' He picked up his pencil case and warbled into it, '*Oooh, you'll never know what it's like to walk in a woman's shoes!*'

There was a stunned silence. 'You have reached whole new depths,' Spike muttered.

Dan shrugged, totally unconcerned. 'High heels must really hurt to walk in. Why do girls do it?' He shook his head, mystified. 'Their minds are different. You probably have to *be* a girl to understand how they think.'

'We could get The Bulb to do that.' The idea, like most brilliant ideas, was sudden and simple. Adam had a flash of wicked exhilaration. 'You know, now that he's helped an enemy and all. The final hurdle could be to walk in a woman's shoes for a day. To really get inside the female mind!'

'He'll never do it,' Dan said, torn between disbelief and longing. 'I mean, he just wouldn't . . . would he?'

Adam grinned. 'Depends how badly he wants what the sensei's got. Secret, ninja-wrestling knowledge. I think The Bulb would do pretty much anything to learn that.'

Spike stared at him for a long moment, then gave a grudging nod. 'It's not a bad idea,' he admitted. 'But I'm not sure it's enough of a challenge. Maybe we should make him dress up as a woman.'

Dan shook his head. 'Even The Bulb has his limits. We

don't want to push him too far. I mean, we actually *want* him to pass the test, remember? So we can go to Japan?'

Spike sighed. 'Yeah, I know.' He pulled some dried skin off his lip and inspected it. At last he nodded. 'OK. Shoes it is then. I'll fire off the email later. Seems a pity to finish it all so soon but I suppose we need to give him time to rearrange the trip.'

There was a sudden panting sound behind them. They turned in unison to find Archie in a state of nervous collapse and extreme oxygen deprivation. He managed to spit out his words in staccato bursts. 'The Beast. Coming here. Adam. Looking for you!' He sank onto his knees, adding unnecessarily, 'I ran. All the way. Here.'

Spike snorted. 'Great. What does that nutter want?'

The blood had drained from Dan's face and he was already reaching for his inhaler. 'I told you not to go out with the fish! And now Jaws is coming!'

Adam's stomach clenched, though not with fear. After all, even Michael Bulber wouldn't be mad enough to attack him in the school library. Mrs Nostel would fight him off with her dried weeds. No, what was really worrying Adam was what the Beast might say in front of his friends. He hadn't spent the last three and a half years telling lies and keeping his life a secret only to have his cover blown now. He could just imagine his friends' faces if the Beast started babbling about Adam vanishing into thin air . . .

'You should probably go.' Spike was staring at his laptop screen as though his life depended on it. There was just the faintest hint of a smile playing across his lips. 'At least, if you want to take Melissa out again without crutches.'

Adam weighed his options rapidly. He couldn't let Bulber blab in front of his friends – but he couldn't let Bulber corner him either. It was too risky escaping into the Hinterland in the middle of a corridor. Mad as it seemed, he could only see one solution. 'Yeah, that's OK. I'm going to go and find him.'

Dan's face turned the colour of yoghurt. He took a quick hit from his inhaler. 'Are you mad?! Are you completely insane?!' He gaped at Adam, wheezing a little. 'I mean, all right, you took his fish – but when the great white is coming for you, you should at least *try* to escape! You don't just *throw yourself* straight into its jaws!'

Archie was squinting at Dan as if he had never seen him before. 'Fish? What fish? What are you *talking* about?'

Adam rolled his eyes. As he walked away, he could have sworn that he heard Dan whimpering behind him.

Typically, now that Adam actually wanted to see Bulb junior, his nemesis was nowhere to be found. Adam wandered the corridors without success. He had hoped to find the Beast somewhere fairly public but with a sinking heart he realised he was going to have to hunt further afield.

He wandered through the playground, clutching his blazer to his chest. The sky was heavy with the threat of snow and the wind cut through his thin shirt. Adam paused and stared towards the back of the sports hall. He knew that the Beast and his cronies sometimes went there for a sneaky cigarette but it was a bit too private for Adam's liking.

Sure enough, as he approached he could smell smoke. He stayed in the playground but walked to the very edge of the wall, where he spotted the Beast surrounded by his minions. They hadn't seen him yet, which gave Adam time to plan his strategy – which was basically not to let the Beast kill him. Deciding that fear would be fatal, he took a deep breath and tried to keep his voice steady. 'Heard you were looking for me.'

The whole group jumped including Michael Bulber. Then one of his friends, a slight, spotty boy nicknamed Weasel, gave a yelp of surprised laughter. 'I don't believe it! *He* came to *you*!' He leered at Adam. 'You really are thick, aren't you?'

'I'm not the one hanging round with Bulber,' Adam retorted. He turned away from Weasel, trying to keep his expression casual. 'What do you want?'

The Beast was studying him, his face unreadable. One of his eyes was bruised and swollen. 'Just a little chat.'

Adam shrugged. 'Well, here I am.'

The Beast's face darkened but he managed to smile. He turned to his friends and jerked his head. 'Take a walk there, lads.'

Adam shook his head. 'You know, I fancy a walk myself. So why don't you leave your friends there and we'll take a little turn around the playground.'

The Beast laughed. 'Very romantic.' He stared at Adam, obviously wondering whether he should just beat some answers out of him. In the end, his curiosity got the better of him. 'OK, lead the way.'

Adam tried to hide his relief. He started walking, letting the older boy fall into step beside him, keeping a wary eye turned towards him. 'So what do you want?'

The Beast smirked. 'You know, I should have kicked your

head in back there but I decided to give you a fighting chance. So why don't you just tell me about your little magic trick the other night and I might not break your arms.'

Adam shrugged. 'There was no magic. It was dark. I hid and made a run for it. You just didn't notice.'

The Beast smiled. 'You're a nob, not a ninja. So let's just cut the fairy tales and tell me what happened.'

Adam shrugged. 'Believe me or don't believe me. I told you what happened.'

Before he could react Michael Bulber had lunged and wrapped one meaty arm around his throat. He bent down until Adam could feel the other boy's breath hot in his ear. 'In about five seconds I'm going to start squeezing and I'm not going to stop until you answer my question.' He tightened his grip, grinning when Adam coughed. 'That's right. Hurts, doesn't it? Bit like this did.' He gestured towards his black eye. 'I'm going to give you one of these as well, just to keep things even.'

Adam didn't know much in the way of self-defence. One thing he *had* learned though was how to break out of a headlock. When you had an older brother like Aron it was a useful skill to have.

He grabbed the Beast's little finger and pulled it sharply in the wrong direction. Bulber gave a yelp of surprised pain and loosened his hold just enough for Adam to wriggle to freedom. Wheezing a little he scuttled to safety before the Beast had a chance to catch him again. 'What are you *doing*? We're in the middle of the playground!'

The Beast's face had darkened with fury. 'You're going to tell me what I want to know.'

Adam felt an answering fury quicken in his chest. Michael Bulber seemed to have a gift for finding a temper Adam hadn't known he possessed. 'No, I'm not – because there's nothing to tell!' He could feel himself shaking, more with anger than fear. 'I told you what happened. If you don't believe me, tough.' He forced himself to take a step closer. 'And that gives you a problem. You're basically saying I can make myself disappear. So the question you need to ask yourself is: do I *really* want to threaten someone who can make himself *disappear*?'

For the first time, the Beast's expression changed and something that might have been fear crossed his face. He took a step away from Adam, eyes narrowing, calculating. 'You're full of it,' he sneered, but both of them knew that something had changed. 'I could tear your head off right here.'

'You could,' Adam agreed. 'But if I have some kind of superpower maybe I can stick it back on.'

The Beast glared at him uncertainly, then forced himself to laugh. 'You're mental. I don't even know why I'm wasting my time on you. So why don't you run back and hide under your little table in the library?' He backed away a few paces, then turned and jogged back to safety.

Adam watched his retreat until his breathing had returned to something like normal. Then he grinned, thrust his hands in his pockets and sauntered back towards his friends. He had just had the most brilliant idea.

Back in the library Adam's friends were huddled over the table top, caught in a heated debate. They didn't see him at first. Archie was glaring at Spike. 'We can't just sit here and do nothing. The Beast probably has him dangling from a hook in the changing rooms by now!'

Spike shrugged. 'Who are you going to tell, The Bulb? He would probably go and join in! We all warned him to stay away from Melissa.'

'Thanks for watching my back, mate,' Adam said, resisting the urge to throw himself across the table top and strangle Spike.

The effect was electrifying. All three of them leaped to their feet. Dan's chair hit the ground with a thunk. 'You're alive! You've escaped from the jaws of death!'

'Of course I'm alive,' Adam said, trying to pretend that he wasn't as surprised as the rest of them. 'His dad might be The Bulb but he's not actually allowed to kill me, you know.'

Spike was watching him coolly. 'So what did he want? And how did you live to tell the tale?'

Adam kept his expression neutral. 'Nothing much. He just wanted to talk to me.'

Archie stared at him with saucer eyes. 'It didn't seem like nothing much! He said he was going to kill you. He was pretty detailed about how he was going to do it! I drew it.' He pushed a piece of paper across the table towards Adam, revealing a perfect diagram of how Adam might look with no limbs and his head on a stick.

Adam winced and looked away. 'It was all just a misunderstanding. But it did give me a great idea. I hope you haven't emailed The Bulb just yet.'

Spike eyed him from across the top of his laptop. 'We were just about to. Why?'

Adam shrugged. 'No reason. I just thought maybe we could make things a little more . . . ambitious.'

Dan chewed his lip. 'I think seeing The Bulb in high heels is ambitious enough for me!'

Adam grinned. 'Yeah, I guess. I was just thinking that maybe we could keep it in the family. Get both the Bulber boys dressed to kill. You know, a bit of father-son bonding.'

They stared at him. Dan's mouth was hanging open. 'Isn't one brush with death enough for you?' His voice was faint. He cleared his throat and pointed an accusing finger. 'I've heard of people like you! People who looked death in the eye and started getting a buzz from it! They're addicts! Adrenalin junkies!'

For a moment Adam almost yelled that he was the *opposite* of an addict to death. He controlled himself and turned to Spike. 'I'm game for it if you are.'

Spike gave him a long appraising glance. At last he shook his head regretfully. 'I'll mess with The Bulb's head but the Beast is a different matter.' His fingers tapped madly across the keyboard for a few moments and then with a flourish he hit send. 'It's done. Bulb senior only.'

Dan looked nervous. 'Michael Bulber will already kill us if he finds out we're setting up his dad.'

'No he won't,' Adam said grimly. He thought about the Beast's face; how freaked out the older boy had looked when he realised Adam might have superpowers. Then he smiled.

Chapter 14

In spite of his fighting talk Adam decided to lie low for the rest of the week. He'd seen what the Beast and his friends were capable of – he wasn't going to stay freaked out by Adam for long. But Michael Bulber kept a low profile and Adam began to relax. He knew that if he made it to the weekend he would be safe. After that there would only be one more week to go before the half-term break.

He had another reason to be cheerful. On Tuesday when he walked into biology he expected Melissa to be absent. It was their last lesson working together and probably his last chance to really talk to her. But to his delight Melissa was sitting in her usual place. Whatever had happened to her mum couldn't have been serious, although Adam still felt a pang of unease for reasons he didn't quite understand.

Melissa had swivelled round on her stool and was chatting to the girls who sat behind them. Adam tried to walk towards them nonchalantly but completely ruined the effect by crashing into a bench and knocking a pile of textbooks over with his bag. He muttered an apology and scrambled to pick them up. By the time he finally made it to his seat Melissa and her friends had fallen silent. One of them, a girl with blonde hair and trendy specs, looked him up and down and shook her head.

Feeling paranoid, he crept onto his stool and muttered hello with his face in his school bag. What had Melissa been saying? He tried to run a mental replay of Friday night. Things had gone well until they left Petrograd. Admittedly the evening had gone downhill pretty rapidly from that point. Maybe Melissa had told them about his disappearing act or the fact that he didn't like coffee or the funny smell that had followed him into the pizza place. Maybe she had found out about his frogmarch to the cashpoint at the hands of the angry Italian. He felt cold sweat break out beneath his shirt and fought a sudden, desperate desire to run for the door.

'Hi, Adam,' Melissa said.

He grunted something in return. What did she mean with her 'Hi Adam'? Was it the voice of pity? Had she just been telling all her friends what a loser he was? That he smelled of bin bags? That he hadn't texted her once all weekend even though he knew her mum wasn't well? Heat was rushing up through his body and into his face. He had pretended to look in his bag for what felt like an hour. No one on earth had a school bag containing anything *that* interesting. She was going to expect him to pull out the lost treasure of the Incas soon. There was nothing he could do but sit up and accept his fate.

When he finally turned his burning cheeks towards her she was smiling perfectly normally. 'Did you have a good weekend?'

He stared at her. 'Erm . . . Yeah. I mean, kind of. Big family thing. You know, really boring.' *Apart from the bit where Auntie Jo insulted Darian, Darian threatened me with the death penalty, Heinrich announced that he was going to die . . .* 'What about you?'

She shrugged. 'I've had better.' She was trying hard to keep her voice light but her face was strained.

Adam hesitated, feeling like he was prying. 'What happened with your mum?'

Melissa kicked at the bottom of the bench. 'She was in the hospital for a few hours but then she went home. They wanted to do some kind of test on her but she said she felt better.' She shrugged. 'She needed to go to work on Saturday morning. So did I.'

'Oh right.' Adam felt awkward. He also felt pretty sure that Melissa's mum must be nuts. Didn't she realise how fragile humans were? How fragile their *lives* were?

Maybe Melissa could read his thoughts in his face. She scowled. 'Look, I know it's OK for your dad, since he's got such a great job.' She managed to make it sound like an insult. 'If he needs to go to a doctor he can probably just take time off. But I told you, if my mum misses work she gets kicked out. And then we get kicked out of our flat. So it's a no-brainer. We don't *all* live in a big house.'

Adam glared at her. 'You don't know anything about my father. He works really long hours. I mean *really long*. He gets called out at night all the time!'

For a second she looked confused. 'I thought you said he was a businessman.'

Adam cursed himself silently. 'Yeah . . . he is . . . you know, like a . . . a troubleshooter! He deals with unexpected problems.' *That's a nice way of putting it. Unexpected problems like death.*

Melissa sighed. 'Look, I didn't mean to start on you. I'm just . . .' She shrugged. Her eyes were tired and sad.

Her hand was resting on the bench, beside a pencil case with lots of graffiti on it. Without thinking Adam put his hand on hers. It was a lot smaller than his. It seemed to disappear, apart from her fingertips. Her skin was very pale. They both stared for a long moment.

About a millisecond later, Adam realised what he was doing. There was a tiny man at the back of his mind hopping about and shrieking insults. He sounded amazingly like the angry Italian. Adam snatched his hand away from Melissa's as though her fingers had just bitten him. 'Sorry. About everything. You know, your mum. And the hand. And taking so long the other night.'

Melissa grinned at him. 'I had a nice time the other night.' She looked away suddenly, fidgeting with her pencil case. 'I thought you would have texted.'

'I was going to . . .' Adam tailed off, not really sure why he hadn't.

'It's OK, I think I know why you didn't. I heard that Michael Bulber was giving you hassle. I'm really sorry. He's such a . . .' She struggled to find the right word, then settled for rolling her eyes. 'We only went out a couple of times and it was back in September.'

Adam's heart contracted all over again at the thought of Bulber taking Melissa on a date. 'I'm sure he's a nice guy underneath all the . . . erm . . . violence,' he said, not sounding remotely convincing.

Melissa sighed. 'No, not really. I know what people say about him but I kept thinking he must have hidden depths.'

Adam managed to suppress a snigger – but only just. 'And does he?'

'I never got a chance to find out. Every time I tried to talk . . . Well, let's just say he was more interested in mauling me.' She shuddered delicately.

Adam took several deep calming breaths. 'Yeah, great guy.'

Melissa rolled her eyes. 'He never gets the message. He asks me out again every so often – like this morning. You know, because it's Valentine's Day on Friday.'

'Oh, right,' Adam said, snarling inside at the Beast's continued and blatant interest in her.

'Yeah, I was going to go to Cryptique. They're having a big Valentine's night. They always play brilliant music.'

'Great,' Adam mumbled. He had a sudden miserable image of Melissa dancing in the coolest club in Flip Street, surrounded by gaggles of admirers. He gave a heavy sigh.

'Yeah, it'll be really good,' Melissa said.

She was staring at him expectantly. It was making him nervous. Did he have something between his teeth or dangling from his nose? Her eyes were doing the laser thing. It was different though this time. He stared back at her. It was like she was trying to communicate something to him by the power of thought . . .

A brief look of frustration passed across her face. 'So do you think you'll be going? On Friday?'

Adam almost snorted with mirth. Yeah, of course he was going to Cryptique because he was so famously cool . . . He glanced away, pretending to look at his textbook. 'Nah, probably not. I have a lot of other stuff to do.'

'Oh, right.' Her face fell. 'It's just I was going to see if you fancied coming but if you're too busy –'

'Nothing I can't put off,' Adam said, snapping his head up so fast he almost dislocated his neck. 'I'll have to talk to some people, move some things about but I can take care of it. And Cryptique is great. Always a good night there.' He was babbling like a maniac. He made himself shut up.

'I didn't know it was your kind of place. I've never seen you there.'

'Oh yeah,' Adam said, nodding violently and trying to look nonchalant. 'I used to go there a lot more but I'm pretty busy these days.'

Melissa raised an eyebrow. 'Wow, I didn't know that! You must know the right people. They're *really* strict on the door. I only get in because one of the girls at work is dating the manager. I was going to see if she could get you in too but it sounds like you're sorted.' She beamed at him.

'Well, it might make things easier –' Adam began.

'No, to be honest it's better if I can just go on in with her instead of waiting. I can meet you inside. It should be a good night.' She gave him a sidelong smile and looked away, busying herself with their experiment. Her smile made Adam feel warm and excited and sick, all at the same time.

The Buzzard appeared behind them with a frown at

their lack of progress so there was no further opportunity to talk. She hovered while they hurried to finish and record their results. It was only at the end that Melissa was able to speak to him again. 'Well, I'll probably see you around but if not I'll see you on Friday.' She hesitated, as if she was trying to pick her words carefully. 'And listen . . . I don't want Michael giving you any grief. Do you want me to have a word with him?'

Adam stared at her, horror stricken. How could she *possibly* think that would help? He couldn't imagine anything worse – getting a *girl* to ask the school bully to leave him alone! She might as well just chop his goolies off and get it over with! Michael Bulber would never let him live it down! He could almost picture the joy on Spike's face if handed an opportunity like this . . . There would be posters, badges, websites in his honour . . . '*No!!!* I mean . . . There's no need. He'll be fine. He'll get the message.'

She looked at him doubtfully then shrugged. 'Well, if you're sure. So, I guess I'll see you on Valentine's Day.' Her eyes were glinting.

Adam swallowed hard and watched her walk away. It was like winning the lottery. Melissa had just asked him out on Valentine's Day. All he had to do now was get into Cryptique, not get killed by the Beast and not make a complete tit of himself. No problemo.

As he made his way home from school Adam knew that everything he had hoped for with Melissa was within his grasp. There was only one hurdle standing between him and success – and that was how the hell he was *ever* going to get into Cryptique.

He knew where it was because *everyone* knew where it was. Flip Street was packed with clubs and bars but Cryptique was a legend. Everyone wanted to be there on a Friday night. Of course Adam had never actually been *inside* and on his own he never *would* see inside. Luckily there was one person he knew who might be able to help. The question was – would Luc be feeling generous? And if he was, what was it going to cost Adam?

He knew he needed to get Luc on his own and in a good mood. He also didn't want to give too much away – the last thing he needed was Luc tormenting him about having a girlfriend. Could he actually call Melissa his girlfriend? Probably not. Better not to run before he could walk. He would probably have to have kissed her before he could say she was his girlfriend. *And* she would have to like the kiss and want to kiss him again. It was all so complicated.

His head swam. It was unbelievable. He might actually have a *girlfriend* soon! A real-life girlfriend like a normal guy! All that stood between him and success was Luc's goodwill.

Luck was on his side. When he got home he could hear music thumping so loudly that the whole house seemed to be vibrating. There definitely weren't any adults on the scene. Sure enough, when he walked into the den he found Luc lying on the sofa playing computer games, dance music hammering out around him. The noise was incredible. 'I take it you're home alone,' Adam bellowed.

Luc didn't even glance in his direction, still shooting

things with one hand, but he did turn the sound down to something approaching a normal level. 'What?'

'Nothing,' Adam muttered. His question was answered. If Auntie Jo had been there she would have been watching her daytime soap operas. 'Is Aron on call?'

'Yeah, I was on last night.' Luc paused his game and flung the controller down, yawning. 'Father and I only had one call-out but it took a while. My guy wouldn't believe he was actually dead. I had to make him jump up and down on his own body. He cried a bit but I made him see the funny side.' He rubbed his eyes with the heels of his palms and slumped back against the sofa. 'I couldn't sleep.'

Adam did some rapid calculations and tried to keep his tone casual. 'So does that mean you're off on Friday night?'

Luc shrugged. 'Unless something major happens.' His eyes narrowed, his face suddenly suspicious. 'Why, what's it to you?'

Adam hesitated. He had reached the moment of truth. If Luc decided not to help him it was game over. He didn't *want* to tell him anything about Melissa – but did he really have a choice? He was relying on Luc's pity. 'I need your help with something.'

Luc gave another enormous yawn. It wasn't really the reaction Adam had been hoping for. 'What exactly do you want me to do?'

Adam stared at his feet. 'There's this girl –' he began.

With startling speed Luc leaped to his feet, clasped his hands to his bosom and pretended to hop up and down with excitement. 'A girl! A girl! There's a girl!'

Adam scowled. This was going to be even worse than

he had thought. Still, he needed Luc so he struggled on. 'We're supposed to be going out on Friday night – you know, because it's Valentine's Day.'

Luc pretended to swoon back onto the sofa. 'Well, I can give you a few tips but if you're expecting me to give you any demos you're out of luck.'

Adam took a deep breath. 'I need you to come with me. On the date.' He tailed off at Luc's stunned expression but forced himself to continue. 'Not for the whole date, just the start of it. It won't take long at all and then you can go and do whatever you want.'

Luc raised an eyebrow. 'I know you're a bit of a non-starter with the ladies but I thought even *you* would realise the whole point of a date is that it's just the two of you.'

Adam slumped onto the arm of the sofa. 'I know that. The problem is . . . where the date is happening.' He paused, trying to figure out some way of saving his dignity – then gave up and blurted out, 'I'm meeting her in Cryptique and I'll never get in if you don't help me!'

Luc stared at him, then started to laugh. He laughed for a long time. Then he laughed a bit more. Finally, his mirth apparently sated, he lay back on the sofa and pillowed his head in his hands. 'Dear, dear Adam, you *are* in a mess, aren't you?' He gave a little chortle of delight. 'So let's just imagine for one second that I *was* inclined to help you with this. What's in it for *me*?'

Adam pondered for a moment. 'Erm . . . brotherly bonding?'

Luc rolled his eyes. 'Yeah, I'm not really *feeling it*, Adam. Try again.'

Adam stared at him with a mixture of frustration and desperation. What could he offer Luc? He thought about his friends in school and the little trades they made with *their* siblings – help with homework, doing the dishes, repairing a bike. Luc didn't need any of those things. Luc had his life exactly how he wanted it. There was nothing Adam could do that would make his life any better; nothing that he could offer that Luc didn't already have. Every person who knew Luc was wrapped around his little finger . . .

Except one. Like a spark igniting behind his eyes Adam saw one chance of convincing Luc without falling on his knees and begging. He hadn't actually ruled that out but maybe there was another way. He pretended to sigh. 'It's OK. I knew you wouldn't want to do it. It's probably for the best anyway. I don't want to be relying on you and then you not be able to go out at all on Friday. Then I'd be stuck.'

Luc snorted. 'Why wouldn't I be able to go out? I mean, short of a tsunami or something –'

'Oh, you know, just with Auntie Jo,' Adam cut in. 'I don't know how she found out about the motorbike but –'

'She *what*?!' Luc was suddenly on his feet, goggle-eyed. 'There's no *way* she could know!'

Adam pretended to frown. 'Well, I *thought* that's what it was about. She said something in the kitchen the other night about how she'd had enough of your disappearing acts and she was going to have a word with Father. She said nobody ever knows where you go or what you're up to and you're obviously hiding something. So she thought it was high time you got betrothed and stayed at home more.'

The colour drained from Luc's face and he stared at Adam glassy-eyed. 'And what did you say?'

Adam shrugged and fidgeted. 'What could I say? It's not like I'm ever out with you and she knows that. I suppose if we hung out a bit more it would be different. I mean, at least if I went out with you on Friday I could say everything was harmless enough. Or maybe you could take Auntie Jo out with you some night. She'd love it!'

Luc gave him a beady stare. 'This is all very convenient for you, isn't it? Maybe I should go and discuss this with Auntie Jo myself.'

Adam nodded, trying to keep his face serious. 'Sometimes it's better to get things out in the open. Just tell her the bike is *totally* safe. Let her get her worries off her chest before she speaks to Father.'

Luc sighed. 'No. I can't risk it. She always knows *everything*! She's like a witch!' He rolled his eyes resentfully. 'I guess I'm going to be your Valentine on Friday night.' His face brightened. 'At least your pathetic attempts at romance will give me a laugh.'

Adam fought hard to stop himself doing a victory dance. 'Great. Thanks.'

Luc's finger appeared in front of his face. 'I haven't finished yet. There will be terms and conditions. I'll have to think about them but they will be numerous and non-negotiable.'

'No problem,' Adam said.

'And what goes on tour stays on tour. You won't see a

thing. If anyone asks I drank lemonade and danced a bit. Then I came home and went to bed like a good boy, understand?'

'Yes!' Adam was starting to get nervous. What exactly *did* Luc do on a normal night out?

Luc eyed him appraisingly. 'You're not much of a wingman but I guess you'll have to do. I was going to Cryptique anyway.'

'Should be a good night.' Adam couldn't believe how casual he sounded.

Luc gave him a sharkish grin. 'Oh, it's a very good night. Valentine's Day does something to girls. You'll see. You'll walk in there on Friday night and you'll smell it in the air.' His grin widened. 'The sweet smell of desperation!'

Adam shook his head. 'You're an incurable romantic.' He considered his options, then realised he didn't have any. He left Luc shooting things and headed upstairs. Sometimes you just had to play the hand you were dealt.

Roll on Friday, he thought.

Chapter 15

f course the weekend was a long way away. Adam found the rest of the week dragging by. He had mixed feelings about Friday. On the one hand if he made it he would get to see Melissa and wouldn't have been killed by Michael Bulber. On the other hand . . . he would get to see Melissa – and after the last time he was determined to get it right.

He wished there was someone he could ask for help. Luc was the obvious choice but it had been embarrassing enough talking to him once. Besides, he didn't trust Luc not to tell him some fairy tale just to get him into trouble. He had once persuaded Adam to give Elise a spider in a jewellery box for her birthday. Adam's ears still rang at the memory . . .

His friends were even more useless than he was. Archie's ideal woman was a ninja in a bikini and only existed in his cartoon strips. Spike seemed above the whole romance thing, aside from occasional stalking, and Dan's idea of the perfect woman had pointy ears and spoke Elvish. What were *they* going to be able to tell him?

In spite of that, Dan and Archie's enthusiasm was

touching. Dan in particular was almost as excited about Adam's date as Adam was himself. At lunchtime on Wednesday, Adam arrived to find their usual table in the library covered with an assortment of garish pink cards. The sound of frantic scrabbling emanated from underneath. He took a wary step sideways and found Dan pulling yet more cards out of his bag. 'What are you doing?'

Dan sat up so fast he cracked his head on the table. 'Ouch! Doing what any friend would do – helping you get the girl! I brought some cards for you to choose from.'

Adam blinked. 'Cards for what?'

Dan rolled his eyes. 'For Valentine's Day of course! You can't go on a date with the fish if you haven't got her a card!'

Adam sighed. 'Stop calling Melissa a fish!'

Dan was beaming. 'You landed the prize catch! But catching her was only the first step. Now you have to keep her hooked!'

'Dan, it's only one date –'

'I wasn't sure what she liked so I got a few different types.'

'Yeah, just a few,' Adam muttered. All the kittens and roses were making his eyes burn.

Archie arrived whistling – then came to an abrupt stop. His whistle tailed off and he backed away, blinking. 'Why is our table pink?'

Dan scowled. 'Stop whingeing and help Adam pick a card for his date.'

Archie edged closer. He flicked through the nearest offerings with an expression of deep scepticism. 'Have you gone off her, Adam? Because if you want rid of her one of these will do the job nicely.' He picked up a card covered in frolicking pink chicks and clutched it to his chest. 'Oh, Melissa, you are as cuddly-wuddly-fluffy as these chicklets! Come home with me to my girlie pink cave so I can shower you with rose petals and my own tears!' He cackled at his own wit.

Dan was getting angry now. 'You didn't even read it!'

Archie rolled his eyes. 'I didn't have to! You may as well just stick a pink wig and some fake boobs on him! He can't send her one of these!'

Adam realised he should probably say something calming. 'So, Dan, where did you get all these cards?'

'My great-aunt used to have a card shop. We have boxes and boxes of her stuff in the house. Just because they're a few years old . . .'

'Well thanks but . . .' Adam struggled to find a way of combining honesty and tact. 'I'll probably just have a look round the shops first. You know, see if anything jumps out.'

'I could draw you one if you want,' Archie volunteered. 'It would definitely be personal then. Chicks dig personal.'

Adam frowned. 'What sort of card would you do?'

'Depends what you want.' Archie sat down, suddenly businesslike. He swept his arm across the table, clearing a space and opening his ever-present sketch pad. 'I mean, you want to make your intentions pretty clear so you draw her . . . and you and some . . . other things.' His pencil flew across the page and came to a standstill. '*Voilà!*'

Adam and Dan stood stunned. It took Adam a minute to find his voice. 'It's . . . erm . . . only a second date, you know.'

Dan was more direct. 'You can't send her a porno Valentine's card! Give that to her and all you'll get at the end of the night is a slap!'

Archie glared at him. 'Well, better that than her falling about laughing!'

Adam stared at them helplessly. This was awful! Dan might have really poor taste in cards but at least he had thought about actually getting her one. Adam would have turned up at Cryptique empty-handed. 'Do you think I should get her a present too?'

'Of course!' Dan said at the exact same moment that Archie said, 'No way!' They looked at each other accusingly and opened their mouths to speak at the same time. Archie got in first. 'You don't want to look desperate.'

Dan looked at Adam with despair in his eyes. 'You're taking Melissa out on *Valentine's Day*. You have to be a *gentleman*!' He shook his head. 'I bet you haven't even started thinking about what you should wear. Maybe we should come round to your house and help you pick something.'

Archie squinted at Dan for a long moment. 'Are you sure you're not an actual girl? Or have you just gone completely mental? Anyway, when have we ever been to Adam's house?'

Adam froze. He had been just about to make one of his tried and tested excuses. Now it sounded even weaker than usual. 'Yeah, you can't come round anyway. My mum wanted a new kitchen so the builders are in. You know, big extension.'

'Again?' Dan raised an eyebrow. 'You always have builders in. Your house must be bigger than Buckingham Palace.' He paused and tried to get back on track. 'Anyway, forget about that. Think about the present. You *need* the present. Girls love that romantic stuff.'

'Since when are you such an expert on girls?' Spike had appeared behind them. 'What are you doing?'

Adam shifted from foot to foot. He still couldn't figure out if Spike had ever liked Melissa. Dan could have been mistaken – but lurking outside the art room was classic Spike. He was always a bit obsessive about things.

Dan as usual had no sense of when to stay quiet. 'We're helping Adam figure out what present to get Melissa.'

'Glasses would be a good start,' Spike said, then smiled in a way that didn't quite reach his eyes. 'Only joking, mate.'

'You could get her art stuff,' Archie chipped in. 'She's really into art. She likes manga too – she's not bad. I mean, not as good as me obviously, but not bad.'

'Very big of you to say so,' Adam muttered.

Spike was looking at the drawing and grinned. 'I think you're being a bit generous.'

Adam's patience had finally run out. 'OK seriously, what is your problem?' His temper, this new and dangerous thing, was once again bubbling just beneath the surface. There was something about the way Spike was sneering. It made Adam want to punch his stupid teeth down his stupid throat and sod the stupid consequences. 'Melissa is really nice. If you want to go out with her, go ahead and ask. Just stop slagging her off.'

Spike turned to him with a strange expression on his face, jaw set. '*I'm not interested in her!*' A little bit of spittle flew out of his mouth. The air between them crackled and for some reason Adam's thoughts flew back to Saturday night, the moment when Darian had insulted his father. A moment that could lead to violence . . .

'Get her a toothbrush!' Dan exclaimed, astonished at his own brilliance. 'That's it! It's the perfect gift!'

Adam and Spike blinked and the tension was broken. They turned in unison and stared at Dan, who was burbling on happily. 'A toothbrush shows you care *and* if you snog her she'll have minty fresh breath.'

Spike rolled his eyes and held up his hands peaceably. 'Look, I didn't come here to start something. There's something I thought you would like to see. Coming?'

Adam exchanged glances with the others and shrugged. 'Depends what it is.'

Spike grinned. 'Oh, believe me, you won't want to miss this.'

They followed him along the corridors. Bonehill was an old school and its layout was as eccentric as its founder. Sometimes the building was more like a maze than a school. As they walked their destination became clear.

The Bulb's office was on a glassy corridor opening into the quad, a large, stony area paved with cobbles and dotted with benches and tubs of flowers. In summer it would be packed – even Adam would desert the library – but at this time of year only a few diehards sat in the cold. Glass-lined corridors and doors ran along all four sides of the quad so The Bulb could step out of his office and survey not just the quad itself but the corridors beyond.

They slouched on one of the outdoor benches and waited. Dan swallowed nervously. 'Why have you brought us here? You know he hates us. It's like being a rabbit and hopping up to a fox's den.'

Spike smiled. 'Last period I was in the computer room

so I thought I would check my email – or should I say the sensei's email. Our friend The Bulb had been in touch. He's been a bit reluctant to finish the job. He actually said no at first but the sensei sent him a few tantalising emails about all the ninja wrestling moves he's going to learn and it must have convinced him. He decided that today was the day he would fulfil the sensei's last command.'

Archie dug into his pocket and whipped out a pencil. 'I have a feeling I'm going to want to capture this for posterity.'

Dan was rifling through his bag and swearing under his breath. 'I *knew* I should have kept the spy pen camera with me!'

'Ssssh!' Spike commanded and flapped his hands in warning. 'The door's opening!'

The Bulb emerged from his office and closed the door. He locked it and hesitated, looking up and down the corridor. Finally, he took a deep breath, pushing his shoulders back and thrusting out his chest. His mouth was moving a little, as if he was giving himself some kind of pep talk.

'I can't see his feet!' Archie hissed. 'The stupid flowerpots are blocking them!'

Spike seemed unruffled. 'Don't worry. I just wanted to make sure he wasn't going to chicken out.'

He led them out the door on the far side of the quad and headed off down the music corridor, a mirror image of The Bulb's corridor. Adam scuttled behind, feeling a mixture of guilt and excitement. This was it! If The Bulb really did this then they couldn't ask for more. They should have been walking in parallel to him across the quad but at first there was no sign of him. They stopped and turned back towards his office. There he was, moving slowly with a strange bobbling motion, keeping one hand on the wall. Spike's eyes glinted. 'I think it's safe to assume that he's wearing heels.'

Dan gave a squeal of delight, then clapped his hand to his mouth when they turned and glared. 'Sorry. I just can't believe he's actually doing it!'

'I can't believe how much you sounded like a girl there,' Archie grumbled, rubbing his ear.

'No need to wait,' Spike said cheerfully. 'I know where he's going and based on his current speed it's going to take him a while to get there.'

They followed him until they reached the main foyer. It was right in the centre of the school and always packed with students heading into the assembly hall and dinner hall or just hanging out away from the cold. Half the school seemed to be there – including Melissa.

To Adam's horror she wasn't alone. Her friends were over near the assembly hall but Michael Bulber was standing beside her. They were talking – or rather he was talking. His face was intent and one enormous hand rested possessively on her shoulder. Adam wanted to go over and punch him.

Spike was talking. 'He's going to do his usual walkabout for maximum exposure. He told the sensei he wasn't afraid to inspire his pupils so he wanted everyone to see him.' He sounded cheerful but maybe that was because he was looking at the Beast and Melissa.

Something odd was going on in Adam's chest. His heart was curling up, like a snail retreating into its shell. Maybe it was the Beast's hand on Melissa's shoulder. Maybe it was the way she was looking up at him like she was really listening. He was probably telling her that Adam was a loser and she would be better off going out with him instead.

And then, just when Adam might have started to howl with despair, two separate miracles occurred. First, Melissa shrugged Michael Bulber's hand off her shoulder and snapped something at him. His face changed but she had already turned her back on him. Turned towards Adam.

Secondly, The Bulb hobbled into the centre of the foyer and came to a standstill. The conversation around him ebbed and died as students turned to stare. A murmur passed through the throng. As The Bulb lurched forward the pupils around him parted silently. As he approached Adam held his breath.

The last pupils cleared the way and The Bulb was revealed in all his glory, tottering towards them with a beneficent expression on his face and bright red high heels on his feet. Archie swore softly under his breath while Dan simply stared slack-jawed with wonder. Adam stood frozen beside Spike, both of them taking in Michael Bulber's face as he watched his father approach.

The Beast thundered past them and grabbed his father's arm. 'What are you *doing*?'

The Bulb frowned. 'I'm having my lunchtime walkabout. Nothing for anyone to worry about.' He seemed perfectly at ease – at least until Miss Lumpton hurried towards him, did a comedy double take and turned on her own (rather more subdued) heels, fleeing into the assembly hall. His expression faltered a little but he gave his son a brave smile. 'You'll thank me later.' He hobbled away with surprising dignity.

Needless to say, the moment he disappeared from view

it was like some kind of spell was broken. The air rang with howls and shrieks of laughter. Pupils fell to the ground clutching their stomachs. The Beast stared around him like a man possessed. His face was truly psychopathic but there were so many targets for his rage that it seemed to have flipped a switch in his brain and turned him to stone. As his huge head swivelled from side to side his eyes locked on Melissa, who was laughing but trying hard not to. Clearly this was the final straw. He stormed out of the foyer, first years bouncing off him like ping-pong balls.

'Gentlemen, our work is finished.' There was something almost priest-like in Spike's countenance. 'I'll wait for his inevitable boasting email to the sensei but I think we can all agree that he's done enough.'

There were nods of agreement. Adam didn't really notice. He was too busy watching Melissa, who looked over, smiled and rolled her eyes, pointing in the direction of The Bulb's exit. He smiled back, torn between ferocious joy and terrible guilt. The Bulb *was* a monster but maybe they had gone too far. 'I think he's done plenty. In fact, we should find him a real sensei to teach him actual ninja moves. He's earned it.'

Spike shrugged. 'Japan is a big place. There might even be a real live ninja sensei who's mental enough to take The Bulb as a pupil. Who cares? All I know is that in a few months' time I'll be sitting in Tokyo surrounded on all sides by supercomputers!'

Adam grinned. Spike was right. In a few months' time he might well be in Japan. But before that, Adam would be on a real-life Valentine's Day date with Melissa. Things were definitely looking up.

Chapter 16

he big night had finally come. Adam had made all the usual preparations – showered, changed, pinched Aron's aftershave, blocked all premonitions and sent up a desperate prayer to the Fates that no global catastrophe would occur in the next six hours. He was as ready as he was ever going to be.

He felt nervous. He'd been thinking about Melissa a lot, not just because he didn't want to mess things up. She had started to steal into his thoughts at the oddest moments. He'd even dreamed about her the night before. She had been walking up a long flight of stairs holding a bunch of flowers, her face tight with misery. At the top of the stairs was a long corridor and suddenly nurses appeared, passing on either side of her like silent ghosts. Melissa turned into a side room and sat down beside a woman lying on a bed. The woman had Melissa's pale skin and dark hair but her hand lay on the pale blue sheet, thin and wasted.

Adam had jerked awake then in the darkness, overcome by the same sick, sweaty feeling his premonitions gave him. Clutching his keystone helped settle his stomach – but what was *that* all about? It felt a little like his doom sense but that only kicked in right before someone died unexpectedly. The woman in the bed looked like she'd been ill for a long time. If she died she wasn't going to be a sudden death – any Luman could look after her. Some Lumen were specialists in hospital work. The woman wouldn't need a fast-response Luman so why was Adam even thinking about her?

Even now, hours later, Adam shivered at the memory. Who was she? Could she be Melissa's mum? But if she was . . . then she had bigger problems than missing work to see a doctor. It was probably just a freaky dream – nerves about his date. He pushed the woman out of his mind and tried to focus on the evening ahead. It was going to be the best night of his life – and for once he wasn't going to ruin it thinking about death.

Luc was already waiting for him in the garden, pacing up and down like a caged tiger. He grabbed Adam's shoulder and propelled him up against the wall. 'We need to talk.'

Adam gulped. Surely he wasn't going to back out now! 'OK, I'm listening.'

Luc hadn't loosened his grip. 'There are some ground rules for tonight. Number one, whatever I tell you to do you do it, without asking questions or crying like a girl. Number two, once inside you do not approach me under any circumstances. You pretend not to know me. That means no looking at me or leering at me or popping over to say hello.' He gave a simpering girlie wave by way of example. 'Number three, you never ask me to do this again but you will pretend you've been out with me as required. You are now my official alibi.'

Adam thought about the last one. It could work out well if he was going to be seeing Melissa again. 'OK, deal.'

Luc gave him a long stare, then nodded, apparently satisfied. 'Good.' He disappeared into the bushes and emerged holding what looked like a bowling ball. 'Now put this on.'

Adam stared down and gulped. He was holding a motorbike helmet.

Half an hour later, he staggered off Luc's motorbike, jelly-legged and resisting the urge to fall to his knees and kiss the ground. Luc rode a bike the same way he did everything – with a mixture of gleeful abandon and supreme arrogance. Adam's ears were still ringing from the blare of a thousand car horns. 'You're . . . mental!' he spat.

Luc shrugged. 'It's faster than the bus. Pity I can't stash a Keystone round here somewhere and then we could have swooped. Mother counts them every day though . . .' He took Adam's helmet and stashed it with his own behind a row of commercial dustbins. They were in an alleyway. Adam didn't recognise it, although that was hardly surprising; he'd kept his eyes screwed shut for most of the journey so they could have been anywhere. But as his hearing returned he became aware of a low, bass thud that seemed to come up out of the ground itself. 'What's that noise?'

Luc held up one finger with a beatific smile. 'That, bro, is Cryptique.' He pulled out a dust sheet from behind the bin and threw it over the bike. Clearly this was just one of its many hiding places. 'If we get a call-out I'll meet you back here. Just keep your fingers crossed that the Fates are smiling on us. Well, on me anyway.' He led Adam through a maze of small alleys until they emerged into a larger road.

Straight ahead of them was what looked like Dracula's mansion plonked onto a normal city street. It had a massive stone front and huge wooden doors, arching to a Gothic point. There were no windows on the ground floor and only a few on the floor above. Already there was a huge queue snaking along the front of the building and halfway down the street. The same bass thud reverberated through the sharp night air.

Luc gripped Adam's arm painfully. 'Now, this is the bit where you follow me and you don't say *anything.*' They crossed the road and sauntered straight to the front of the queue. Luc ignored the mutterings of the people around them and grinned at the bouncer. 'All right, Ripper?'

Adam stared in disbelief at the man mountain before him. He wasn't much taller than Luc but what he lacked in height he more than made up for in girth. He was basically the size of a small car – a small car with a black leather jacket, a shaved head and piggy eyes.

As Adam watched, Ripper grinned through a mouthful of broken teeth and exchanged some kind of complicated thirty-second handshake with Luc. There was a lot of fist bumping and palm sliding. 'All right, mate? Knew I'd see you here tonight – I know your MO.'

Luc grinned. 'You know me too well. This is my brother.'

Ripper's tiny eyes narrowed until they became squint lines. He jerked his head but thankfully didn't offer his hand. Adam had tried to follow the sequence but he had lost track after the first seven moves. Ripper turned to Luc and his face was less friendly. 'We're not running a playgroup here, mate.'

Luc sighed. 'I know. Thing is, I promised I'd bring him out tonight so I have a little proposition for you.' He leaned in closer and muttered something in one of the bouncer's cauliflower ears. Ripper's eyes widened until they were almost half the size of a normal human eye and he bared his scary teeth in another trademark smile. 'All right then. Just this once – and only cos it's you.'

Luc step back and grinned. 'I owe you, mate.' There was another endless handshake and then Adam watched Ripper step aside and wave them in the door. He tried to act nonchalant but it was impossible. He was in Cryptique! He was actually *inside*!

He watched Luc greet the girl in the booth and she waved them through without paying. Luc murmured something to her and she laughed and kissed him. Adam stared at his brother, flushed with something between pride and envy. Luc just . . . had something. He didn't know what it was. He just knew that Luc had it and he didn't. He waited for Luc to finish and muttered, 'Thanks.'

'That's OK,' Luc said cheerfully. 'I now own you, simple as that.'

'What did you tell Ripper you would do?'

Luc's face darkened. 'That is something you really don't want to know.' His eyes widened. 'Holy crap, who's this?'

Adam turned and felt his heart skip a beat. Melissa was walking towards them beaming. She was wearing some kind of white knee-length dress with puffy, lacy sleeves. It looked really old, like something from a black and white film. Her hair was pulled to one side and pinned in some kind of knot. She looked amazing. 'Hey,' she said and kissed him on the cheek. 'So you made it.'

Adam's cheek was burning. He gave her a lunatic grin. 'Yeah, sure did. You look like –' He tailed off, struggling to find the words.

'He's trying to say you look fantastic,' his brother cut in and stepped forward. 'I'm Luc.' He held out his hand with his most charming smile.

Great. Now Luc would work his magic. Adam took a moment to wallow in bitterness. In his mind's eye he pictured Melissa throwing herself into Luc's arms and staying there.

Instead she shook Luc's hand, smiled and said, 'Hi, I'm Melissa.' Then she turned to Adam. 'You should see it inside! They've gone mad with sparkly things. It doesn't even look like Cryptique.'

Luc cut in before Adam got the chance to speak. 'You come here a lot, don't you? I think I've seen you here before.'

'Have you?' Melissa said politely. 'Yeah I do come here but I don't recognise you to be honest. Nice to meet you though.' She turned back to Adam and smiled. 'So – you ready to show me what you've got?'

'*What?*' Adam swallowed hard. What exactly did she want to *see*?

Melissa grinned. 'On the dance floor, Adam. Show me what you've got on the dance floor. Your funky moves.'

Luc sniggered. 'He'll be right in. I just need to have a word with him first.' He watched her walk back into the main room and grabbed Adam's arm. 'OK, I have no idea how you got her to come here tonight but Do. Not. Mess. This. Up!'

Adam shrugged his hand off and scowled. 'I'm not planning to.'

Luc eyeballed him with uncharacteristic sincerity. 'I'm not joking. She's hot. What did you do, use some kind of Jedi mind control?'

There was no way Adam was going to admit that he was just as mystified as Luc. 'We just like each other.'

Luc clutched at his heart and pretended to swoon. 'That's lovely. I give it an hour tops before you make an arse of yourself. But that's not my problem. It's time for us to go our separate ways. I'll meet you back here at the end of the night. I'll ignore your tears and you'll ignore the lipstick all over my body.' He waggled his eyebrows and leered.

Adam made vomiting noises and watched his brother swagger away. 'I will not arse this up,' he muttered. He squared his shoulders, took a deep breath and marched inside.

Cryptique was even better than he had dared to imagine. The main room was dark and cavernous with strange little niches and side rooms. It was oddly like the crypt underneath his garden but the bright lights and occasional puff of dry ice took away the creepiness. There was an endless bar running the length of the room and a DJ booth on a stage at the front. Seats were few and far between; this was a place where people came for a serious dance.

The thought of dancing made Adam nervous. He was a

competent ballroom dancer – like all Lumen – although he would eat his own arm before admitting this to his friends. But club dancing was different. He tried to surreptitiously observe the crowd but most of the dancers so far were girls.

He found Melissa at the bar perched on a stool and chatting to the guy behind the counter. She had somehow managed to keep another stool for Adam. He hopped on, suddenly feeling shy.

Melissa seemed perfectly at ease. 'So you made it then. You haven't really been here before, have you?'

Adam considered lying for about a millisecond, then realised he would only cave in under the laser eyes. 'No, I haven't. But I've always wanted to come.'

She took pity on him and didn't press him on why he'd lied. 'Who was the guy you were with?'

'My brother, Luc.' Adam watched her closely, waiting for some flicker of interest but there was nothing obvious. Heartened he continued. 'He got me in. He knows one of the bouncers – Ripper.'

Melissa shuddered. 'God, Ripper's such a creep. What's your brother doing hanging out with that psycho?'

The question bothered Adam. Luc was just Luc – but what *did* he do all day when he wasn't on call? Aron mostly hit the gym in his time off but Luc was different. As far as Adam could see he spent most of his free time out and about, probably with people like Ripper. What other unsavoury characters did he know? The thought was unnerving.

He shared some kind of fizzy red concoction with Melissa and tried to chat over the music. It was hard. The dance floor was filling up and the DJ seemed to have made it his mission to send everyone home with perforated eardrums. Adam found himself getting fidgety. Somehow it wasn't very romantic in spite of the Valentine's theme . . .

Thinking about Valentine's reminded him of something. He scrabbled in his pocket, pulling out a slightly battered and bent pink envelope – although thankfully it wasn't one of Dan's offerings. Adam slid it along the counter towards Melissa, trying to look casual. 'I brought you a card.'

Her eyes sparkled. 'Thanks. I should have brought you one but I haven't got a bag with me. I hope you don't mind. I'm sure you got plenty of other cards.'

'Oh yeah,' Adam muttered. Auntie Jo was very reliable like that. Another thought occurred to him. 'I thought girls *always* had bags. Where do you keep all your stuff?'

Melissa arched one eyebrow. 'Do you really want to know the answer to that?'

Adam choked on the fizzy red stuff and Melissa laughed. She took his hand and pulled him off the stool. 'Keep the card in your pocket for me, will you? Go and hit the dance floor. I'll meet you in a minute.'

The dance floor had filled up while they were talking. Adam took his time, sliding between dancers, watching what they were doing. No waltzing or foxtrotting here, that was for sure. He made his way into the centre of the dance floor, reasoning that if he was going to make a fool of himself it was better being hidden by the crowd.

He'd never really been into dance music. Luc loved it – but then Luc's music sounded like a drug-crazed wood-pecker beating on metal pipes while apocalyptic sirens wailed in the background. Every time Adam heard it he felt like his eyeballs were going to start melting and running down his face.

This music was different. It was fast but the beats and sounds and voices were merging and looping, rising higher, then falling low. Tentatively Adam began to dance. He felt awkward at first but gradually he realised that no one was paying any attention to him. Eyes closed, he let the music surround him and engulf him, until in a strange way the music and the dancing became the same.

He wasn't sure how long he had danced for when the music changed, becoming more trance-like. There was a roar of approval from the crowd and he joined in. More people were moving towards the dance floor, pushing and pressing. Adam found himself being swept along by a wave of bodies. Lights pulsed and swirled and dry ice hissed out, filling the room with a haze, softening the shapes and colours. Adam felt a simple, uncomplicated happiness.

Over the beats and bass a woman's voice rose, clear and crystalline, and the lights died, plunging the room into darkness until white strobes shattered everything, almost blinding Adam. Everything slowed down. He stared mesmerised as the figures around him transformed into puppets, faces transported, smiling or frowning with concentration.

At that moment the bodies shifted and a figure appeared in front of him, recognisable but still far away across the crowd. Melissa was moving towards him, the lights turning her into a series of strobe-like photographs, her eyes wide and bright, smiling, her skin as luminous as her dress. She was dancing not walking, and Adam watched as she raised one pale arm towards the ceiling, fingers stretching, hand angled like a ballerina. She was frozen for just a second and then the moment was gone. Every strobe brought her closer until one final flash of white brought her face almost to Adam's. He stood still. He could smell sweat and perfume, feeling her breath faintly. She stretched a little towards him, smiling and his chest was doing something strange, expanding and contracting at the same time . . .

And then a hand seized his shoulder and pulled him round. He pivoted on one foot, stumbling and almost falling until his captor saved him. The lights changed, returning to the same bright flashes of colour, the music speeding up and all around him people were moving like a vast flock of birds. He stared up bewildered and to his horror he was no longer looking at Melissa. He was looking at Michael Bulber.

Chapter 17

he Beast's face was twisted with rage but he was trying to smile. 'You're having a laugh, aren't you? Bringing Melissa here right in front of me. So now I'm going to sort you out once and for all. I don't know what you did in the alley but I don't think you're going to want to try it here.' His fingers tightened on Adam's shoulders, digging in painfully. 'I told you to leave her alone.'

Adam felt a surge of despair. Was Michael Bulber never going to get the message? How could he persuade the Beast that he wasn't *trying* to annoy him? He just kept managing to do it by accident! Things had been going so well! It made Adam feel like punching him on the nose – but that would lead to certain death. His options were shrinking by the second . . .

At that moment a familiar voice drawled in Adam's ear and a mixture of humiliation and relief flooded through him. 'Well, well, if it isn't Mickey B! And I see the romance of the evening is bringing out your touchy-feely side. Thing is though, I don't think you're Adam's type.'

The Beast's surprise was comical. 'All right, Luc?' He

loosened his grip and jerked his chin towards Adam. 'Didn't know you knew this little tit.'

Adam gaped up at the Beast. The change in him had been instant and unexpected. How did he know Luc? Or maybe he should be asking the question the other way round. After all, Luc hadn't been to school since he was eleven.

Luc stepped forward and threw a casual arm round Adam, surprising Adam as much as the Beast. 'This little "tit" is my brother and we usually keep names like that in the family if you know what I mean.'

The Beast was staring at Luc. 'Oh yeah, right. Just having a laugh.'

Luc shrugged. 'Everybody likes a little laugh. I heard Baz had a bit of fun with you last weekend. Now that *did* make me chuckle.'

Michael Bulber gave him a thin smile. 'Baz doesn't like people messing him around. You should remember that.'

Luc yawned with great relish. 'I'll try. It's just that I have so many more interesting things to remember, you know? Anyway, good to chat. Now that you know Adam's off the market you better run along and find someone else to play with tonight.'

The Beast sneered. 'Yeah, I might just do that. See you around, Luc.' He gave Adam a last glowering look and barrelled his way through the crowd, disappearing into the darkness.

Adam turned to Luc, not sure whether to strangle him or fall on his knees with gratitude. 'OK, how the hell do *you* know Michael Bulber?'

Luc shrugged. 'We move in similar circles. Or rather, different circles that occasionally overlap.' He sniggered and called the Beast something unmentionable. 'I don't know him that well – but *he* knows *me* well enough not to try anything when I'm standing right beside you. You may kiss my feet later.' He paused and frowned. 'Still, I can't stand guard over you all evening – I'm at a delicate stage in proceedings. Maybe you should call it a night.'

Adam glared at him. 'There's no way I'm going home! I didn't do anything to him!' *Or to Melissa*, he added silently. He thought about how close they had come to actually kissing and could have groaned with frustration.

Luc rolled his eyes. 'It's your funeral. I'm going to be too busy to save you.' He nodded towards a cute brunette in leather trousers who was smiling hopefully over at them. 'You're on your own, bro. Try not to get killed.'

Adam watched him disappear into the crowd and prayed that the Beast would leave him alone. He peered around, wondering where Melissa had gone, when suddenly she appeared to his left. He sighed with relief. Maybe she hadn't even noticed . . .

'Sorry! Everybody kind of moved at the same time and I got swept along. Was that Michael Bulber?' At Adam's subdued nod, she groaned. 'Seriously, what is his problem?'

'Oh, it's OK,' Adam said, trying to hide his indescribable relief. 'He knows my brother so everything's sorted.'

Melissa was less ecstatic than he had expected. 'So your brother hangs out with Ripper *and* Michael Bulber?'

'This is a great place!' Adam exclaimed, desperate to change the subject. 'The music's brilliant!'

Melissa smiled, thankfully distracted. 'Yeah, I love it. It's like when you're here . . . you forget everything else. Oh, I *love* this song!'

She started dancing and Adam danced next to her. Looking around, he could see that people were pairing up and dancing closer, faces touching. In fact some of them were touching quite a lot more than faces. The pressure was on.

The thing was, everything was going so well. Should he really risk messing things up? They had *almost* kissed – but that had been a *moment*. Everything had been perfect – the music, the lights, the way Melissa was looking at him . . . You couldn't force a moment like that. Maybe he should just wait. On the other hand, when was he ever going to be out with Melissa again if he didn't make his move . . .?

He inched in closer, trying to look casual. He felt like a big cat stalking something tiny and edible. The trouble was, he was getting in the way. Melissa's elbow kept hitting him in the side and after a couple of clunks she looked at him with vague irritation. He backed away a few paces and closed his eyes, pretending to be lost in the music. As children Elise had dragged them all to lessons with a French dance mistress so they wouldn't shame her at Luman balls. Adam tried hard to remember what Madame Gauche-Pieds had taught them in their dance lessons. '*The man must lead his partner! The woman must feel lighter than air, as soft as a summer breeze!*'

In other words, just grab her and move her! He took a deep breath and pounced, seizing Melissa's waist with one

221

hand and her fingers with the other. It was more of a waltzing stance than a club slow dance but still . . .

He suddenly realised that Melissa was staring at him with honest confusion. Her mouth was hanging open slightly. 'What are you *doing*?'

The music changed tempo, the beats increasing. The couples around them tore themselves apart and began to jump on the spot, hooting and screeching with approval. The moment was lost – to Adam's incalculable relief. 'Nothing! Just messing! Erm . . . I'll get us a drink, shall I? Back in a minute.'

He slithered through the crowd, cheeks burning at the memory of her bewildered expression. He was almost desperate enough to go and ask Luc for advice, until he remembered that he would have to surgically remove his brother from leather-trouser girl. Great. He was on his own.

He had nearly reached the bar, when something large and heavy tapped his shoulder. Before he even finished turning he knew what he was going to see. 'OK, seriously, give me a *break*!'

The Beast gave him a sharkish smile. 'That's not very friendly.'

Adam was staring death in the face – and suddenly realised that he didn't care. The evening had started so well and now it was turning to ashes before his eyes. 'Listen, I like Melissa. I didn't bring her here to rub your face in it. I didn't know you'd *be* here. If I'd *known* you would be here I would have taken her anywhere on earth *apart* from here.'

The Beast shrugged. 'Yeah, I know that. I didn't realise

222

you were Luc's brother. So, you know, no worries. Any friend of Luc's and all that.' He held out his hand.

Adam stared at him with deep suspicion. Michael Bulber wanted to shake his hand. This was quite a change of heart – and Adam wasn't buying it. He wasn't quite ready to trust the older boy with his fingers. He was pretty attached to them and he wanted to stay that way. 'How do you know Luc?'

The Beast smirked. 'I've seen him around and . . . Let's just say I owe him one. So, let me buy you a drink.' He held up one enormous hand, quelling Adam's protests. 'It's just a drink. I'm not proposing. Just let me get you one drink and we'll call it quits. Name your poison.'

Adam eyed him warily for a moment, waiting for some cruel double bluff. When nothing painful happened he nodded slowly. 'OK, thanks. Just lemonade's cool.'

Bulber shrugged. 'Hey, if that's all you want . . .' He sniggered and stormed off towards the bar, bodies ricocheting off him.

Adam shook his head in wonder. Did Luc know *everyone*? Why couldn't he have mentioned that he knew Bulber? It would have saved Adam a lot of grief! He didn't want to be *friends* with the Beast but maybe this way they could just ignore one another, rather than being sworn enemies. It would definitely give Adam one less thing to worry about . . . Of course he would have to spin the story for Melissa. Maybe make it sound more heroic than, '*He's scared of my big brother.*'

The Beast reappeared beside him and handed him a glass. 'Here. Cheers.'

Adam raised his glass in a silent toast. He took a sip and winced. His lemonade was disgusting. Probably some cheap, nasty brand that no one had ever heard of. He didn't really like it but the Beast was watching him and it didn't seem sensible to jeopardise their truce. He pasted a smile onto his face. 'Thanks.' He managed to drink half of it in one gulp and felt a great wave of relief when the other boy smiled back. 'So . . . we're cool now?'

'Oh yeah,' the Beast said. For some reason he seemed to be trying not to laugh. 'Things are going to be great. We'll be the best of friends after all this.' He raised his own bottle and drained the contents in one gulp.

Adam's smile wavered but he made a brave effort to finish the lemonade. It took a few attempts. Bleugh! The thing was, the Beast didn't seem in any hurry to go anywhere. He was suddenly getting friendly, pointing out people that he knew, showing Adam his new mobile and generally being so . . . *normal* that it was completely freaky! Adam tried to play it cool but he felt twitchy. After all, as Dan would say: who turned their back on a great white?

But as the minutes slipped away he began to relax. The Beast hadn't killed him yet. He just had to finish his drink to be polite then make his excuses and find Melissa. He'd been gone so long she'd be wondering where he was – and Adam knew he wouldn't be her only admirer tonight. His lemonade tasted awful but he managed to swallow the last gulp. He felt slightly sick but it was a relief handing Bulber the empty glass. 'I better go but you know . . . cheers for the drink.'

The Beast grinned from ear to ear. Adam blinked. OK,

that was weird. Michael Bulber was actually, *literally* grinning from ear to ear. His mouth was enormous, like some deranged Cheshire cat's. He blinked again and Bulber's face returned to normal. Bizarre!

The Beast was looking at him, concerned. 'Are you OK?' When Adam nodded he laughed and clapped his shoulder. 'Well, can't stand around chatting. You should get back to Melissa. Can't leave her all on her own. I'm sure she's ready for some action.'

Adam nodded. He felt a sudden powerful wave of affection for the Beast. The guy wasn't so bad after all! It was exactly like Melissa had thought – he was just misunderstood. He held his hand up and attempted a Luc-and-Ripper-style handshake. He mostly seemed to end up just slapping the other boy's fingers but the Beast didn't seem to mind. In fact he was laughing. This was great! They were friends! 'Thanks, man,' Adam said.

The Beast's face loomed up close to his. 'Go and find Melissa. It's time you showed her your moves, Romeo.' His eyes were wide and the pupils were black and bottomless. Adam stared into them, mesmerised. 'This is going to be a memorable evening.'

He turned and walked away. Adam stared after him, feeling sad. *Come back, new friend*, he almost cried but then he remembered how much he loved Cryptique and the music and Melissa . . . He stopped and giggled. He loved Melissa! He lurrrrrrrrrrved Melissa! That was so *funny*! He could imagine himself writing her name and drawing a little heart over the 'i', the way girls did! Ha ha ha!

He squinted at the bar, feeling vaguely concerned. There

was something he was supposed to have done but he couldn't remember what it was. Or why he had forgotten it. He still felt a bit sick and he didn't understand that either. Didn't matter though. Nope, not one bit. He was going to go and kiss Melissa, he was sure of it. Romeo was ready!

Adam turned and stumbled off into the crowd. People were dancing and they were all so *happy*! They were so happy that he wanted to *hug* them! In fact he was going to! He was going to hug some people! Only . . . they looked less happy now – but that was OK! He was going to go and hug Melissa instead.

Where had she gone? His stomach flipped over. The lights were pulsing all around him, like a rainbow, and there were so many people, all dark and shadowy against the lights. It was a bit scary, until he saw the dark shadows were dancing and the dancing was making them happy. They were whirling and twirling, just like his head and Cryptique. Whirling and twirling like a merry-go-round.

And then, like a vision . . . he saw Melissa. Her white dress stood out beneath the lights. It was so colourful and then it was so white and then it was a million colours again. She had her arms up in the air, dancing, and her hair had fallen down a bit and she looked so happy, like a beautiful fairy.

He decided to tell her that. 'You look like a beautiful fairy,' he said, but she didn't seem to hear him over the music, so he stumbled closer and said it again and then again and then again. The music changed and Adam's heart beat faster and faster in time with it and he was so excited he had to jump up and down because the music was brilliant! And Melissa was brilliant! And life was brilliant!

And now Melissa had seen him and that was even more brilliant because she was smiling. She was saying something but he couldn't hear her because his heart was too loud and all he could hear was the blood rushing through his veins. The lights were all around her like a rainbow and she was in the centre of the rainbow.

He stopped, awestruck. This was the moment. This was the perfect moment, the moment when he was going to kiss her and she was going to like him back. It all made sense now. He had to like her right now! She knew it too because her face had changed and she wasn't smiling any more, she looked serious and her lips were moving and he was finally brave and he was going to kiss her lips RIGHT NOW!

Adam took a deep breath, moved towards her – and pitched headfirst into darkness.

Chapter 18

omething was wrong with Adam's eyes. They felt funny, like someone had glued them shut. He forced them open and an agonising shaft of light hit him in the eyeball. There was a terrible groaning sound. It took a moment before he realised that *he* was making it.

When he finally found the courage to open his eyes again he was lying in his own bed, wearing his clothes from the night before. His head was throbbing and there was blood on the front of his shirt. Adam blinked and tried to remember how he had ended up there. A series of images flickered across his mind in rapid succession – the motor bike ride to Cryptique, Ripper's smile, Melissa in her white dress, the Beast grabbing him. Then – nothing.

His bedroom door creaked open and Luc slipped inside carrying a glass of water. 'Ah, Sleeping Beauty's awake at last. Here – you'll want these.' He dropped two white tablets onto the bed. 'For your head. Trust me, these will help.'

Adam took the water from him and swallowed the tablets. They stuck in his throat and he gagged a little. 'What happened? How did we get back here? Why don't I remember?'

Luc pulled a chair over, turned it round and sat on it with his legs astride, resting his chin on the back of it. 'You don't remember *anything*?'

Adam frowned. 'I remember dancing.' He closed his eyes and concentrated hard. 'And Melissa was there.' Something was wrong with the picture of her. There were rainbows all around her and her mouth was moving soundlessly. He shook his head, frustrated. 'Then everything goes sort of black.'

Luc's expression was unreadable. 'Well, maybe that's not such a bad thing. Drink some more water.'

Adam glared at him. 'Why? What *happened*? Why can't I remember anything?'

His brother looked at him almost kindly. 'Well . . . probably because Michael Bulber slipped you a mickey.' He rolled his eyes at Adam's bewilderment. 'He spiked your drink.'

Adam choked mid-gulp of water. 'He *what*?'

'He told Ripper he bought you a drink and dropped something into it. Don't worry, it wasn't anything really serious – some herbal thing he got on the Internet. Just enough for you to make a tit of yourself.' Luc shook his head, almost admiringly.

'A tit of myself?' Adam whispered. He had a sudden feeling of deep foreboding. 'Tit of myself how?'

Luc shifted uncomfortably in his seat. 'I didn't really see everything. I was a good bit away from you at first.'

Adam glared at him. '*What did I do?!*'

Luc was trying to keep his face straight. 'Well, you were dancing a bit weirdly for a start – kind of pogoing – and you seemed to be babbling a lot. Your mouth was like . . .' He stopped and slapped his thumb and fingers together at high speed. 'And then Melissa came up and I got a bit closer because I could see something was wrong. So you started making this . . . face.' He began to laugh.

'What kind of face?' Adam shrilled hysterically.

Luc struggled to control himself. 'Sort of like a . . . kissy face. Like an amorous goldfish.' He collapsed and laughed until his eyes overflowed.

Adam felt the bottom of his stomach drop out. 'And Melissa saw all this?'

Luc frowned. 'Well, she seemed OK up until then. But then –'

'There was more?!' Adam screeched.

Luc tried and failed to look serious. 'Well, then you decided to kiss her – or at least I think that was your plan. You sort of *dived* at her. Only you got a bit . . . sick. On her shoes.'

Adam stared at him aghast. He tried to speak as slowly as possible because clearly this was all a terrible misunderstanding. 'You're trying to tell me that I *threw up* on Melissa's *shoes*?'

'You mostly missed them,' Luc said cheerfully. 'It kind of landed in front of them. Only a few spatters really. You pretty much collapsed. Luckily I was right beside you by then. I caught the back of your shirt so no broken nose. Big brother to the rescue! Oh – for the record, someone else snagged leather-trouser girl while my back was turned. You owe me.'

Adam looked down at his shirt, the blood and missing buttons. 'Why was I bleeding?'

Luc shrugged. 'I had to swoop us home. There was no way you were going to stay on the back of the bike. At least you hadn't lost your keystone.'

Adam played with the edge of the quilt for a long time, waiting for Luc to jump up and laugh; say it was all just a cruel joke. As the seconds rolled by it became clear that it wasn't going to happen. 'I really did all that, didn't I?'

'Well, strictly speaking Bulber did it. If it's any consolation I asked Ripper to sort him out. Now there's a man who enjoys a bit of violence! Trust me, Mickey B will be walking crooked this morning.'

Adam buried his face in his hands. 'My life is over.'

Luc sniggered. 'Stop being so dramatic. At least you didn't throw up on Ripper because in that case your life really *would* be over and we'd be burying you about now. Plus there were no call-outs. I would have had a lot of explaining to do.'

Adam stared sightlessly at the ceiling. 'I've totally messed up with Melissa.' There was only one good thing – he hadn't known anyone else there. The Beast would torture him but Melissa was too nice to make a big deal about it. With one week left in school before the half-term holiday, he would probably survive the scandal. By the time they all went back after the holidays it would be old news. 'It's a nightmare but at least only Melissa and Michael Bulber actually *saw* it.'

Luc hesitated. 'Yeah . . . about that. Thing is, Mickey B had his phone out. I told Ripper to get it off him – but to be honest he isn't the brightest. He gets too excited at the prospect of tearing heads off. So . . . there *might* be a video or two.'

Adam stared at him, horror-struck. He could feel his mouth moving but somehow no sounds were coming out. He lay down and pulled the quilt over his head. 'Go away. Just leave me to die in peace.' He stayed there, mind reeling, until he heard Luc leave the room and close the door. How could Michael Bulber be so *evil*? Did he really want Melissa *that* badly? If so he would be feeling pretty happy this morning. She certainly wasn't going to want any more romantic evenings with Adam.

'*I threw up on Melissa*,' he whispered, the words finally sinking in. How was he ever going to face her again?

Going into school on Monday took more courage than Adam even knew he possessed. He'd slept badly, not least because he'd been plagued by more dreams about Melissa. All of them had involved either the woman in the hospital bed – or Adam throwing up on Melissa in the middle of school, surrounded by jeering crowds. When the alarm clock went off, the temptation to hide beneath the covers for the day had never been stronger. Only the thought of Luc's merciless needling forced Adam into his uniform and out the door.

It had frozen hard overnight and everything looked cold and dead as he trudged up the long Bonehill driveway. To add insult to injury, when he put his hands into his jacket pockets for warmth he felt something hard and sharp-edged. It was Melissa's unopened Valentine's card. Adam's heart twisted painfully. He skipped registration – there was no way he was ready to face Melissa just yet.

He found himself slinking through the corridors like a criminal. First period no one seemed to notice him but by second period a few people were whispering, staring and sniggering. Hiding in the toilets during break only gave him the opportunity to hear the story spreading. By lunchtime things were becoming desperate. Scuttling towards the library he could see a group of sixth-formers at the end of a corridor huddled round a laptop. Their howls and hoots of mirth were still echoing as he crept through the library door.

His friends were already there, throwing Dan's macadamia nuts at each other and laughing. As he approached they fell silent. Adam's stomach was flip-flopping but he sat down and gulped. 'OK, just say whatever you need to say and get it over with.'

He braced himself for the worst but it didn't come. Archie grinned and shrugged. 'You win some, you lose some, mate.'

'Yeah,' Dan piped up. 'Plenty more fish in the sea. Even *nicer* fish! Fish with . . . longer tails! And bigger fins! She'll be sorry she jumped out of your bucket!'

Adam sighed. 'I *threw up* in the bucket! No *wonder* she wanted out of it!'

'At least you didn't actually throw up *on* her.' It was the first time Spike had spoken. 'You mostly missed. I slowed the video down to check. No major damage.'

'Bet you enjoyed that,' Adam said through gritted teeth. He felt his fists clenching beneath the table. 'She's all yours now. You can have a cosy night in together watching me make a complete arse of myself!'

'Actually I was watching the video to see if I could *edit* it,' Spike said. 'Unfortunately I can't so I've just been tracking it and taking it down. I found about forty copies online at break time. There are only a couple left now.'

Adam felt a twinge of guilt for expecting the worst from Spike. This was quickly replaced by complete despair – because if *Spike* felt sorry for him he must have *really* messed up! 'Thanks. But you can't take them down forever. They're just going to keep putting them back up.'

Spike gave a grim little smile. 'No they won't. They're all having a bit of bother with their computers. It's funny how every time people upload that video their laptops and phones get attacked by a particularly nasty virus . . .'

Adam could have wept with gratitude. 'Thanks. Seriously.' He hesitated, then blurted out before he could change his mind, 'Can I see it?'

There was a pregnant pause. 'That's probably not a great idea,' Dan said. For once in his life he seemed to be struggling not to put his foot in his mouth. Being Dan, he failed spectacularly. 'I mean, if you see how awful it is you'll probably want to go and kill yourself.'

There was a strange, strangled sound from Archie. 'Sorry, mate,' he croaked at the sight of Adam's glare. 'It's just the dancing.' He chortled explosively. 'You were jumping about like your feet were on fire. And waving your arms about.' He gave a vivid demonstration of a mad man frantically swatting invisible bees. 'I tried to draw it but I couldn't capture it somehow.'

Adam turned to Spike, who was trying and failing not to laugh. 'Please. I need to see it.'

The other three exchanged glances. Dan nodded. 'I think he needs this. You know, for like, closure or something.'

Spike turned the laptop towards Adam and raised an eyebrow. 'You sure about this?' At Adam's nod he hit a key and the video began to play.

Adam spent the next three minutes of his life in an agony of embarrassment. He watched himself bounce and flail about like a man possessed. He watched Melissa's smile as he approached, then observed the smile faltering and a look of concern appearing on her face.

The camera shook a little at this stage, as if the cameraman was laughing himself sick. He thoughtfully pulled himself together in time to move sideways and capture Adam's 'kissy mouth' followed by a spectacular swan dive towards Melissa. Bulber had even been considerate enough to zoom in on the moment Adam puked and Melissa's desperate leap to safety. There was a final thrilling scene as Luc lunged into the frame and caught Adam's shoulder, breaking his fall. Melissa was staring at her feet and looking as if she might cry.

Archie shook his head in wonderment. 'What were you *on?*'

Lemonade. And something herbal, Adam thought bitterly. He groaned. 'Michael Bulber set me up. He spiked my drink.'

Dan was squinting at the laptop screen. 'Who's the guy at the end? The one who caught you?'

'My brother Luc. He helped get me into Cryptique in

the first place.' So Luc *had* actually saved him. Adam grudgingly conceded that he owed him one after all.

Dan's face had brightened. 'Maybe he can get us all in some time!'

Adam stared at him in disbelief. 'Do you honestly think that Luc will *ever* take me *anywhere* again after that?'

Dan's face fell. 'Well, maybe not for a couple of weeks but . . .'

Adam rolled his eyes and turned to Spike. 'Is the Beast in today?'

'Nope. I heard The Bulb talking to Lumpton earlier and telling her how poor Michael had been jumped and beaten up while he was out. Two black eyes and a cracked tooth.'

'That's terrible,' Adam muttered, feeling faintly ashamed of the warm glow this news gave him. He chewed his lip. 'Have any of you seen Melissa?'

'Nope.' Archie's mouth twitched. 'She's probably still in the shower.'

Adam rolled his eyes a sudden, explosive snort of laughter. Everyone jumped, including him. The thing was, the whole ridiculous situation *was* funny. If he'd seen it in a film he would have wet himself. So would his friends and Chloe and Luc and Auntie Jo . . . Unfortunately this was his actual life; his life, that endless parade of blundering incompetence. He was like some kind of prehistoric animal dropped into the modern world, crashing about Godzilla-style, causing mayhem wherever he went.

He sighed. 'I should probably talk to her. What the hell am I going to say? What do you *say* to a girl when you've *puked* on her?'

Spike grinned. 'You tell her to keep her hair on – but to take her shoes off.'

It was the following day before Adam saw Melissa. He had spent another night of sweaty dreams and another hellish morning scuttling about the school, listening to jeers and sneers wherever he went. On the bright side nobody was looking at laptops; presumably they were all in repair shops thanks to Spike's counter-attacks. Once again Adam reminded himself never to fall out with Spike.

He slunk into the biology lab, half relieved and half sad that he was no longer partnered with Melissa. He knew she liked to sit at the back so he swallowed his pride and sat at the front, much to the surprise of Stinky Pete (whose nickname was pretty much self-explanatory). When Melissa walked in Adam hit the floor, throwing his pencil case down first by way of excuse. He counted to twenty before he dared to reappear.

The Buzzard was in foul form and for once Adam was nothing but grateful. She was tiny but terrifying and when she was in a rage a cloud of dark energy seemed to follow her round the room. Nobody dared to lift their heads for fear of meeting her malevolent gaze so Adam was able to spend the period copying his textbook into his lab book. He almost relaxed – a mistake under the circumstances.

The bell went too soon and he swept his books off the bench and into his bag, planning to make a rapid exit. He almost made it but a scent in the air around him made him freeze. It was slightly sweet and slightly fruity and definitely not Eau de Stinky Pete. At the same time he heard Melissa's familiar voice just behind him. 'Are you planning on avoiding me forever?'

Adam swallowed and turned slowly on the spot. Her face was pale but there were two high spots of colour in her cheeks. Her eyes had gone from lasers to . . . something stronger than lasers. Maybe alien lasers. Whatever they were, they could strip skin off a human face. She arched one eyebrow. 'Well, are you?'

And quite suddenly Adam felt tired. It wasn't a 'stayed-up-too-late' tiredness. It wasn't even a 'morning-after-the-night-before-when-you-were-spiked' tiredness. It was a kind of weariness that seemed to rise up from the very depths of his soul. All this time he had told himself that he could be normal. He could be an ordinary guy with an ordinary life, an ordinary job, an ordinary girlfriend. The choir in his chest almost sang at the thought and he screamed at it to shut up, like some demented Russian conductor. It fell into stunned silence.

He wasn't ordinary and he never would be. Something had changed, filtering in past his usual stubborn optimism, forcing him to see the truth. There was a kind of grim relief in the realisation. Maybe now it was time that Melissa realised that too. 'Yeah, pretty much.'

She stared at him. 'What, you *are* going to keep avoiding me?'

Adam sighed. 'Look, I'm sorry about your shoes. If you tell me how much they were I'll give you the money. Really – sorry. Now I've got to go. I'm going to be late.'

She was looking at him incredulously. 'So that's *it*?'

Adam scowled. 'I said I was sorry. What more do you want?'

'Why are you being like this?' Her voice was quiet. There was something fragile in it.

It was like a needle in his heart. It made him feel helpless and embarrassed and sad and stupid and guilty and then finally angry. 'Because I threw up on you! And first time round I stood you up. And *then* I took you out and abandoned you for half an hour. I'm a tit and you're really nice. So go and hang out with someone who doesn't puke all over you!'

She blinked. 'I know throwing up wasn't your fault.' She rolled her eyes. 'Michael Bulber never knows when to keep his mouth shut. He's the tit, not you.'

She was so nice. Adam looked at her and felt a pang for the life he was never going to have. Who knew what might have happened . . . ? The Russian conductor interrupted these wistful thoughts and fixed Adam in his demented gaze. No point prolonging the agony. 'See you, Melissa.' He hesitated, not sure if he was doing the right thing, trying to pick his words carefully. 'And those tests your mum needs at the hospital? Tell her to go and get them. Seriously.'

Her mouth opened and closed soundlessly. As he walked away, he reflected that Dan would have been pleased. Adam had finally made Melissa look like a fish.

Chapter 19

he rest of the week in school promised to be long and miserable. Thanks to Spike the videos had at least disappeared but the sniggers and stares hadn't. A few enterprising first years had even begun to re-enact the whole scene, until Archie threatened them with violence and embarrassing nude portraits plastered all over the school.

As for Melissa . . . Well, it was like she and Adam didn't exist on the same plane of reality. He had become invisible. She ignored him so completely that he might as well have been in the Hinterland. He felt a strange mixture of sadness and relief. His friends weren't impressed but Adam couldn't tell them the truth – that *he* had pushed *her* away.

As if his sufferings weren't great enough he was coming down with something. As he moved around the school he would have to stop, feeling his head go light and swimmy. Sometimes he felt nauseous for just a second but the feeling disappeared as quickly as it came. Lumen hardly ever got sick so on top of everything else that had happened Adam was starting to get paranoid. Maybe the Fates had their eyes on him after all . . .

School felt different. It had always seemed like a sanctuary for Adam, a safe refuge in the general madness of his life. Now he felt detached from it all. Finally the penny was dropping. Like Melissa, it was just one more thing he wasn't supposed to have. Adam knew that it was time to accept what his family had always told him. On Wednesday night, just a day after his last conversation with Melissa, Adam stunned everyone. He announced at the dinner table that he wanted to go on a call-out that night.

Nathanial put his knife and fork down carefully. 'You want to come out tonight? On a job? Instead of Luc?'

Adam nodded and tried to feign enthusiasm. 'Yeah, I'll be on holiday next week so I don't have as much homework as usual. I just thought I could help.' He did *owe* Luc for getting him into Cryptique. And for not letting him squash his own nose.

Nathanial nodded. 'I see. Well, I'd be delighted if you would come with me tonight.' He hesitated, staring at Adam's heaped dinner plate. 'Although . . . maybe you've had enough to eat for now.'

Hours later, as Adam put his vomit-spattered trainers in the washing machine, he wished that he had taken his father's advice. He watched his battered shoes and slimy socks begin their resentful trundle through the wash cycle, still thinking about the three souls they had guided after a fatal house fire. It had been pretty horrific. He heard Nathanial approach the kitchen door, presumably to say something comforting, but the footsteps stopped, hesitated and finally retreated towards the study. Adam sighed. He

241

couldn't blame his father. He wouldn't know what to say to him either.

He mooched into the den. Auntie Jo was still up, crunching through a slice of toast and watching some kind of zombie film. She glanced at his bare feet and grinned. 'I told you – you should have donated your pudding to me.'

Adam scowled. 'Yeah, OK, rub it in, why don't you.'

She stared at him not unkindly. 'You gave us all a bit of a surprise tonight. Why the sudden change of heart?'

Adam shrugged. He felt oppressed, as if a great weight was resting on him. 'It's my job. I'm going to have to do it for the next fifty years so I guess I better get used to it.'

Auntie Jo snorted. 'Fifty years is a long time. You're a bit young to be thinking that far ahead. Anyway, who knows what might happen?'

It was Adam's turn to snort. 'Yeah, who knows? Oh . . . wait a minute. I *do* know. I'll come of age, be a Luman, get married, have kids, guide souls and then die. Hopefully someone will be good enough to guide me through my Light, although I guess it won't really be necessary, what with me already knowing the directions. They'll only want me for my Keystone.'

Auntie Jo had a strange expression on her face. 'Not everyone finds it easy being a Luman.' She faltered and cleared her throat. 'Don't give up on school just yet.' Her mouth opened and for a moment Adam thought she was going to say something else. Instead she sighed and shook her head, tugging fiercely at the locket round her neck. 'Anyway, go away. You're distracting me. I've missed the best bit, where the zombies eat that annoying girl with the blonde hair.'

The next day after school he had to beg Nathanial to let him go on a call-out. He took quite a bit of convincing. For once Adam wasn't sick, which was quite surprising given the fact that he almost choked to death on his own blood. His nose didn't so much bleed as haemorrhage. The soul they were guiding was an elderly woman who had fallen off her bicycle. She was more concerned about Adam than she was about herself, much to Nathanial's embarrassment. Adam was sent home to clean himself up and he was glad to escape. He fled upstairs and spent the night in his room, nauseous and mortified. No one came to bother him.

Friday passed in a blur of misery. It was the last day of school before the break and everyone else was full of excitement. Adam avoided people as much as possible. At lunchtime he sat in the canteen alone, picking at a sandwich without appetite. His stomach had churned on and off all day, as if angry at missing out on the chance to throw up the night before.

He felt exhausted and limp. All he wanted to do was put his head down on the table and have a little doze. Of course he would probably wake up to find his eyebrows missing, especially now that Michael Bulber was back in school. In fact with the Beast back he might find his whole head missing. He hadn't seen him but people were talking about his two black eyes. By all accounts he looked like a raccoon. *Thanks, Ripper.*

Dan appeared not long before the bell went. 'You didn't come over to the library!'

Adam yawned. 'Yeah, didn't feel like it.'

Dan grinned. 'You missed out on hearing the good news. The Bulb has just emailed the teachers to confirm that the Japan trip is go!'

Adam stared at him. He knew he should be happy. After all, this was everything they had worked for. So why was it that all he could think was *who cares?* He probably wouldn't even be here by then. He'd be making a full-time career as the world's worst Luman. He forced a smile. 'Brilliant.'

Dan was burbling away happily. 'I know, it's great! I emailed the role-play convention people in Japan and there are still places left.' He wiped imaginary sweat from his brow. 'I could probably get you a ticket if you're interested.'

Adam made a non-committal sound. 'Yeah, I'll wait and see.' *Because if I make it to Japan I can think of at least ten thousand more interesting things to do . . .*

'We're going to meet up at Spike's on Tuesday. He's getting *Zombie Nightlords 4* tomorrow and he reckons he'll have it completed by then if he pulls a marathon session.'

Adam sighed. 'Look, mate, I'd love to but I'll be busy. Loads of family stuff.' He rolled his eyes in an attempt to convey his contempt for this state of affairs. It wasn't entirely an act.

Dan shrugged. 'Well, never mind. There's no such thing as a bad holiday. And in a week no one will even remember you chucking up on the fish.' He scrabbled in his pocket and pulled out a tattered flyer. 'This probably isn't your thing but it's on tomorrow. It's like a flash gig. All these bands are just going to turn up all over the city and play. I'll be around so just text me if you're going.'

Adam managed to keep a smile pasted on his face until Dan was out of sight. Only then did he finally slump onto the table and close his eyes. In a couple of hours he would be free.

When the final bell went Adam felt nothing but relief. He ran for his bus and managed to get a seat, pressing his face against the window. The cold glass made his head hurt less. The chatter around him became a soothing backdrop and he hovered somewhere between sleep and wakefulness.

Images flashed through his mind, dreams dancing around at the edges of his vision. It was a sunny day and people were swarming through the city. A band was playing on a temporary stage, against a backdrop of fountains and statues. A woman was laughing and holding a baby up in the air. The baby was laughing too. People were milling about with cameras. Then a great blast of heat and ferocious light blew Adam backwards and the scene disappeared into black smoke and screams.

He jolted in his seat, head fuzzy and confused. It took a moment to remember where he was and only a mad scramble for the door got him off the bus at his stop. The walk home seemed to take twice as long as usual and he felt dizzy and weak. Maybe he had lost more blood the night before than he had realised . . .

He limped through the iron gates and paused. All day long his only thought had been the need to make it home. Now that he was there he wasn't sure what to do. If he went inside someone would be waiting for him with questions, demands, pity. He wasn't ready to disappoint anyone just yet so he decided to go and hang out with the dogs.

They were in their pen, awake and happy to see him. Sam wagged his tail enthusiastically as he approached and Morty gave a deep wuffle of welcome. He let them out and took them into the paddock behind the house. It was surrounded by a high hedge, which sheltered it from view.

This probably explained why Luc was there, lurking behind an ancient yew tree. He leaped up, shoving something into his pocket out of sight as Adam rounded the corner. As soon as he realised it wasn't Nathanial he cursed. 'What are you doing?'

Adam scowled. 'What does it look like I'm doing?' He kicked a soft football for the dogs and they tore off in pursuit. He was seething inside. All he had wanted was ten minutes of peace and quiet with no one else around. 'More to the point, what are *you* doing?'

Luc smirked. 'Nothing for you to worry about. So, another job well done last night by all accounts.' He laughed without malice when Adam unleashed a torrent of abuse on him. 'I'll give you one thing, you're not a quitter.'

'It's not like I have any choice, is it?'

Luc shrugged. 'Not really. You might still grow into it. Maybe when you come of age everything will fall into place. Although let's face it, you're going to be about *fifty* before that ever happens. Anyway, how's the girl?'

Adam blinked at him. He was so used to people asking him how the fish was that he had to think about who Luc meant. 'Dunno. We're not really talking.' He gave the football an especially vicious kick, much to Sam and Morty's delight.

Luc raised an eyebrow. 'I take it back. You are a quitter after all, at least with the ladies.'

Adam was too exhausted to think of a fantastically witty retort. His head swam and for a second he thought he might collapse. He crouched down and gave Sam a rough hug to hide it. 'Will you look after the dogs?'

Luc was staring at him oddly. 'Are you all right?'

'Oh yeah,' Adam muttered as he stumbled off towards the house. 'I'm brilliant, me. King of the world.'

Two hours later Adam staggered downstairs for dinner. It had taken Elise, Chloe and finally Aron's booted foot against his bedroom door to rouse him from a thick, soupy sleep. His head was still buzzing with bizarre dreams. Faces, music, fountains, screams . . . It was like a haunted merry-go-round had been spinning the whole time he slept. It left him feeling shivery and weak.

Elise had already served everyone else and he tried to sneak in unobserved. It didn't work. 'Are you well, Adam?' Nathanial enquired.

Adam swallowed hard, trying to keep the sick feeling at bay. What was he doing here? There was no way he was going to be able to eat. Elise dished up some kind of red meat with vegetables and tiny potato pieces. She always cooked the meat rare and the blood mingled horribly through the yellowish sauce at the side of the plate. Adam averted his eyes and nodded at Nathanial. He didn't trust himself to open his mouth.

Aron began to recount his adventures with Nathanial earlier in the day. Apparently they had swooped over to Germany for a massive Autobahn accident, then called on Heinrich for lunch. Adam watched Aron as he spoke. His eldest brother was Luman to the core. He had never wanted to be anything else. They had never been close but as they got older the distance between them grew ever greater. They were just too different. Aron found Adam an embarrassment now.

In spite of this Adam felt a grudging admiration for his eldest brother. He was totally single-minded about being a Luman. He wasn't as quick-witted as Luc but he was slow and steady and got the job done. Nathanial and Elise were proud of him. In fact Elise was positively beaming at him as she spooned a second helping of bloody meat onto his plate. Adam looked away and tried to turn his retching into a cough.

It didn't work. Auntie Jo was watching him from the end of the table. 'What's wrong, Adam? You're not sick, are you?'

The conversation came to a shocked halt and six pairs of eyes swivelled towards Adam. He cleared his throat. 'I'm fine. Just . . . I think I must be getting a cold or something.'

Elise raised one eyebrow. 'Really?'

Adam could understand her scepticism. There were lots of different theories about why Lumen didn't really get sick. Some thought it was because of the frequent trips into the Hinterland; others that the keystones protected Lumen. Either way, as soon as children learned to swoop they were generally blessed with good health all their lives until the Fates cut their threads. He tried to shrug the whole thing off. 'Look, half my friends in school are sick at the minute. I've probably just picked up a bug.'

'It's lucky you don't have a girlfriend,' Luc said, looking completely innocent. 'I mean, just think of the germs people exchange kissing and stuff.'

'Of course he does not have a girlfriend!' Elise hissed, sounding more Gallic than ever in her wrath. 'I will not have this kind of talk at our table! We are a respectable family!'

'Sorry, Mother,' Luc murmured with every appearance of humility. He ruined the effect by leering at Adam from behind his napkin.

Nathanial was looking worried. 'Maybe we should take you to see John. I hadn't thought about the dangers you might face still being at school at your age.' John Murphy was a doctor and one of the very few non-Lumen who knew a little about their world, though even he had only the sketchiest details.

Adam resisted the urge to roll his eyes. 'It's just a little bug. I'll probably throw up for a day or two and then it'll be over.'

'Hmmmm, throwing up. Nothing out of the ordinary then. Although you usually save it for when you're working,' Luc muttered. Adam kicked him beneath the table and had the satisfaction of seeing him wince.

'You were such a sickly child,' Elise said suddenly. 'Every night I was changing your bed, washing your pyjamas.' She shrugged in a manner that implied Adam had been sent to her as some kind of trial.

Adam frowned. 'I didn't know that.'

'Well, it stopped as you got older,' Nathanial said kindly. 'We think it was just when you were very young and still showing some promise as a Seer. Of course, when you grew out of it . . .' He paused and tried to hide his disappointment. 'Well, I suppose every cloud has a silver lining. At least your health improved.'

Adam stared at him. He realised that his mouth was hanging open and quickly snapped it shut. This was new information. The beginnings of an awful suspicion were taking root . . .

Auntie Jo confirmed his fears. 'Do you remember that night when we had to call John out to the house?' She turned to Adam. 'You were only about four. We couldn't understand what was wrong with you – it was like a scene from *The Exorcist*. You kept screaming about the train. Then the next day there was that railway crash. Sixty people killed. It was only a few miles away. We realised you'd been having a premonition – you were picking up on what was going to happen. It's probably for the best that you aren't a Seer. You're sick enough when you're swooping!'

'Yeah,' Adam whispered. His head was spinning. His stomach still churned and his mind was full of a kaleidoscope of images; the smoke, the sunshine, the baby's face . . . He stood up so quickly that his chair fell over and clattered onto the flagstone floor. 'Sorry. I feel really sick. I just need some fresh air.'

'Adam . . . ?' Nathanial began and Elise stood up, her face unusually concerned.

He waved them off. 'Seriously, I'm OK. It's just a bug.

You should probably stay away from me. I just need . . .
some air.'

He fled into the garden. It was a cold, starry night and
a full moon was shining down on the trees and hedges,
throwing long shadows onto the grass. Adam jogged a little
way from the house, hoping no one would come out. He
knew now what was wrong; the reason the sick feeling had
been growing all week. Auntie Jo and his mother had given
him the last missing piece of a jigsaw.

All week he had been keeping something at bay without
even meaning to. That's why he'd been feeling sick. He
knew now what he had to do. He needed to let down the
barriers he had spent a lifetime building up – getting so
good at it that he barely knew he was even defending
himself. This premonition wasn't just one death. It was
something big.

Adam took a deep breath and allowed the images to
flood in. Within seconds he was on the ground.

Chapter 20

he square was full of people, most of them tourists. Adam recognised it immediately – the great column, the fountains, the statues. People of every colour and race were pointing cameras and chattering in an assortment of languages.

It was sunny and unseasonably warm, with not a scarf or heavy coat in sight. There was a carnival atmosphere, not least because of the temporary stage assembled at one end of Trafalgar Square. Families were posing for photos and groups of people his own age were just hanging out and having fun. A dark-haired girl walked past in clumpy boots and a vintage dress. She looked a little bit like Melissa.

Adam turned and surveyed the scene, half knowing that he wasn't really there; knowing this was a moment that hadn't happened yet. Some quality in the light reminded him of the Hinterland, a layer of something else laid over the 'real' world, 'real' time.

Worlds within worlds and moments within moments. He knew he had seen this exact scene before. A faint memory of it lingered from his dreams, from his vision on the bus. He was trying to remember but there were just so many people. Something bad was going to happen. The music starting and the crowd cheering; the great flash and the screaming . . . He turned on the spot, chewing his lip. Something happened to change everything.

He jogged towards the temporary stage. The band were getting ready to play, finishing their sound checks. The lead singer had spiky hair and lots of piercings. He was grinning at the gathered crowd and blowing kisses at a girl with long green hair. She was waving a homemade sign with 'Septic Kisses' and her mobile number scrawled across it. Adam paused and frowned. There was something familiar about that name.

He had just turned his back on the band when a sudden cold shock of recognition ran down his spine. Without warning, directly ahead of him, he saw the woman with the baby, at the back of the crowd. She had dark hair, pulled back with a bright red scarf. Her baby was wearing tiny jeans. Adam's stomach twisted. It was going to happen! Any second now she was going to lift the baby up and it was going to happen.

He ran towards the woman, desperate to get past her. In his vision the light had come from behind her, obliterating everything around her in the sudden rush of flame and black smoke. Something had to cause it. His eyes danced along the ground, searching for a bag, a parcel, *anything*.

As he reached her the woman lifted her baby. She was laughing. Everything slowed down. Adam wanted to scream a warning but no sound came out. The baby was staring at her with wondering eyes and then its mouth moved, opening in a joyful gurgle. At the same moment the crowd shifted and Adam saw him for just a second – a young man, pale face, eyes staring and intense, his mouth moving rapidly as he lifted his hand . . .

Then the great light flashed and Adam fell back into nothing.

Adam came to on the cold grass. The stars were bright against the night sky and he lay blinking, trying to get his bearings. He was lying in the shadow of one of the yew trees. Everything was still.

Where had the sunshine and the people gone? It seemed impossible but Adam knew that every moment of it was real. The sick, weak feeling had gone. A small premonition could be kept at bay but something so big, so close to home – well that was a different matter. It had to make itself known and already Adam felt a kind of relief.

Of course his relief was short-lived. This was something that was actually going to happen. He still hadn't dared to intervene in any more deaths, knowing that Darian could be watching for anything unusual, putting his Seer's ability to use for the Concilium. But this was *different*! This wouldn't just be one death – Adam could feel it. This would be lots of people – maybe twenty or thirty souls, not to mention all the injured who would be left behind. There was no way he could sit back and do nothing.

He crawled upright and used the yew branches to pull himself onto his feet. The leaves were soft in his hand. He took a few deep breaths before he risked walking back to the house. At the kitchen door he met Nathanial coming out, his face worried. 'Are you OK?'

'Yeah, I'm fine,' Adam said, grinning like a lunatic to show how fabulous he was feeling. 'I told you, I just needed to walk around and get some fresh air.'

Nathanial frowned. 'You couldn't have walked very far. You've only been gone for a minute.'

Adam cursed silently. Looking inside the kitchen, everyone was sitting where he had left them. It felt like he had been gone for ages but obviously the vision had only lasted seconds. 'Well, it's like you used to say. Fresh air, exercise – the great healer!' He slid inside and smiled at his family. 'I'm all right but I'm going to go upstairs if that's OK.'

Elise was staring at him through narrowed eyes, looking almost concerned. She pursed her lips but after a second she nodded. Presumably she was afraid his recovery would be short-lived and didn't want to risk a full-scale chunder attack on the kitchen floor. 'I will look in on you shortly –'

'No! I'm OK, I just need to go to bed, I'm *really* tired.' Adam feigned an enormous yawn. 'I'll be *fine* in the morning. Goodnight, everyone! Sweet dreams!'

He fled upstairs before he could look any more insane. His mind was racing. OK, so he knew what was going to happen and where – but so far he didn't know exactly *when*. He did however have a nagging suspicion growing at the back of his mind . . .

In his bedroom Adam ran to the chair in the corner and grabbed his school blazer. An image from his vision was gnawing at him. He could still see the band and the girl with the green hair. There was something familiar about her sign, the name above the phone number. He pulled out Dan's gig flyer and uncrumpled it, eyes darting over the names and places until they locked onto the last name.

There was the venue – and the band name. Adam's chest felt hollow. The Septic Kisses were playing the following afternoon in Trafalgar Square – which gave him less than twenty-four hours to figure out how to save a whole lot of people.

Adam spent a sleepless night making his plans. An hour after leaving the kitchen he heard his mother's light footsteps approaching the door and he leaped into bed, turning off the lamp and feigning the sleep of the innocent. After she was gone he paced up and down until something approaching a plan fell into place.

There were lots of things to think about. Firstly, there was no question of letting the bomb go off; he had to do something to stop it. But with Darian snooping about, there was no way he could let *anyone* know about his premonitions. He picked up Dan's flyer and smoothed it out again. It was going to be his alibi.

Secondly, he needed to look like he was just there for the gig. There would be CCTV everywhere, not to mention people taking videos on their mobile phones. He needed to find something that would help him blend in but hide his features. Piercing his face or dyeing his hair green wasn't on the cards. With sinking spirits he thought of the perfect items. Dan had been on holiday in America the previous summer and had brought Adam back a baseball cap. It was stuck at the back of a drawer unworn, along with some giant sunglasses Auntie Jo had bought him a few years before. They would have to do.

His plan was simple. He was going to be like anyone else, heading to a gig on the first day of the holidays. It just so happened that while he was there he was hoping to stop a massacre. He flopped down onto his bed and tried without success to get some sleep.

A few hours later he was back at the kitchen table, crunching through toast soldiers and a boiled egg. For once he was grateful that Elise was an early riser. His stomach churned as he ate but he had to look normal.

His father walked in, freshly shaved and looking less tired than usual. He kissed Elise on the cheek and accepted a cup of coffee. 'Morning! Any plans for today, Adam?'

'Yeah, just going to meet one of my friends at a gig.' Adam tried hard to look like someone planning a pleasant day out, not a lunatic going to confront a suicide bomber. It was harder than he thought.

Elise frowned. 'You should be helping your father.'

I will be, Adam thought. 'Yeah, I think I've thrown up enough times for one week, thanks.'

Nathanial gave him a wry smile. 'Yes, we'll give that stomach of yours a rest. All better this morning, I take it?' At Adam's nod he looked pleased. 'Good. Well, go and enjoy your day. You're only young once and it doesn't last long.'

Adam gulped and tried to smile. If he messed things up this afternoon his youth would be even shorter-lived than Nathanial imagined.

*

An hour later Adam was on a bus. He had trawled through his wardrobe in search of his most bland and unremarkable clothing – jeans and a plain black hoodie. The baseball cap and sunglasses were tucked away in his backpack.

He was going to be early but that was OK. It would give him time to scope the place out – and figure out where the bomber would be. In an odd way Adam felt almost happy. The awful sick feeling was gone and now that he was on the move he at least felt like he was *doing* something.

He left the bus and jumped on the Underground. Speeding and rattling beneath the city, he imagined the bomber's preparations that morning. Had *he* sat down for a last breakfast? Was he on a bus or train at this very moment, looking for all the world like any other backpacker?

The Fates seemed so cruel sometimes. What sort of creatures could allow a woman and her baby to be killed by a madman? How could *anyone* think it was better to stand aside and let the Fates have their way? Maybe it was better to stand up to them, even if it meant risking execution. After all, they could always kill you on a whim. A short-circuit, a stumble on the stairs, a piano falling from the sky . . .

A woman's voice interrupted his thoughts, announcing the next station and warning him to mind the gap. As the train pulled away, he hesitated, closing his eyes and letting the warm, fumey air wash over him. Once he was above ground . . . it was game on. He rode the up escalator and bought some drinks and snacks before heading out into the sunlight.

It was only a short walk to his destination but he didn't want to get there too soon, conscious of the CCTV cameras. If he failed in his mission every scrap of footage would be pored over by the police. He couldn't risk any knocks on their family door so for a while he just wandered, past churches, museums, shops and theatres, weaving through tourists and traffic until he could circle back towards his target.

The square unfolded below him. Adam stood at the north end, in the shadow of the huge gallery rising behind him. Ahead, the two fountains flanked the great column directly south of his position. He hadn't been here since he was a little kid, trotting obediently behind his primary school teacher.

It was still early but already the square was filling up with tourists. People were perching on the edges of the fountains, pointing out the statues and making peace signs for cameras. Stalls were selling souvenirs and candied nuts and everyone looked happy. Directly ahead, between the two fountains and the column, men were working to build the temporary stage. The familiar sight made Adam shiver.

Knowing he had a wait in store, he found a vantage point and sat back, trying to figure out his next move. He had only the loosest idea of a plan. The bomber was facing south in Adam's vision, coming from Adam's own vicinity, moving towards the crowd around the stage. Somehow Adam had to stop him getting close to that packed mass of bodies. He had an idea that if he could meet the bomber *before* he reached the fountains they might give some kind of shelter to his intended victims.

The details of how he was going to stop the man were still hazy. It would be so much easier if he could just sneak up in the Hinterland, then pounce on the bomber in the physical world. The only downside of this brilliant plan was that he would probably scare the bomber into detonating himself.

Adam ate his crisps and drank a can of fizzy stuff just to pass the time. The sun was rising ever higher, working its way round behind the column. The light was somehow . . . familiar. As if to prove his point the men building the stage climbed down, one of them speaking into a walkie-talkie. It was almost show time.

Adam's heart was beating faster. He stood up, already regretting the fizzy drink. A sudden wave of panic threatened to engulf him. He could still just go. Just turn and walk away; let the Fates or the bomber have their way. His father and brothers would quickly appear. A couple of the northern Lumen could deal with sudden deaths. Maybe there would even be some French or Irish fast-response Lumen if the body count was high enough. Darian might be with them, snooping around and checking up on Nathanial. Adam would have broken no laws and it would be obvious that no one had been interfering with the Fates' plans.

But those scenes, fresh and terrible in his mind . . . Adam sighed. It was never going to happen. You couldn't see that smoke or hear those screams and walk away. How could you live with those images in your mind, knowing that you could have stopped them? All right, he was scared of messing things up – but in reality no matter what he did he couldn't make things any worse! He rifled through his bag and put on his baseball cap and sunglasses.

Superhero disguise complete, he walked down into the square on numb legs. The people around him drifted past, ghostly and unreal. The world itself seemed to be changing, sounds and people and colours revolving, like a haunted carnival. Somehow the more hyper-alert his senses became, the more the physical world began to resemble the Hinterland.

There were whoops and catcalls ahead of him. To Adam's horror the band were walking towards the stage, pushing through their fans, carrying guitar cases. The spiky-haired guy with the piercings was waving and grinning. Adam hurried to the back of the crowd. There was no sign yet of the woman with her baby but he couldn't have more than a few minutes to find the bomber.

What was he going to do? He couldn't just run up to people and tell them there was a bomb. They would either laugh at him, think he was a nutter or jump on him until the police arrived, assuming *he* was the suspect. All he could do was persuade the bomber to stop.

Adam turned back to the north end of the square, towards the National Gallery, scouring the crowd, trying to recall his brief glimpse of the bomber. A pale face, intense eyes, a huge rucksack on his back . . . In other words the bomber looked just like hundreds of other people in the square!

Think, he commanded himself. Most of the backpackers were in pairs or groups, not walking alone. The few who were on their own were taking their time, strolling around soaking up the atmosphere and snapping photos. They weren't walking across the square, pale and purposeful, mouths moving silently in pep talk or prayer.

There was a roar of approval from the stage behind him and Adam's heart jumped up into his throat. He turned and saw the band on the stage. At the same moment he spotted two people coming from separate directions – the green-haired woman pushing through the crowd with her sign and the woman with the red scarf. The woman was lifting her baby out of a buggy, wrestling with the straps. A man was helping her. Adam hadn't noticed him before. A family on a day out, about to be wiped out of existence.

But as he watched them the strangest feeling passed over him. Tiny hairs on the back of his neck rose and a shiver rippled down to the base of his spine. He turned slowly on the spot, knowing before he even looked around that the bomber was approaching. It was impossible to explain his certainty; something more ancient than reason was at work.

And as he finally turned his back on the crowd the man came into view. He was standing at the far end of the square, looking straight towards Adam. He seemed supernaturally still, totally focused on his target – the crowd who were yelling for the band to start playing. Adam didn't dare to turn around. He knew the baby would be free of its buggy by now.

He started to walk, one foot in front of the other, mechanical. As he came closer the bomber began to walk too. It was almost comical. Adam looked around, feeling a sudden hysterical urge to laugh. It was like high noon in a western film, the sheriff confronting the villain, ready to see who was fastest on the draw.

The distance between them was closing too fast. Adam could see the bomber more clearly now. He was younger than he had expected, with wispy brown hair and a sparse goatee. He was smaller than Adam and thin, almost stumbling beneath the weight of his rucksack. Thinking about what was inside that bag almost brought Adam to a standstill but he forced himself to keep walking.

The bomber was jumpy. He ignored Adam at first, focused on the mob behind him, but as he got closer his eyes darted from side to side. They were going to meet just north of the fountains, in a zone that was relatively empty of tourists. Adam stared desperately around, searching for ideas. If he scared the bomber the young man would hit the button before Adam even opened his mouth.

They were five metres apart . . . four metres apart . . . The bomber was looking edgy . . . and finally Adam had a flash of inspiration. He cleared his throat and tried to channel Elise and every other French relative he had. '*Excusez-moi? Monsieur?* Could you possibly take *un photo?*'

The bomber stopped. This close Adam could see how young he really was – only a few years older than Adam himself. His eyes were hollow but he paused and stared at Adam as if he was an alien. 'What?'

Adam's throat was dry. He forced himself to smile and kept his best accent going. 'Please? You can take *un photograph* for me, *oui?*'

The bomber glared at him and started to walk past. 'Piss off.'

Without thinking about it Adam seized his arm. 'I know who you are.'

There was a frozen second as the bomber deciphered his words and a look of utter panic flashed across his thin face. Adam realised that grabbing him was pretty much the worst thing he could have done – only the bomber's terror was keeping him paralysed. He dropped the young man's arm and stepped away, holding his hands up peaceably. 'Sorry, mate! I'm not going to do anything. It's just . . . I know what you're going to do and . . . I've been sent to tell you . . . don't do this!'

The bomber's mouth was moving but no words were coming out. Maybe he was wondering if one of his co-conspirators had betrayed him.

Adam adopted Auntie Jo's thrilling horoscope voice. 'I was given a vision! I saw what you planned to do – but it's not too late!'

The bomber was staring at him wide-eyed. Finally he blurted out, 'A *vision*? How . . . how did you know? Are you . . . an *angel*?'

Adam almost snorted but managed not to. 'Yes . . . well, kind of. I'm a messenger. A messenger who can see the future! And this isn't the right thing to do!'

The young man paused, confused. His right arm was tense, hand hidden in his pocket out of sight. 'God wants me to do it.'

Adam shook his head, trying not to look at the hand in the pocket. If he thought about it for even a second he would turn and run for his life. 'NO! God doesn't want you to do this!'

The bomber stared at him and a look of utter exhaustion passed across his face. His body sagged a little. 'God wants me to do it. They told me. You can read about it in the book.' He was rambling, eyes a little unfocused.

Adam was beginning to feel desperate. Who was this guy? Who had told him this stuff? 'Seriously, God doesn't want you to do anything. God wants you to . . . go home! Go home and get some sleep!'

For just a second the bomber looked at him almost hopefully and Adam's heart soared. Then a flicker of doubt narrowed the young man's eyes and twisted his mouth into a sneer. 'I know what you are! You're a . . . a *devil*! A tempter!' He looked like he was going to cry.

'No! I'm not!' Adam looked around in despair. A tour group was walking towards them, coming from the National Gallery. They weren't too close yet but they would be soon. He saw a woman in heels, holding her daughter's hand, and an elderly man snapping photos. He pulled off his sunglasses. 'Please,' he whispered. 'Don't do this.'

The bomber looked at him with a kind of weary triumph and pulled his hand out of his pocket. 'This is God's will.'

And in the last possible second, as the young man pressed a key on his mobile phone, Adam clutched his keystone and stepped forward – just as the bomb roared and detonated.

Chapter 21

dam flew backwards off his feet, feeling the breath punched out of his body, even here in the Hinterland. A hot wind blasted across his face like sandpaper and he kept his eyes closed tight until he felt it subside.

There was a moment of stunned silence, before the first screams came. He lay for a second, not wanting to open his eyes. *I don't want this life any more. Please. Let me be someone else.* Then, as the screams were picked up by others, he felt a great wave of shame. When he stood up there would probably be souls all around him – souls who would give anything to be back in their bodies. He didn't deserve any pity right now.

He opened his eyes and risked a glance. He looked left – and recoiled. He was staring at a woman's leg, a slim calf still wearing a strappy, high-heeled shoe. The woman herself was some distance away, lying on the ground stunned; but her arms were moving. Slowly Adam crawled up onto his feet. In the physical world there were bodies on the ground, some bleeding – but all of them still held their soul safely inside. He hadn't saved these people from injury but he had – for now – kept them from death. Already he could hear a siren wailing dimly in the distance. In a few minutes there would be people here to help those injured.

There was only one soul visible, perhaps fifty metres away – the soul of the bomber himself. He was standing wide-eyed and slack-jawed, as if he couldn't believe he had actually pushed the button. He stared around the Hinterland, eyes widening even further as he watched Adam walking towards him. 'It's you!' He stared at the scene around him, expression somewhere between revulsion, guilt and satisfaction.

Adam's jaw was clenching painfully, in time with his fists. He wanted to grab the bomber by the throat, punch him in the face and kick him somewhere painful, preferably all at the same time. He knew he should stop and get himself under control but he couldn't. His anger was so great that his body felt too small to contain it. For the first time he understood his father's maddening composure – how he always managed to hide his emotions. After all, it was usually Nathanial who dealt with these kinds of jobs. He'd had a lifetime to practise keeping his feelings to himself.

The bomber was staring at him. 'Are we really dead? Like, properly dead?'

Adam glared at him. '*You* are.'

The bomber's face fell. 'So . . . *this* is heaven?'

Adam snorted. He waved a hand at the injured lying on the ground behind him. Some of them were crying now or moaning softly. 'Does this look like heaven to you?' The bomber chewed his lip and Adam laughed. It sounded odd and brittle. 'What, not living up to your expectations?' He shook his head, caught somewhere between fury and sorrow. 'Why did you *do* this?'

For the first time some of the bomber's defiance returned. 'I did it for God, the Lord and Creator of this world! We've been abusing God's creation – we deserve to be punished! And now God is going to reward me!'

'*Really?*' Adam almost snarled. When the bomber nodded Adam took a step closer, until their faces were only inches apart. 'Thing is, if some Creator *made* the world and all these people, don't you think it's going to be pretty pissed off that you just tried to *blow it all up?*' He waved his arm around the scene. 'These people are tourists! There's a little baby over there! What the hell is the *matter* with you?'

The bomber's face grew shuttered. 'It doesn't matter what you say. I'm going to heaven now. *You* won't be going there.'

Adam stared at him and all his rage suddenly drained away. 'I don't know where you're going, mate. I'm just glad I don't have to go there with you.'

'You're going to hell!' the bomber hissed but his face was a little frightened now. 'I'm going to heaven and you're going to hell.'

Adam pointed at the injured. 'That's hell. Those people are already there, thanks to you.' He looked at the people helping them and some of the tightness around his heart lifted. 'But maybe *that's* heaven. Your head is all messed up. You don't understand *anything*.'

The bomber set his lips but they were trembling a little. 'I want to go to heaven now.' He looked like he might cry.

Adam blinked and shrugged. The anger was back but now it was a cold, bright, hard thing in his chest. He didn't know what lay in store for this guy but the time for talking was over. He took a deep breath and tried to push air past the cold, bright thing inside him. 'You have to go on a journey now. Do you see a Light?'

As his voice lilted the bomber's face relaxed. 'I see it,' he whispered. 'There it is!'

Adam was trying very hard to concentrate. In the physical world he could see the first ambulance arrive, rattling and bumping as close to the carnage as possible. He needed to remember the steps, the sequence, but the bright, hard thing was getting bigger; a great cold ball. He couldn't see, couldn't think. A woman screamed as someone tried to help her onto a stretcher and her scream echoed and echoed.

He took a deep breath, his mind empty, putting one hand on the bomber's shoulder. 'Just step into your Light,' he heard himself say but no more words would come out. The young man had already forgotten him, was already moving. He didn't even hear Adam's last words. 'You're going on a journey now and I'm not giving you directions. It's going to take you a long time – but you'll need it. Think up some excuses. You're going to have a lot of explaining to do.'

And before the soul had even disappeared, Adam was already walking away.

Adam emerged from the Hinterland just beyond the square, conscious that his father could appear at any moment. Back in the physical world there was nothing to muffle the screech of sirens. They were a long-drawn-out wail of pain and fear echoing around the old buildings. It was still bright and sunny, the morning chill long gone, far too nice for this time of year. Far too nice for tragedy.

His chest felt hollow and he moved like an automaton, one foot in front of the other. He was in so much trouble he couldn't even imagine it. No Luman could work alone before they came of age. Nathanial wouldn't know that there were supposed to be lots of other souls there but he *would* know that *somebody* had died. Any second now he was going to follow his death sense to the scene – only to find the bomber's soul gone. At first he might assume it was Aron, trying to prove something – or maybe even Luc. But when they protested their innocence eventually his thoughts would turn to Adam.

Of course he wouldn't believe it at first. Adam smiled wryly. Who would have thought that *he* would be volunteering to send souls on, all on his own? No puking on his trainers today. But when Nathanial realised what he had done . . . Adam sighed. Better make the most of the sunshine. He wasn't going to be seeing the light of day for a long time.

The bright sharpness of his anger had faded completely now, leaving only tiredness. He passed a quiet memorial park, set incongruously at the intersection between several busy streets. No one was there. People were already getting news about the bomb and cutting their shopping trips short, knowing the chaos to come.

There was an old stone bench in the centre of the park, speckled with bird droppings and overshadowed by naked trees. Adam sat down on the cleanest spot and closed his eyes, trying to make his mind go quiet. There were fewer sirens now; the ambulance crews would have raced off to hospitals. Police would be sealing off the scene, searching for clues, not knowing how much worse things could have been.

He thought about the woman with the red scarf. She had set out that morning, looking forward to a nice day with her family. Now she would always remember it as the day the bomb went off. *But what will she do?* Adam wondered. *Will she sit in her house, too scared to go out? Or will she go out into the world and keep doing what she likes to do?* The thing about hiding was – death always found you in the end. It could claim you at home just as easily as it could on the streets – but that was OK. It was what you did before you died that was important. You had to make it count.

There was a war memorial in front of Adam, a simple pillar of polished granite. Adam expected the usual verses about not growing old, not being forgotten – but instead there were only two words. *Carpe diem* – seize the day. The day ahead was all that you knew you had. His thoughts wandered. If the Fates were to cut his thread that night, what would he regret? What would he wish he'd done differently? What would he wish he'd done *full stop*?

He stood up, filled with a sudden sense of purpose. He knew what he had to do.

It took a long time to walk to Flip Street. By the time Adam reached Alter-Eden it was late afternoon. It was a

271

riot of colours inside, mad assortments of clothing festooning the walls and crammed onto rails. Behind the counter he spoke to a girl with blue hair and feathers stuck over her eyelashes. She deigned to let him slip round the counter and along the narrow corridor behind, out into the yard.

The fire exit was propped open. The corridor led him out into a weedy yard, carpeted with fag butts and empty diet cola cans. At the far end was a rickety bench, squeezed in between the wall and a huge blue recycling bin. Melissa was sitting there with her head tipped back, eyes closed. One impossible sunbeam had slipped between the tall buildings all around, bathing her face in light. Adam stared, transfixed. She looked tired and unhappy and beautiful, like a sad angel.

He might have stood there forever but she sighed and twisted the cap off her water bottle. As she raised it to drink her eyes opened and locked on his. She became very still. 'What are you doing here?' She didn't sound angry, just indifferent. Somehow that was worse.

Adam shrugged. 'I just came to say hello.'

Melissa gave him a blank stare. 'Oh right.' She turned her face back to the sun and closed her eyes.

He shifted, a little uncertainly – then remembered the courage that had brought him here. *Seize the day*. He'd already made a mess of things so he might as well finish the job. He walked over and sat beside her.

She made an irritated noise. 'What do you *want*, Adam?'

'I wanted to see you.'

'Why?'

Adam took a deep breath. 'Because I like you. I mean, I really, *really* like you.'

Melissa laughed. 'Yeah, of course you do. That's why you were so nice to me in biology the other day.'

Adam hung his head, wishing he could explain. 'I'm really sorry. I just . . . Look, I don't have any kind of good excuse. But I'm sorry.'

'Yeah, you told me. Is that it?'

Adam nodded, feeling miserable. He wished she would look at him but for once her eyes were burning holes in the ground, rather than him. She pulled out a pot of something and rubbed it on her lips, studiously ignoring him. All his words seemed to have disappeared. 'There was a big bomb earlier,' he heard himself say.

At least now Melissa was looking at him, eyes wide. 'Where? You mean near here?'

Adam nodded. 'I guess you didn't hear about it. I was there when it went off, right nearby. There was a gig on.' He paused, trying to find the right words. 'It made me think. You know, how funny life is. You don't know what's going to happen. I guess I just wanted to see you.'

She was staring at the ground again, a faint flush of colour in her pale cheeks. Adam waited for her to say something – *anything* – but she stayed quiet. He sighed and stood up. He'd done what he came here to do – the rest was up to her. 'I'm sorry I messed everything up. Maybe we can talk some time back in school.'

Time to go, before he made even more of a fool of himself. He was almost back at the fire door when she spoke. 'Adam.' When he turned round she was on her feet,

273

the sunlight still playing over her face, softening it. 'What you said the other day. My mum's going to the hospital for her tests.' She looked like she wanted to say a lot more but couldn't find the right words.

Adam felt cornered. He couldn't afford questions. He tried to smile. 'That's good. I'm sure she'll be fine but you know – better to get things checked.'

Melissa shrugged. 'Yeah, I guess. And . . . we'll talk. Maybe next weekend?'

There wasn't going to be a next weekend because he was going to be under house arrest until he was at least seventy. Maybe that was why he did it. He strode across the yard, put his hands on her shoulders and kissed her. Her mouth was soft and damp and surprised. She tasted like cold water and warm strawberries.

He pulled away after a few seconds, bracing himself for outrage or a right hook, but she only blinked and touched her bottom lip uncertainly. Adam swallowed hard. 'Sorry. You just looked really nice and . . . I wanted to do that for ages. That night at Petrograd, and then at Cryptique before I . . . well, you know what I did.' He tried to smile. 'And I'd really like to go out but I'm kind of grounded forever so . . . maybe we can hang out at school. After the holidays?'

She looked bemused. 'Yeah . . . I guess.'

'OK.' How did he sound so casual? He'd kissed her! He'd seized the day! He was a rock star!

'Adam.' When he turned Melissa suddenly looked more like her old self. There was a glint of wickedness in her eye. 'That was pretty good. At least a six out of ten. You just need to practise.'

Adam grinned. 'I'll bear that in mind.' And as he walked back inside, the corridor didn't seem dark at all – because in spite of everything the world was still a shiny, happy place.

It took Adam a long time to get home. The whole city knew about the bomb now although the casualties were still unclear. Adam could have reassured the authorities on that score but it just wasn't possible. Buses and Underground services were disrupted but people were doing their best to go on as normal. Saturday shoppers and tourists alike were holding up street plans and trying to navigate home on foot.

Adam wasn't in any rush. He could have swooped – what was one more broken law at this stage – but he made the most of his freedom, walking for over an hour. It was almost dark as he finally approached the high gates around the house. The trees stood out black against the dusk. One of the dogs barked, perhaps in welcome.

He wasn't sure what waited for him inside. Would they have figured out what he had done yet? Maybe. He didn't regret it though. There was no reason why Darian or anyone else would know that he had saved so many lives. As far as other people were concerned it was just good luck that the bomber hadn't killed anyone else. Only he knew the truth.

Adam looked up at the house and sighed. Love it or hate it, this was his home – his world. The thing was, standing here on the street outside was his world too. Life was funny like that. It was all about the choices you made

275

and the things you valued. Good things happened and bad things happened. Some people were nice and some people weren't. Some people were *really* nice. He thought about kissing Melissa and it made him feel warm inside.

He touched his palm to the electronic pad and watched the gate swing open. He tried to imagine his family, pretending that this was just any other Saturday with a few quiet hours between call-outs. His mother would be making the dinner. Nathanial would be in his study and Auntie Jo would be crunching through her endless pile of toast and watching a horror film. Luc and Chloe would be bickering good-naturedly beside her while Aron pumped iron up in his bedroom.

They would all be doing what they enjoyed. That was the thing about being alive – it was brilliant! Everybody deserved the chance to live on their own terms, for as long as they could. If he could help people do that for longer, then that would be his mission. Whether he did it as a doctor or a rogue Luman . . . only time would tell. Either way, he'd found what he had to do; how to live before he died.

As the gates closed behind him Adam grinned. One thing was for sure. Life was always surprising.

Epilogue

aris was always at its most beautiful by night. Even with snow on the ground the crowds were out on the streets, bundled up in stylish coats and scarves. Restaurant windows gleamed like jewels, revealing magical worlds behind, where people talked, ate, kissed and poured wine. The aromas of steak, garlic and bitter chocolate were overwhelming.

Darian ignored the crowd as he hurried towards a less salubrious district. Of course no one would dare to question him now – just one of the many perks of finally being safely on the Concilium. He allowed himself a brief smile of triumph. Still, old habits died hard. It was always better to be cautious – at least until the moment came to strike.

He slipped into an alleyway and satisfied himself that he was truly alone. Only then did he pull the object out of his pocket. It looked insignificant, as indeed it was in all respects but one. This tiny, black, pearl button was his ticket into another realm – a realm where even a Curator could not enter without the proper key.

Without even pausing for breath he shifted his focus

and stepped forward into the Hinterland. The physical world around him faded and he found himself in the empty borderland. No one had died so no Light nor frightened soul was waiting for him. He was looking at a paler version of the physical world, the colours more muted in the night.

He began to walk, straight through buildings and cars, crossing roads and rivers. He clutched the button between his finger and thumb and as he focused his mind on it alone, Paris began to disappear. *Everything is energy*, he reminded himself. Even a Luman's mind clung to order and the familiar. It took something special to help him see the Hinterland as it truly was – a vast and endless twilight.

He swallowed hard, angry that even now after all this time the place could still make him fearful. Not much further. He could feel the heat growing in the tiny pearl; see a faint light begin to glow between his fingers. The doorway would appear soon. All he had to do was keep walking, keep concentrating . . .

And there it was, quite without warning, a street's length away. As he approached, the door opened and a woman's silhouette appeared. Darian smiled, a small, secret smile. It wouldn't do to be too bold with this woman. Like him, she was a newcomer, proud of her position, still tetchy and quick to take offence. Darian understood that. Power freshly won had to be maintained. It was like wearing in a new pair of shoes. Soon, they would both be more comfortable with their new status – and they would walk more confidently in their world.

For now, he would tread carefully. She was clever – but not as clever as him. He was going to tell her a story, weaving a web of truths and half-truths. Soon the wrath of the Concilium *and* the Fates would fall on Nathanial Mortson and his family. Perhaps then he could pluck through the wreckage of the Mortsons' lives and salvage the one thing he held dear.

For now though he had business to attend to. He pushed Elise from his mind – it was too soon to think about the prize. Instead he gave his most charming smile to the woman in the doorway, burying his hatred and mistrust deep inside him.

'My dear Morta, how lovely to see you. If only all the Fates were blessed with such beauty. And if only I brought you better tidings . . .'

Acknowledgements

No book is written in isolation. Special thanks to my fabulous agent Gillie Russell for keeping the faith. Thanks also to all at Hot Key, especially my editors Emily Thomas, who 'got' the book right from the start, and Georgia Murray for getting me through the edits unscathed.

My colleagues and pupils at Sperrin Integrated College showed huge enthusiasm for the book. Mary McClelland, Lucien St Aubyn and the Flowerfield Writers, Portstewart all gave timely encouragement. And huge thanks to the PWA for all the cheerleading and craic along the way – Julie Agnew, Mandy Taggart and most of all Bernie McGill – tutor, mentor and friend. This book would not exist without her.

Thank you to my family and friends, especially my parents Derek and Patricia and my parents-in-law Michael and Gretta. Most of all though, thank you to my husband Colm Murphy for unfailing love and encouragement.

And a special mention for our daughter Ellen. You're already our greatest creation.

D.J. McCune

D.J. McCune was born in Belfast and grew up in a seaside town just north of the city. As a child she liked making up stories and even wrote some down, including a thriller about a stolen wallaby.

D.J. McCune read Theology at Trinity College, Cambridge but mostly just read lots of books. She lives in Northern Ireland with her husband and daughter – and two cats with seven legs between them.

If you'd like to know more you can find her at:

www.facebook.com/djmccuneauthor

www.debbiemccune.blogspot.com

Twitter @debbiemccune